The Well-Tempered Clavier

William Coles

William Coles

Based on a true story

Legend Press

Independent Book Publisher

Legend Press Ltd
13a Northwold Road, London, N16 7HL
info@legendpress.co.uk
www.legendpress.co.uk / www.myspace.com/legendpress

Legend Press publishes contemporary, high-quality fiction
for the modern mainstream market. Our list is rich and varied
and aimed at providing readers with a different, thought-
provoking perspective. All of our titles are available to buy
directly (with exclusive discounts and special extras) at our
popular online shop www.legendpress.co.uk/23301

British Library Catologuing in Publication Data available.

ISBN 978-0-9551032-7-8

Set in Times
Printed by Gutenberg Press, Malta

Cover designed by Gudrun Jobst
www.yellowoftheegg.co.uk

Legend 🕮 Press
Independent Book Publisher

To Margot, my wife

Acknowledgements

I hesitate from turning this into a teary-eyed Oscar speech, but there are a number of people I need to thank.

Ever since I embarked on this novel-writing venture – some years ago, I can tell you – I have had a coterie of stalwart cheerleaders. These are the ones I would especially like to thank:

My brother Toby, Charlie Bain, Jerv and Angela Cottam, James Cripps, Mike Hamill, Sebastian Hamilton, Jeremy Hitchen, Tim Maguire, Charlie Ottley, Giles Pilbrow, Mark Pilbrow and, a rose among all these thorny men, Louise Robinson.

I am much indebted to the heroic efforts of my agents Jenny Brown and Darin Jewell, as well as my editor Tom Chalmers, who were all formative in getting this book into print.

Although this book is a novel, I do share at least one trait with its hero – in that I truly was one of Eton's most indolent loafers. So my thanks to my two tutors Michael Meredith and Nick Welsh, outstanding English teachers the pair of them. I hope this book brings them some small amusement to see how, despite my tabloid wanderings, a few kernels from their lessons may actually have taken root.

To my parents, Bob and Sarah (who will doubtless cringe when they read this, so I'll keep it short), I say a special thanks – not least for their perpetual bullishness.

My two boys, Dexter and Geordie, will one day, I hope, realise how they have been an unending source of good cheer to me.

And lastly, *merci mille fois* to Margot – a great wife and, as it happens, a great friend also.

BOOK 1, PRELUDE 17, A-flat Major

I am not given to emotion.

But even now, 25 years on, the sound of Bach's *Well-Tempered Clavier* makes the hairs bristle at the nape of my neck. My stomach spasms, my heart jolts, and in an instant I am back there, back in a small music room with lime-green walls and a scuffed upright Steinway.

The Well-Tempered Clavier comprises 96 preludes and fugues that Johann Sebastian Bach wrote for the Clavier, or piano as it is now called.

I know each one. And once, when I was in my musical prime, I could play a number of them too.

There is one prelude, however, that I only play on the glory days, on the anniversaries. And that is when I start to choke up.

I used to be able to play this prelude from memory, note perfect, every finger knowing exactly where and when they had to be on the keyboard. But those were in the palmy days when I was prepared to devote two hours to practising a single bar of music.

Today all I have left are the relics of my indifferent musical talent. I can only manage five bars before my fingers clunk onto the wrong notes. Everything ends in discord.

Though if I were note perfect, it would make no difference. For even years back I could never finish the prelude without crying.

It's the Prelude 17, in A-flat Major.

When I write it like that, it sounds so stark.

But you should hear it. Hear all 90 seconds of it. Even first time round, right off the gun, you'd think it quite charming. Delightful.

5

Second time it's even better.

The purists might claim Bach wrote many better preludes. But then memory is everything, is it not? And when I hear this prelude, I dream of a woman who was, is, and will always remain, the most beautiful woman I have ever seen.

When I think of her, she is never static, like in a photo. For as I remember her she is always laughing, really laughing, mouth open, with the most perfect white teeth.

First I recall her mouth and then her hair, a dark mane that cascaded over her shoulders in a glistening wave of silk; and her lips, always kissable red, erotic moist; and her flashing walnut eyes; and her fingers, long sensual fingers with exquisite buffed nails, tailor-made for the piano.

I've had other loves since – extraordinary passions. Though their stories are for another time.

This woman was my first great love.

And her name? Her name was India.

I know that what she did was wrong, that it is immoral for a teacher to seduce her 17-year-old pupil. But at the time that was not how I saw it. I thought I'd been given the greatest gift of my life.

My memories though run in sequence. And always, after remembering the magic of India, I recall myself 25 years ago.

These days everything has mellowed into easy come, easy go.

But then I was all things and everything: exuberant and truculent, moody and energetic, sporty and slothful, gangly and assured, witty and graceless, sensitive and obtuse, and charming and callow in equal measure.

I was also an emotional iceberg, while at the same time being riddled with the most insane jealousy.

I was, like another ignorant, self-obsessed lover before me, a man who loved not wisely but too well. But, unlike Othello, I was only 17 at the time.

And why am I going back there? Why do I feel the need to relive all these old memories and put them to paper?

Something happened last month, and since then I have found

that when my mind is idling I start to reminisce. The more I delve, the more it all comes back to me – about the love, about *The Well-Tempered Clavier*, and, above all, about the folly of a schoolboy who, like the base Indian, threw a pearl away richer than all his tribe.

The year was 1982 and the school was Eton College, a seething cauldron of pubescent boys and humming testosterone. It was everything you've heard about it and more. But all you need to know for now is that there were some 1,238 boys dressed up in their black tailcoats, black waistcoats, tight starched collars, stained black pin-stripes and scuffed black lace-ups, and with not a girl in sight.

The school does not have a walled campus but sprawls over the town, and has done so since 1440. By rights it should be busy, abuzz with the everyday activities that you see in parishes all over Britain. But Eton is like some vast schoolboy prison camp where every trace of blooming girlhood has been excised off the face of the earth. Without exaggeration, a boy could go weeks at a time without seeing a single female under the age of 50.

This being the case, the arrival of any young woman into Eton's rarefied male stratosphere was inevitably going to cause a great pulse of interest; akin to a howitzer being fired into the middle of a piranha-pond.

And, as I have already alluded, India was not just any young woman.

That April morning in 1982 when she walked out from the School Hall into the blazing sunshine, it was as if a pristine white peacock had strutted out into a monstrous horde of soiled black crows.

I was 17, with still another year to go before my A-levels. Another rank and file Etonian destined for a spectacularly mediocre school career.

I have forgotten so many things over the years. But of that particular day I can recall everything to the last detail.

It is a glorious cloudless Friday, the second day of the summer term, with the sun burning high in the sky, leaving my stiff collar wet and a slim trickle of sweat slipping down my back. For once, I am immaculate. My shoes still gleam with first-day-of-term polish, my waistcoat, tailcoat and trousers are fresh from the cleaners, and my hair still hums with the scent of barber's gel.

It's just after 11am and I am in the midst of a pulsating mass of Etonians. We stand on the pavement outside the School Hall beside an ornate streetlight, known as the Burning Bush.

There are more than 100 boys, nattering and chattering, a black wave of twitching adolescence. It's Chambers, the only time in the day when you can be guaranteed to find a master – useful for chits that need signing and work that needs handing in.

Inside the School Hall, the scores of gowned masters – or beaks – are small-talking and sipping tea. When they are done, they exit the hall to face the black-and-white sea of schoolboys.

The tourists, who roll past in their air-conditioned coaches, watch in amazement.

A few of my friends are about, and, like a large well-ordered penguin colony, we all know where we stand in the pecking order.

At the top end of the Eton spectrum is our house captain, the Honourable Charles Savage-Leng, second son of one of Scotland's oldest peerages. He goes by the name of Savage and has the olive looks of a Greek God. He is tall, even for an Etonian, at six-foot-four and his dark hair curls back over his ears. As a prefect, or popper, he wears a wing collar and bowtie, and a resplendent red silk waistcoat with gold buttons.

Right at the bottom of the Eton muckheap are the fags, or F-tits, the 13-year-olds in F-block, scurrying around in their over-sized tailcoats.

And I am squarely in the middle of Eton's panoply of different ranks. Not a member of Pop, nor of Sixth Form Select, nor a member of the Eight, the Eleven, the Association, the Field, The Mixed Wall, or the Monarch. No – I have done nothing of note that might earn me a bowtie and a fancier uniform.

Beside me is Jeremy Raikes, as unkempt as ever, with a thick hedge of black hair that would have had the school barber salivating. We joined the school on the same day in 1979, and are destined to leave on the same day in 1983.

There is only one thing to talk about.

The whole school is talking about it.

The whole country is talking about it.

And for the space of two months it dominated our lives: The Falklands.

Those two words access such a raft of different memories for me. The pictures of the Coventry as she died in the sea, heeling over like a stricken beast; the evocative names, Goose Green, Bluff Cove, Tumbledown, Port Stanley, the Malvinas; my first introduction to the Super Etendard jet, the Mirage III and the AM.39 Exocet missile; and a Lieutenant-Colonel, an Old Etonian, shot in the back of the neck and awarded a posthumous VC.

On 2 April, Argentina had invaded those tiny inhospitable islands in the South Atlantic, and within three weeks the Falklands had become Britain's one universal topic of conversation.

I had been devouring the news for many reasons. My father was ex-army and every meal at home had been spent tuned in to Radio Four or the World Service to pick up every morsel of news as and when it happened. But my father and I were viewing the Falklands from polar extremes. He was facing a long and leisurely retirement and would have given his eyeteeth to be there in the thick of the action. Conversely, I was due to become a soldier and…I didn't know what to think about an actual war.

"With all your dad's contacts, you've probably seen the plan of campaign," Jeremy says.

"Of course." I look at his smeared glasses, thick and crusty with grime. "Steam into South Georgia, mop up there and head for the Falklands. Two months, that's all it'll take."

"Two months? Fat chance."

"The Argentinian army is made up of conscripts. Every one of the soldiers is a conscript."

"Whereupon?"

"They're like us, aren't they? Got no option but to be out there. We're packed off to Eton; they're packed off to the Malvinas.

Their hearts aren't in it."

"Interesting. Very slightly interesting." Jeremy pushes his glittering glasses back up the bridge of his thin nose. "Stretching it a little with the conscripts?"

"It's a perfect analogy." I warm to the theme. "We both have to wear a very dull uniform. There's not a woman to be seen. We quickly learn to keep our heads down. And all of us are just obeying orders, though none of us really knows why."

"Though the conscripts probably get better food than us."

"Without doubt."

He fishes around in his stained waistcoat pocket and wordlessly passes me a grimy Polo. "Bet you wish you were out there."

"Don't know," I reply. "Never really thought about putting my life on the line."

He pops three Polos into his mouth, chewing them one after the next. "I thought the army was the family trade."

"Cascading through the generations. Thank you for reminding me."

I scratch the back of my chaffed neck, trying to distil a month's worth of ambivalence into one sentence. For the truth was that, since the start of the Falklands War, I had never stopped thinking about the army, and I was not a jot closer to coming to any conclusion. "There's one thing I dread more than being killed on the battlefield."

"Something worse than death?" Jeremy raises his eyebrows. "Coming back here as a teacher?"

"That would be bad." The Polo snaps against my tongue. "Would I have the guts to kill someone? Would I be able to shoot them in cold blood?"

"Look them in the eye and pull the trigger?"

"Too bloody right." I squint up at the sun, looking for answers. But there are never any answers to war. And in a way, war is almost akin to a love affair, for when they're finished all you're left with is questions. Even years on, you're still asking yourself if you did the right thing, still wondering if you made the right choice. And invariably, because the grass is always greener, you come to the conclusion that you did not; that when it came to the critical point, you fluffed it.

Jeremy touches my arm. "Enough of that. Here he comes."

We shoulder our way through to our housemaster, Francis Frederickson. For eight months of the year, Frankie was our Victorian father, our spiritual counsellor, our affable mentor, our judge, jury and part-time executioner. He probably knew more about me than my own parents; although that may have been more of a reflection on my parents than Frankie.

"Morning boys," he says as we give him a couple of book chits for signing. He has the look of a jaded police sergeant; his thinning hair greased back straight over his head and gleaming in the sun; his shoe-laces frayed at the ends; his grey suit already crumpled; and his white bowtie just an inch off-centre. "Any news from the front?"

"Nothing since this morning," Jeremy replies.

"South Georgia, eh? Until a week ago, I'd always thought that was in the Deep South." Frankie signs the chits with a flourish. "Almost makes me wish I'd signed up for a full 15 years."

"The Eton Rifles must be a pretty good second though, Sir?" Jeremy says.

"Might have made Lieutenant-Colonel by now."

"Brigadier at the least."

Frankie laughs. "Quite so."

"But it's got to be more fun ordering us around, isn't it Sir?" Jeremy continues.

"It might be," Frankie says. "If you ever obeyed any of my orders."

He chortles to himself as he tucks his pen away.

Then, as if by osmosis, a frisson ripples through the boys. Not a word is said, but we are aware of an alien presence.

A slight nudge at my elbow from Jeremy and, from looking at Frankie, I find that my gaze is drawn to the huge doors of the School Hall. The collective sigh is just audible.

I turn, I look, and I stare transfixed. All thoughts of Frankie, the Falklands, are erased from my mind.

A woman, a young woman in her early-20s, has glided out of the hall. She stands for a moment on the steps, basking in the sunlight, smiling for the sheer joy of having the sun on her face, and all the while oblivious to the extraordinary reaction she is generating.

Even then, her teeth seem whiter than any teeth that I have ever seen before; lightly-tanned skin that sets off her scarlet lipstick to perfection and that wave of brown hair. She wears a creamy cotton skirt, white shirt and a cream jacket, and carries a small leather attaché case. A total vision of loveliness in a pool of murk.

It's like a physical blow to the stomach. She's winded me. She is the most perfect woman I have ever seen. Of all the fantasy girls that I had raked over in the glossy magazines and lusted after on screen, there is not a single one that could hold a candle to the woman standing in front of me.

I am devouring her with my eyes, searing every detail and every nuance into my memory banks so that, even if I never seen her again, I will always be able to recall that one sublime moment.

She stands on the School Hall steps for just one second, two, and briefly surveys the scrum of schoolboys at her feet. With one click of her fingers she could have had us do anything she pleased.

However, she seemed to have this innocence; a lack of awareness of the effect she was having on the boys before her; a Queen Bee that imagines herself one of the drones.

She flicks her head back, hair streaming behind her, and flits down and disappears into a morass of blackness. I watch her path through the parting tailcoats.

I stare and I stare, wanting to snatch up every moment of this awesome being. When I'm finally quite certain she has gone, I turn back and become aware that other boys are starting to talk again.

Frankie raises an elliptical eyebrow. It means everything and nothing. Jeremy slips his arm through mine and we slope off. I am in a daze, unmasted and unmanned. But there is one sour spot in a moment of unalloyed joy.

Savage makes a point of coming over to us.

"Have a pound in my room by lock-up, the pair of you."

"Are you fining us, Savage?" Jeremy says.

"Make it two pounds each."

"On what grounds?"

"Having a stiffy in public," Savage says. "School rules expressly forbid out-of-house erections." He guffawed, the F-tits scattering as he strides through them.

I can think of nothing to say. Savage's remarks seem unsavoury, like a blunt scratch on a perfect record.

For at that time, the thought of sex together with this woman had not occurred to me. She was so unattainable that the very concept of sex had not registered on the horizon.

"Jerk," Jeremy says, steering me through the boys. "What a total jerk."

We have a couple more lessons, or divisions, before lunch – humdrum English and even more humdrum Economics – but not a word sinks in. My mind is on holiday, time and again running over the memory of that woman on the step, her smile and hair toss before she melted into the blackwash of tailcoats.

For three days, I hugged the memory to myself. It was my talisman, my default mechanism. If ever I were daydreaming, up she would pop, standing there in the sunlight. (Although Savage would crop up too; how I came to loathe him for besmirching my perfect memory.)

Nowadays I am more proactive. Nowadays, if I had suffered the *coup de foudre* that hit me outside the School Hall, I would have done something about it. Definitely. Anything at all, rather than just sit passively to await the turn of events. I would have discovered her name. I might have turned up for a few more 11am sessions at the Burning Bush. I might have engineered some kind of casual meeting.

There are many things that, older and wiser, I might have done to effect a meeting so we could have got onto first name terms. But back then, aged 17, the idea of actually doing anything about this woman and of getting to know her better...well, it was as absurd as the notion of me building a space rocket for a trip to the moon.

Absurd.

Ludicrous.

Beyond farcical.

But sometimes, you know, fate likes to lend a hand.

My life has been blessed in so many ways. The best education money can buy; great friends; extraordinary adventures; lucky breaks aplenty.

Yes, a lot of good stuff has come my way.

Some of these things I made happen and some were just down to good fortune. But what happened to me that Monday was the most outrageous, the most remarkable lucky break of my entire life. And it all stemmed from the fact that in those days I was a very modest piano player.

When I was aged ten, my grandmother had died and left me her piano. I'd started to have lessons, but I was not in any way, shape or form a natural piano-player.

By the time I was 17, I'd been having lessons for seven years and I had even notched up a Grade Five music exam. But, like all my other endeavours at Eton, my musical skills were outstandingly indifferent. The school was awash with scores of music scholars and I was not of their number. No, I was one of the musical flotsam that drifted on the surface of Eton's music scene, botching away on one lesson a week.

That wasn't to say I didn't have a few party pieces, some tinkling little numbers with which to entertain the troops – Scott Joplin had always been a favourite and I knew about five of his rags off by heart; Beethoven's Moonlight sonata, without the tricky bits; a brace of Chopin waltzes, along with smatterings of Schubert and Mozart. The selection was not exactly mind-blowing, but to the uninitiated (i.e. someone who had never played a note) they could come across as mildly impressive.

After Grade Five, I'd given up taking the exams but I was still plugging away with lessons. I have no idea why. Maybe because it was all part of my weekly school routine; or maybe because I didn't totally object to the drudgery of practice; or just maybe because it had always been my destiny to be having piano lessons that particular summer.

Each week at Eton, I had a few free periods that were ostensibly for study. It was during these times that I had to arrange my piano lessons.

My first lesson of the term had been fixed for noon that Monday and I was edgy. Not because of my general lack of practice, but because I was due to meet my new teacher.

My teacher for the previous four years, Mr Bowen, had quit the school at short notice, and for the summer term I was to be foisted onto some other member of the music staff.

I didn't know who was going to be teaching me but I did know that I was going to be put through my paces – scales, arpeggios, party pieces – so that the new teacher could size up the raw materials on offer.

Another epoch-making event in my life. Click my fingers and I am there.

My house is the Timbralls, though at Eton the houses are known not by their names but by the tutor's initials – in my case 'FF', for Francis Frederickson. The house is just 200 yards from the School Hall and overlooks a great swathe of playing fields called Sixpenny – the fields, according to Wellington, where Waterloo was won. The Timbralls had only one claim to fame, that the creator of James Bond, Ian Fleming, was there as a boy. The entire 007 collection is in the house library and I have read every one of the Bond books several times over.

The Music Schools are a good ten-minute walk away. Out of the house and into Cannon Yard, then past the captured Sebastopol cannon that a grateful old boy, General Peel, had given to the school in 1867. I gave it a lucky slap and made a wish. Past the Burning Bush and right at the lights onto Keate's Lane, named after Dr Keate, the greatest flogger in Eton's history. Keep heading straight and the Music Schools are just opposite the lower boys' chapel. I have made that walk so many times I could still do it in my sleep.

It is another sunny day but now it is more than hot, it is scorching. Not a trace of wind in the air and the sweat seems to bubble off me. I walk past some builders who are dressed in shorts and t-shirts. The absurd juxtaposition of clothing is laughable – for like all the other boys I am wrapped in the worst conceivable clothes for a blazing summer's day. But you get used to it, get used to sweating and stinking throughout the summer, just like you get used to all the other mild annoyances that are forced on you at school.

By the time I reach the music rooms, the sweat is dripping off me and my skin is marinating in an oily slick. I can feel my shirt wet under my thick black waistcoat and my cuffs grimy against my wrists.

The Music School is pleasantly cool and dark, a haven after the noon sun. High ceilings, lino floors and scuffed walls, though the smell is just as it is in all the school buildings: the teenage whiff of sweat and pulsing pheromones.

A look at the noticeboard to see who will be my piano-teacher for the term – a Mr James in room 17.

Up the stairs, slicking my wet fringe off my forehead, and down a dark corridor on the top floor. On either side are a dozen boxy practice rooms with a piano in each. The doors all have a small window at head height, and as I walk I can hear snippets of music – a Beethoven piano sonata, a raucous guitar, some scraped scales on a violin.

Room 17 is at the end of the corridor on the left. I can hear a piano being played, being played with an extreme competence I will never possess. I can hear measured trills and a delicate touch.

I don't know the music, but the style is familiar. It could be Bach. But it's warm and much more graceful than the mathematical compositions I normally associate with Johann Sebastian. I am charmed.

For a moment I linger outside the room, slowly perspiring in the still air. The music comes to a gentle end and then there is silence.

I tap at the door and, without waiting for an answer, walk in.

I am dumbstruck.

It's her, the woman from the School Hall three days ago, sitting at the piano not two yards in front of me. Hands lightly on her lap, she looks at me, looks me straight in the eye, and gives me quite the loveliest smile I have ever seen, starting at the edges and turning into a full 1,000-watt beam.

I hover in the doorway, my hands clutching at my cardboard file, and, although my brain is spinning at the speed of light, I can think of nothing sensible to say.

"You must be Kim." She stands up, puts out her hand. "India James. Do call me India."

India. I had never come across the name before. It is both exotic and lyrical. A name to match its owner.

I shuffle my cardboard file. My fingers are so sweaty that they feel greased. For a second, I think about wiping my hand on my trousers, but I stop myself. We shake hands briefly. The touch of her warm skin is electric. White heat.

"How do you do," I say, as some semblance of formal etiquette kicks in. New sensations are still exploding in my brain; I take in her clothes, a flowing floral dress and dainty brown sandals; and the scent, a smell that I will forever associate with heaven on earth – lily-of-the-valley; and those hazel eyes with black as black eyelashes; and her moist scarlet lips; and that mane of brown hair which looks even more perfect than the first time I saw her.

I am all too aware of myself, of the stinking tailcoat that I'm wearing and my drenched shirt. I'm not fit to be in the same room as her.

She slips over to a grubby armchair in the corner of the room.

She's still smiling; in fact, the smile has never left her lips, as if she's delighted to see me. Can this possibly be happening? It feels like an out-of-body experience.

She gestures to the bench-like piano stool. At this stage, I still can't bring myself to think of her even as India. She is far too exotic to be human and to have a name. She is just 'She' – at that moment, without a doubt, the most astounding, the most extraordinary thing ever to enter my life.

I carefully place my tatty file onto the piano, take a seat, and look at her. All is silence, but inside my head a speeding express train is running at full tilt towards a bridgeless chasm; my brain is going through repeated galvanic convulsions, neurones are fizzing and sparking, and all I can do is look dumbly into her face, unable to say a word.

But I finally manage a smile, a shy, nervous smile that says: "Do with me what you will."

India smoothes the pleats in her dress and I catch sight of her ankles. They are slim and tanned, criss-crossed with brown leather laces that loop into a bow.

She speaks again and for the first time I notice her voice. A melodic purr that caresses my ears. At that moment, all I want to do is look at and listen to her for the rest of my life.

"So Kim..." She's said my name again. From her lips it sounds like the most beautiful name in the English language. "Tell me a bit about your music."

Subconsciously I had started wiping the palms of my sweaty hands on my trousers. Disgusting. Abruptly I stop. I am aware of the sweat dripping off me. My tailcoat and waistcoat feel like a straitjacket.

"Would you..." I start. "Would you mind if I took off my coat?"

"Of course," she says. "It's stifling. I'll open the window."

As I hang up my tails, she opens the window. Her slim figure is in silhouette against the green sward of fields behind, the sun shining through the fabric of her cotton dress. I can see the outline of her legs. It's all far too much to take in.

We are seated again, though I don't know how I found the piano stool. I begin to tell her about my musical career to date. I'm trying to be self-deprecating. I can feel her willing me on, but it's all just a pile of beans; it's nothing.

"Sounds great," she says. I'm rewarded with another smile. "Is there anything you'd like to play?"

I leaf through my scraps of music and find a Mozart sonata that I know well. Only that morning I had played it from memory.

I sit at the bench and rest my fingers on the keys. Is she watching me? Are her eyes staring at the black fingermarks on my starched collar?

I begin to play but I can't concentrate. I'm sitting alone in a room with the most beautiful woman I've ever seen – it is far too much for me to be able to play as well. I have lost all physical control of my fingers. They are so oily that they slip on the keyboard. My timing is shot to pieces. It's horrible.

After a minute, I break down. My brain is simply powerless to move my fingers. I sit with shoulders slumped and hands dead in my lap.

However, there's nothing to be done but have another go. It's not as if I have anything to lose. "I'll try it again." I steel myself for another disaster. Before starting, I turn round to look at her.

But she is no longer in the armchair. Silent as a cat, she has moved to stand at the window, staring out over the fields. A perfect picture of beauty, framed by the lime-green paint of the music room walls. "Take your time," she says.

A deep breath. I breathe in, breathe out, and then take my red polka-dot handkerchief to wipe my fingers. For a few seconds I'm able to focus on the piano and forget the goddess who is standing so close. I start to play. Badly and without emotion, like an ill-tuned machine, a score of missed notes along the way. At least I manage to complete this time.

I lift my fingers gently from the keys. My legs tremor with delayed shock against the piano-stool.

"Very nice," she says. "You've got real potential."

In seven years of piano-playing, nobody has ever said that to me before. I blush, the blood coursing into my cheeks and to the tips of my ears. "Thank you."

"So where would you like to go this term?" she says, still standing by the window. "What would you like to do?"

I have not the faintest idea. What I wanted, more than anything else, was an ice-cold shower and time to think. Everything was happening so fast. I was hurtling pell-mell down a toboggan track.

I stare at my shoes and wish I'd bothered to clean them. "Well...," I reply. I look at her again, full in the face. I would do anything for this woman; I can deny her nothing. "I...I quite liked the piece you were playing earlier."

"The Well-Tempered Clavier?"

I might have heard the name before though I couldn't remember it.

"If that's what it's called." I'm about to wipe my hands on my trousers, but again restrain myself.

"My favourite," she says. "Let me play you some."

And at this, she bends down by the side of the piano and picks up a leather music bag. It looks like a slim briefcase. There are no locks or hinges, just a flap that loops over the trim brown handles. She pulls out a half-inch thick volume, *The Well-Tempered Clavier, Books I and II complete*.

She flicks through the pages. "48 preludes, 48 fugues," she says. "They're known as the 48. Something for your every mood."

"And that piece you were just playing?" I still found it difficult to look her in the face; I had the perpetual feeling that I was not worthy.

She claps her hands with delight. "I love that one," she says, skimming the pages to Prelude 17 in A-flat Major, and then, I still cannot comprehend how, I am sitting in her armchair while she is seated at the piano. Playing *The Well-Tempered Clavier*. For me.

I am spellbound, unable to move, barely able to catch a full breath. It is quite the loveliest music I have ever heard.

The prelude sounds like a babbling brook that ripples and spumes down the side of a mountain before slipping into a sheer, smooth lake. Mesmerising is the only word for it.

I am overwhelmed; not just by *The Well-Tempered Clavier,* but by the sight of India's tanned back, the tresses of hair that curl around her shoulders, and her fingers dancing over the keys. She plays effortlessly. It seems like the easiest thing in the world.

All too soon, the prelude comes to an end. "I love that piece," she says. Before I can reply, she is leafing through the music book. "Let me play you some more. Give you a proper taste of *The Well-Tempered Clavier.*"

The notes and trills cascade over my head, prelude after prelude, fugue after fugue. All for me. I can only sit back and marvel. This is so far beyond the realms of my previous experience that my brain seems to glow as it stretches to absorb every detail and every sensory trace that lands on my ears, my eyes and my nose. The wafts of lily-in-the-valley, the far-off whine of a lawn-mower, the soothing calm of lime-green walls, the sight of India absorbed in her music, and *The Well-Tempered Clavier* itself, which has now become so elevated in my mind it borders on the spiritual.

As she finally finishes, she turns on her seat, demure hands in her lap, and smiles with genuine contentment. I have to get a grip, blow my nose, do anything to get rid of the tear in the corner of my eye.

I clap very lightly. "I would so love to play like that."

"Just practice," she says. "Though I guess it helps if you love the music."

By chance, she has a three-page copy of the First Prelude. "Something to get you started," she says, passing it to me as I leave. "My father gave it to me when I was ten-years-old."

She looks at the front cover.

"It still has all my old notes."

What a day, what a day. I can remember saying a clumsy thank you before stumbling into the street and back out into the brilliant sunshine.

It was life-changing. In one hour, I had fallen in love thrice over – with a composer, a piece of music and a pianist who seemed touched by God.

PRELUDE 1, C Major

For a glimpse of Eton at its most formal, I will take you to lunch at the Timbralls.

At 1.10pm, the whole house had to be standing in silence by their chairs in the dining room. It was a handsome room with wide bow windows overlooking Frankie's garden. When the hubbub had died down, Frankie would sweep through to the top table, his long gown flowing behind him. He would then take his place by the window and say a simple grace, *"Benedictus benedicat."*

The 50 boys in the house were sat at five long tables, Frankie was with the seniors, while our Dame, Lucinda – the sole feminine influence in the house – sat with the juniors. I was always stuck with the rabble in the middle.

There were ten boys on my table, boys who through force of circumstance I had come to know better than my own brothers. We were all in the same year, had known each other from the age of 13, and had endured each other's worst adolescent excesses. They were not necessarily my friends, but they were my most intimate acquaintances throughout my time at Eton.

I had other friends from other houses, but these nine other Etonians were the boys with whom I had three meals a day, who helped me out with my extra work and who were the first port-of-call if I were looking for mischief or amusement. They were my allies and my messmates, the thorns in my side and the butts of my jokes. Some of them I liked, some of them I disliked, but there was rarely open warfare. For, like the Argentinian conscripts in the Falklands, we'd been signed-up for a five-year stretch, and we knew that life was generally more pleasant without too much fighting.

Our year was split down the middle between the Swats and the Scallywags. The Swats, keen to make the most of their Eton education, were fizzing with ambition. My more natural home, however, was with the Scallys.

Jeremy, it was no surprise, was also a Scally; then there was Gervase Street, plump and unloved, with sadly the worst acne of any boy at Eton; and Richard Glynn, a sprite, phenomenally gifted at languages and art.

And then there was Archie.

"See that headline in today's *Sun*?" Archie asked. He was wiry, with a pug-dog face and a yapping brisk voice that tended to grate. "'*Stick it up your Junta!*'"

Richard poured some water for the five of us. "Hilarious."

"Two fingers to the peaceniks." Archie wafted his head to the side as an aproned maid placed a plate of stew in front of him. "Bloody Argies."

"But if we had a peace deal, we might not have a war," Richard replied.

"If we have a peace deal, the Argies will have pissed all over us." Archie planted an elbow on the table and shovelled the stew onto his fork. "Wimpy!"

"Nothing like a bit of jingoism to get the country going." Richard leaned to the side for the maid. "Thank you."

"It's not jingoism, it's commonsense," Archie said. "Thatcher didn't have any option."

"Should certainly see her through the next election, if that's what you mean," Richard responded.

"What's the Falklands got to do with a General Election? It's a point of principle." He crossed his eyes, let his mouth go slack. "Duhhhh!"

Richard tapped his fingers together. For a moment he was about to say something but thought better of it. Instead, with a little shake of his head, he tackled the stew.

"It's principle, see?" Archie ploughed on.

Richard buttered some bread, absorbed by the sight of his sliced white.

"Don't you have principles?" Archie said, straining forward over the table. The veins were popping out at the side of his neck. "Run up the white flag, why don't you?"

Richard looked almost like an artist as he precisely spread the butter, working it all the way to the crust.

"Stop being such an oik, Archie," Jeremy said, to put an end to the conversation.

"Me?" Archie replied. "What, me?"

Jeremy raised his eyebrows at me. For a second his eyelids fluttered, no doubt trying to stifle the urge to hurl his food in Archie's face.

Archie spooned up more stew. "All I'm trying to do is have a civilised conversation about the biggest story of the year. Don't you get it? Dontcha?"

"Thank you for explaining that," Jeremy said. He took a pristine white handkerchief from his pocket and patted his lips before turning to me. "I have always thought it our great good fortune that, when we came to Eton, we ended up in the same house as Archie."

"We are blessed," I said.

"He is the daily grit in our lives that helps create the pearl."

"Grit being the operative word."

"Or maybe he is the mortar that helps bind our happy band together. He is our common link."

"Cheers Archie." Jeremy raised his glass. "We'd all be going crazy without you."

Archie watched us, eyes twitching from left to right, not sure how he'd been sidelined.

Jeremy scrutinised me and for the first time noticed the dizzy, goof smile on my face. I'd been miles away.

"Something's happened to you this morning," Jeremy said quietly. "You look rather happy."

I could only smirk, hugging my glorious memories close; for to have said anything about India at lunch would have been as if to have announced it over the public tannoy.

I raised my finger to my lips. "Later," I whispered.

All Eton's boys have separate rooms, and mine, on the top floor of the Timbralls, had one of the best views in the school, overlooking Sixpenny and in the distance another tranche of playing fields, Mesopotamia.

The room was a good size for a 17-year-old, with a shabby sofa, armchair, bookshelves and desk, or burry as it was known at Eton. On the walls were a few posters of my fantasy girls: two of Blondie with her pouting strawberry lips, one of Cheryl Tiegs, and another of Farrah Fawcett. I also had a poster of a large white Labrador. Before women came into my life, dogs had been my first love.

I kicked off my shoes, hung up my tailcoat and lay down on the bed to give myself a few moments of beautiful reverie. Over and over again, I was re-running what had occurred in the Music Schools. I was trying to digest the huge wealth of raw unedited material that had showered my senses. Different pictures of India kept flashing into my head.

I was distracted by the rumbling sound of a boy-call. It started off very low and went up at the end, "BoooyyyUppp", like a farmer calling his cattle.

For a second my limbs stiffened. It was an involuntary twitch, a hangover from the days when I too had been a fag, running errand after errand for the senior boys, the members of the library.

The boy-calls were as good a way as any to knock any hint of preciousness out of the new boys' heads. If ever a Librarian needed a job doing, he would stand at the top of the stairs and bellow "BoooyyyUppp".

Out the fags would come, tumbling from their rooms in various states of undress, all elbows and knees as they tried to gouge their way to the front. They'd stampede up the stairs to line-up outside the library, and the last boy in the queue would be fagged off, or despatched halfway across the school to wherever the Librarian thought fit to send him.

Boy-calls were an incessant part of Eton life, like the deafening jumbo jets that rumbled overhead. You learned to ignore the calls but God they were barbaric.

Jeremy knocked at the door. He came in – as all boys do – without waiting for an answer and flopped down at my burry, his tailcoat scrunching underneath him. He was remarkably cavalier about the general state of his uniform and would think nothing of going out with stained trousers, rumpled tails and shirts begrimed with three-days worth of sweat. Though it wasn't as if any of the fairer sex were ever going to be near us. Not in a million years.

Hands behind his head, back of the chair leaned against the wall, and with his feet propped on my burry, Jeremy looked like a London club-man at ease.

"Is it me," he said, "or are the boy-calls getting louder?"

"I think Savage is using a loud-hailer."

"All the better to hear him with." Jeremy began unbuttoning his waistcoat and, when that was done, he started on his shirt. "Tell all then. What's happened?"

The smile stretched across my face. It was only the best thing ever to have happened to me.

But, even at this early stage, I knew that the information had to be protected.

"This is a secret," I said.

"Of course."

"No, this is a genuine secret," I said. "Promise you won't tell a soul."

"Of course," he said – and I trusted him. (And thank God I did. But more of that later.)

"Well..." I delicately toyed with the bomb in my hands, wondering how to deploy it with maximum effect. "Do you remember the woman in white we saw outside School Hall last Friday?"

"Comely," he said. "Delectable."

"You're right," I continued, staring at the ceiling to dream of her face. "I met her today."

"You have all the luck." He took off his round wire-rim glasses, breathed on them and then polished them with the hem of his shirt.

I laid out my cards one by one. "We shook hands; she introduced herself. It was very formal."

"So what's her name?"

"India James."

He looked out of the window, but said nothing, giving me my head.

"She played the piano for me." I templed my fingers before delivering the *coup de grace*. "She's going to see me again next week."

"She's your new piano teacher?"

"Correct."

He laughed, clapping his hands to his face. "*Fouquet in Le Touquet!*"

"Lucked out." I coolly blew on my cupped fingernails before buffing them on my waistcoat.

Jeremy chuckled to himself as he absorbed the news. "Savage will be green as beans when he finds out."

"I hadn't thought of that," I said. "An added bonus. Bet he wished he'd taken up the piano rather than his lousy guitar. He'll be gutted."

And so, with all the precision of a clairvoyant, I had unwittingly spelled out the precise turn of events over the next two months.

How different my life might have been if it had not been for Charles Savage-Leng. But maybe, even without Savage's help, I had always been destined to be with India – and always destined to part.

Jeremy stretched to turn the desk-light on, and off, and on and off, and on and off, and will she and won't she, until the light bulb started to flicker and spark. "Well, it will certainly get you practising, won't it? We won't be able to keep you off the piano."

And he was right about that too.

The Timbralls had a piano in the dining room. It was nothing fancy but adequate to lead the way for the hymns at evening prayers.

During the previous four years, I'd practised about twice a week, putting in at best a half-hour session before the next day's lesson.

But that Monday afternoon, my head still spinning with a jumble of snap-shots of India, I played for a full two hours. I'd never done anything like it in my life.

I started with a few scales and arpeggios, four octaves each, just to limber up. My fingers had by now stopped trembling.

Only then did I allow myself to look at the sheet music. India's music, which she had held in her own hands, and which she had owned since childhood.

All afternoon I'd been twitching to have a look. But I'd saved it up, delaying the moment, knowing the wait would make it all the sweeter.

First I studied the cover, in red and black Gothic script, which showed that the music was a classic. *J.S.Bach, The Well-Tempered Clavier, Book 1, Prelude 1, C Major*. Underneath were the words from Bach's original folio:

'The Well-Tempered Clavier,
Or
Preludes and fugues in all tones and semitones,
in the major as well as the minor modes,
for the benefit and use
of musical youth desirous of knowledge
as well as those who are already advanced in this study.

For their especial diversion, composed and prepared by
Johann Sebastian Bach,
currently Ducal Chapelmaster in Anhalt Cothen
and Director of Chamber Music,
in the year 1722.'

In the top right corner, written in faded pencil, was her name. India James. I touched the lettering, imagining how she'd been as a ten-year-old.

I then turned to the first page. The music was strewn with pencil jottings and several hand-written numbers under the notes. These numbers would have helped India learn the correct fingering – and now, just over a decade later, they'd be showing me the way. Note for note, India and I would be learning the First Prelude together.

On the next two pages were some more pencilled numbers and, at the end, just the one word 'Knock-out!' I liked that.

The back-page had no music, but a short history of Bach and *The Well-Tempered Clavier*.

I devoured it, can still remember it almost verbatim. I was sharing a musical Communion with India.

There are several theories about why Bach wrote his two books of Preludes and Fugues. Some say it's an encyclopedic compilation of every possible type of fugue. Others believe it's Bach's celebration of the better-tuned Claviers that were just being introduced in the early 18th Century.

As for the word Fugue, it derives from the Latin '*fugo*', which means 'flee' or 'chase', and, when you listen to the pieces, that's what they often sound like, one hand imitating the other, hunting it down.

Only when I had committed every detail to memory did I start to study the music itself. The notes were well-spaced, which made them easier to read and, better still, it was in the key of C Major. No black notes.

To explain, piano pieces come in 24 different keys, and these keys vary in difficulty. One of the most difficult is B Minor, which has five flats. The easiest by far is C Major, with not a single sharp or flat in the entire octave. For mediocre players like myself, finding that a piece is in C Major is like seeing a bright-green 'Go' light; it means all the sharps and flats will be flagged up along the way and there will be no hidden bogeys.

That isn't to say that a piece in C Major can't be wretchedly complicated, though when I started to study the First Prelude it didn't look too difficult. I hesitate to use the word easy, but it was eminently do-able.

For that and that reason alone, it remains one of my favourite preludes in *The Well-Tempered Clavier*; in fact, second only to Prelude 17, the first piece that India played for me.

The First Prelude was also a delightful introduction to Bach. It was a piece of music that I could tackle with a fair degree of confidence. Only later would I discover that *The Well-Tempered Clavier* contains many, many fugues and preludes that would tax even a concert pianist.

And the melody of that first prelude?

It was sublime. Today you can hear it on any number of radio adverts; Schubert used the tune for his *Ave Maria*.

Just like it says on the cover it is, above all, an even, well-tempered piece, each note carrying the same weight and each bar just slightly different from the one before it. Of all the pieces that I've ever known by heart, it remains the only one that I can still play from memory.

The normal routine when you start to learn a piece is to begin with the right hand (usually with the melody), then practise the left hand (with the beat), and only then do you put the two together.

But, like everything else in my life, I am incapable of any such discipline; always I dive in with both hands together, a bundle of impatience, optimistically expecting that everything will work out just fine.

The surprising thing was that, on this occasion, it did. Maybe India's spirit was standing over me as I plonked away in the Timbralls dining room, but, right from the start, the First Prelude was sounding quite similar to how I imagine Johann Sebastian would have first intended. There were admittedly a few fluffed notes but, although I was only going at half-speed, I found I could keep up a steady rhythm.

The great beauty of the Prelude for an amateur is that, until the final chord, the right hand and the left hand never have to play a note at the same time. Above all, it's a very tranquil piece.

Within 30 minutes, I was smitten. I loved its simplicity.

I was also aware of its intimate connection with India. Like me,

she'd started her *Well-Tempered* career on the First Prelude. She'd
have used the same fingering to play the same notes, would have
practised the same teasingly tricky bars over and over again, and
would have spent a good hour honing the splendid ending.

At times, I was so absorbed with the music that I would forget
all about India.

Then something would gun my memory and I would savour
the marvellous, the monstrous, events of that afternoon. There
were some things, like my greasy hands and my foetid tailcoat,
which made me cringe. But for the most part I basked in my
memories, sunning myself with the recollection of dappled arms
flowing over the keyboard.

Supper, homework, bed at 10.30pm and, when I clicked the
light off, I allowed myself for the first time to dream. To fantasize.

But they were chaste thoughts with nothing overtly sexual.
With clothes staying on and hands remaining dormant in laps.

Nothing could ever come of it I reminded myself – I would
never be anything more to India than another of her gawky pupils.

But, nevertheless, with lips pursed together I blew her a kiss.

The morning alarm rang at 7am and, the moment I woke, I was
aware there was something different about the day, that something
golden had come into my life. Then I remembered; I remembered
India, and in an instant I was skimming through all my memories
once more, which were just as fresh as the moment they were first
minted.

There was no time for dawdling. In the summer, Eton likes to
give its boys a flying start to the day with a division that starts at
7.30am. I had my routine down pat. To have a lightning shave,
brush my teeth and don my uniform took 15 minutes.

The starched collar can be a beast for the junior boys when they
still haven't got the hang of popping the gold stud through the
tight eyelet. But after four years I could do it blindfolded, and
could slot home the short stumpy white tie in two seconds flat.
The first time I wore a starched collar, it almost felt like a shackle.
Its edge chaffed against my skin and the front stud pressed tight

into my neck.

But, like everything else at Eton, you get used to it, and are even left bemused when a gaggle of tourists start hosing you down with their cameras. After just a short while at the school, both the boys and the masters forget what an extraordinary spectacle they present to the rest of the world.

I grab the books and file that I need for the first division, and shrug on my waistcoat and tailcoat in one, doing up the buttons single-handed as I trot down the corridor. To us, the tailcoats were nothing more nor less than a school uniform. Eton's schoolboys had been strapped into this weird garb when they'd gone into mourning at the death of King George III and, so the story goes, some 160 years later they were still mourning the death of Farmer George. I suppose we should have counted our blessings – at least we no longer had to wear top hats.

Cufflinks are also inserted while on the hoof and when I've hit the hall there's time for one quick swill of tea before I'm out of the front door.

Boys have to look the part when they're out of the house, otherwise monsters like Savage take great pleasure in fining them, or administering any number of tedious punishments. Shoes need to be polished black and laces tied; waistcoats must be buttoned, except for the last button which must remain undone (a hang-over from George IV, Georgie Porgie, who was apparently so fat that he couldn't fully do up his waistcoat); the tailcoat has a button, but this is merely for show and must never be used; cuffs must be cuffed; ties correctly tied; socks in keeping with the general assemblage; and hair kempt, well-groomed, undyed, and neither too short, too long, or too *outré*. It goes without saying that all senior boys had to shave.

My early morning lesson was Economics, which, along with Divinity and English, was one of the three A-levels that I was due to sit the next summer. However you slice it, Economics is never going to be a subject that makes your spirits soar.

But, that week, and that term, all my A-level subjects began to strike the most unexpected chords with my personal life.

That particular morning, for instance, we were being told about the celebrated law of supply and demand. And, as it happened, we had a prime example on our doorstep: when the supply of girls is minimal and the number of boy buyers is vast, then demand will go into orbit.

There would also be a strange synchronicity with my Divinity coursework, but most eerie by far would turn out to be the uncanny connection with my English classes. For the play we were studying that term, and the play that fate had decided to mock me with, was none other than Shakespeare's *Othello*.

Now, I find the spectacular irony of it almost laughable.

Twenty-five years back, it was a very different story.

The Economics division ended at 8.20am and it was back to the Timbralls for breakfast. Whenever I entered the house, I would automatically scan the pigeon-holes to see if there was any post for me and, for the first time that term, there were some letters.

One was a plain white card from my father with a second-class stamp. Tiny black writing, clipped and precise, it was a match for the terse army orders that he used to issue. It read: 'I have found that you snapped the stylus of my record player. Your allowance has been docked accordingly. In future, I'd be grateful if you could inform me of any breakages. D.'

Charming. I had indeed neglected to tell him that I'd smashed his rotten little stylus. But there are ways and other ways of reacting to your son and heir smashing a piece of your property.

However, my father was forever incapable of making the stretch from treating me like a junior subaltern to treating me like a son. I was inured to it all. But I still hoped that one day he might be able to unbend enough to sign one of his curt postcards with the word 'Love'.

There was also a second letter, which was expensive blue and altogether more interesting. As I studied it, my heart gave a twitch. A round girlish hand, written in brown ink, and when I put it to my nose I could scent a trace of lavender. On the back, there was the outline of pink lips and the letters 'SWALK'.

I didn't know the writing. But I knew who'd sent it.

Thrilling. In an instant, all trace of my father had gone from my mind.

I raced upstairs and only when I was in the privacy of my room did I open the envelope – not with my finger, but slitting the edge with a pocket-knife.

My hands were shaking. At first I scanned it, eager to find out if I was still in favour or whether I had been supplanted by some other schoolboy love.

But after a few seconds I could relax. The first words, 'My dearest darling Kim', and the close, 'With ooooodles of love', gave me the reassurance I needed.

Taking my time now, I started to read the letter again, soaking up each word, each nuance. I read it once, reached the end and went straight back to the beginning to read it a third, then a fourth time.

She'd written, just as she'd said she would. She was more than up for continuing our fledgling relationship via the Royal Mail. And, when next we met, it seemed there would be more kisses and more hugs. There were even dark hints as to the possibility of...other stuff.

Estelle.

It is true that at the age of 17, I could fancy any teenage girl that came within ten yards of me. Just being in close proximity to a girl could make me shiver with delight.

Not that I knew what to say to them, or how to behave when with them, for that was one area where my Eton education had sadly let me down. But, although their presence turned me into a clueless geek, I loved girls. Any girls.

This said, Estelle was not just any girl. She was 17-years-old and gorgeous, long brown hair in a ponytail, flawless creamy skin, and a trim, perfectly endowed body that had left my eyes on stalks the first time I saw her in a swimming costume on the beach in Cornwall.

The previous month, our families had been staying at the same Cornish hotel. I had spent two days gawking at her from afar, before one morning she'd taken pity on me and started to chat. I blossomed. On the last night, at the hotel disco, we had kissed in the corner. It was my formal introduction to girls and the many delights they had to offer.

Estelle had promised to write, but it was by no means a done deal.

So when I read that letter and realised she'd come good, I was euphoric.

Then and there I replied, returning all her hugs and kisses tenfold, and sowing the seeds for our future together. But I didn't declare my undying love. I didn't want to slay my golden goose.

It was the first time I'd ever sealed a letter with a loving kiss and I posted it after I'd snatched a couple of slices of toast for breakfast.

Estelle! I was a fizzing bottle of champagne, ready to explode with joy.

I know that my attitude may seem fickle; that one moment I should be putting India on a pedestal and blowing her night-time kisses and the next I am fawning after my holiday romance. But that's boys for you, and not all of them grow out of it.

Like almost every other straight 17-year-old boy in the country, I was obsessed with the idea of women in general and girls in particular. I could effortlessly transfer my allegiance from one to the other and back again without a moment's hesitation. My brain was like a fat bumblebee, buzzing from one flower to the next in a perpetual quest for more honey.

Besides, India – stunning, elegant India – could never be anything other than an idle fantasy. Estelle, for her part, almost qualified as a girlfriend. We had kissed and she appeared to be eager for more.

That was the realistic view but there were also certain practicalities to be taken into account, the main one being that Estelle was stuck miles away at Cheltenham Ladies' College. Although her letters might offer me some crumbs of comfort, she was out-of-sight, and therefore usually out-of-mind. Conversely, it was India who was on my doorstep; it was India who, day in, day out, would be stalking through my dreams, plucking at my heart-strings, and firing my soul.

That morning I had a Divinity class, and, like the earlier Economics lesson, it resonated. It made sense. Or more accurately, I made it make sense for the peculiar world that I lived in.

Not that I appreciated it then, but the schoolroom where I was taught Divinity has a quite staggering history. It sounds unbelievable to think of it now, but it really is the world's oldest schoolroom. It is called Lower School and it is in the very heart of the college, just adjoining the schoolyard. Thick wooden beams, long black desks and benches, and two rows of oak pillars, all of it more than five centuries old. Outside, through the small diamond windows, you can just make out the statue of Eton's founder, Henry VI, and, behind him, the enormous buttresses of the upper chapel where the game of Fives was invented.

Lower School came in the colours of black, brown and grey, and the desks were thick with carved graffiti and the names of generation after generation of other bored Etonians. I remember the dust, how it spangled in the stagnant air.

Nowadays, the sheer weight of the room's history seems magnificent. I would love to be back there, back in that dusty, dark room with the ghosts of Wellington, Shelley, George Orwell and Aldous Huxley.

But back then – as with so much of Eton's incredible history – the fact that I was being taught Divinity in the world's oldest classroom barely even registered. At the time, I was far too pre-occupied with India and Estelle.

There were about five boys in the class and our teacher that day was one of Eton's resident priests, Giles Swann. Our subject: St Paul's letter to the Romans.

Now, as it happens, the entire Reformation and the breakaway from the Catholic Church stemmed from St. Paul's epistles. In particular, there was one 16-word text in *Romans* that turned more than a thousand years of Christian theology on its head.

The words themselves seem bland in the extreme. But when

Martin Luther first re-interpreted them, they sparked off an explosion that was felt – and continues to be felt – throughout the Christian world.

This is what St. Paul wrote: 'That through faith alone you shall be justified in the eyes of our Lord Jesus Christ'. Nowadays it is known as 'justification by faith' and for millions of Christians it meant they could abandon the Catholics' predilection for sin and confession. Luther had discovered a much simpler route to Heaven – that since we are all unworthy, faith alone was enough to merit God's love.

The moment of Martin Luther's revelation is known as his 'Tower Experience'. He suffered from chronic constipation and while he was on the lavatory would pore through his Bible. It was here, in the tower, where he had his revelation with *Romans 5*. (Catholics, naturally, say that Luther mistook the moment of physical release for a numinous experience.)

My Tower Experience came in Lower School. My Epiphany was equally blinding.

When I made the connection, it was like a thousand flashbulbs exploding in my head at the same time – Justification through practice.

I, too, was unworthy. But, through practice alone, I could earn India's favour.

Through practice, I could win her esteem.

It sounds crazy. But in that moment it chimed.

The way forward had been revealed to me, and it was to be down the serene path of *The Well-Tempered Clavier.*

Then and there I made a commitment.

I was going to practise till my knuckles ached and my fingertips were red-raw.

And, for a short while, I did.

One of the great joys of Eton in the summer is the huge expanse of afternoons the boys have to themselves. For four days a week, they have a clear five hours to swim, to play games, to do whatever whim took them. The hijinks only ended when they had to be back in their houses at 7pm in time for roll-call, or Absence.

The junior boys had a number of formal sports sessions laid on, cricket for the dry bobs and rowing for the wet bobs. But I had never taken to team sports. I preferred tennis, or a quick round on Eton's nine-hole golf course. Or, ideally, I preferred frittering my afternoons away in a haze of wanton idleness.

That afternoon I chose to spend in the Music Schools. Partly, I suppose, because there was an ever-so-slight chance that I might catch a glimpse of India. But there also happened to be a couple of practice rooms that had Steinway grand pianos, the genuine article, tuned to perfection. Arrive soon after lunch and even a rank amateur like myself could get to play on a Steinway.

Since there are no more lessons, I've changed into jeans and t-shirt. It's spitting with rain. In my hands, clutched tight to my chest, is my file of music and my Holy Grail, the First Prelude. I treat the building with all the reverence of a temple, for it is here that I have come to worship my Goddess. There is not a soul about, not a sound to be heard, and I have my pick of the practice rooms.

It's been a long time since I've played a grand piano. The room is double the size of the other practice rooms, but still comes in the Music School's ubiquitous lime-green. Despite the rain, I open all the windows.

I lift the polished black lid and caress the keys, which once were white but are now yellowing with age. It's a beauty. When I start my scales, the sound fills the room with an explosion of music, so loud that you'd hear it across the street.

From memory, I play that same wretched Mozart sonata that I messed up the previous day. It's note perfect – of course it is, because there is nobody listening to me. I try the sonata again, faster, and my fingers rattle out the trills and the tearing scales.

I'm warmed up, fingers loose and arms relaxed. I place the First Prelude on the stand. My fingers flex and hover over the keys, middle-finger of my left hand ready to strike the first note, middle C. I start slowly, sticking religiously to India's fingering. The ending goes awry, so I try it five more times before I have it perfected. Then I'm away, playing the First Prelude for the first time in its entirety. I dab at the damper pedal; it sounds better if you let the notes run into each other.

It is more beautiful, by far, than anything I could have hoped for.

And then from nowhere, a sudden distinct prickling at the back of my neck. I am not alone.

A light knock at the door, the handle turns, and my heart lurches into my throat. It's her, India, looking lovelier than ever. The reaction is every bit as severe as it was yesterday when first I met her. I'm paralysed.

India is not just smiling, she is openly laughing. As she walks into the room, she is clapping. All I can do is stare like a drooling village idiot – but how else could I react when I am being lauded like this?

She stands at the end of the piano, fingertips light on the lid, and looks at me with this dancing smile on her lips. Her hair is glistening from the rain. I'm melting inside, my heart and brains turning to mush.

"You play much better without me," she says, and again starts laughing.

It's yesterday all over again. India has rendered me into an inarticulate, grunting oaf. "Well...thanks."

"You must have been practising for hours."

There are so many things I could say, but all I can do is stare at my knees. "Er...yeah."

She walks round the piano and looks at the music on the stand. She's standing not three feet from me. I can smell her lily-of-the-valley. Lift my arm and I could touch her.

She looks at the First Prelude. "Strange to see this in front of you," she says. "No one's ever played this sheet music but me."

"I love it," I say. A bit crass, a little clunky.

Out of the side of my eye, I can see she's wearing brown trousers, a cream shirt and a lightweight creamy mac, speckled with rain and cinched at the waist.

She's gliding back to the door now. "Better get that order in for the complete *Well-Tempered Clavier*," she says, hand on the door-handle. "Wouldn't want you twiddling your thumbs next Monday."

Now that she's almost gone, I can feel myself relaxing. It's as if she needs a four-yard exclusion zone around her – any closer and I start to burn up inside. "Thank you," I say, and a question occurs to me. "How did you know I was here?"

She laughs again. How I came to love that laugh. It lit up her eyes and made her hair dance.

"I could hear you out on the street," she says. "It was lovely."

And with a wave she is gone and I sit there in stupefied silence, my mind reeling from the onslaught of the previous five minutes. I chew my thumbnail, still not comprehending what exactly has happened. My Goddess not only heard me on the street, but found me out, praised me, laughed with me.

And there had been one other thing that she'd done when she was in the room.

Just a small thing, hardly anything at all, but even at the age of 17 I was aware that her action was maybe, just maybe, charged with a bat squeak of sexual chemistry.

As she'd stood at the piano, she had frouffed up her hair, sweeping it from one side to the other. It wasn't a come-on. It definitely wasn't flirting. But it would have been described by an anthropologist as a 'preening gesture'. These are not necessarily sexual, but, like my favourite key in C Major, they are a green light for 'Go'. It is usually a woman saying without a word that she would not mind seeing more of you.

PRELUDE 2, C Minor

When I wrote that there were 1,238 boys in the school and not a girl in sight, I was not being strictly accurate.

There were two girls at Eton: both masters' daughters, both in my year and both, by yet another outstanding piece of good fortune, in my English class.

Angela was my personal favourite, with her short tartan dresses and boyish Eton crop. She had a long fringe of brown hair that she used as camouflage so she could surreptitiously inspect the 20 or so boys in the room. I knew this because the class was sat in a horse-shoe shape around Anthony McArdle's desk and for two terms I had been sitting directly opposite her. We rarely spoke, as there were many other boys in the class who were more overtly desperate for her attention. But occasionally we would catch each other's eye, at which I would always be the first to avert my besotted gaze.

As for Marie, she was a blonde, an enthusiastic darling with wavy hair. She, too, had realised there was much to be gained from wearing mini-skirts and sheer stockings. Although Marie and I talked much more than ever I spoke with Angela, she always sat two seats to the side of me, which meant I never had the opportunity to survey her body in the same minute way that I could with Angela.

Before Estelle, and long before India, Angela had been my real-life fantasy girl of choice.

As the beak droned on about Gerard Manley Hopkins ('No worse there is none, pitched past pitch of grief...'), Shelley ('Hail

41

to thee blithe spirit, bird thou never wert…'), and Byron, ('The Assyrians came down like a wolf on the fold, their helmets all gleaming...'), I would while away my time imagining the caressing of Angela's hand and the peppering of her cheeks with kisses. If Marie had sat opposite me, I'm sure I would have been doing the same for her too. But, as it was, it was Angela who was in my line of sight and it was Angela to whom, a thousand times over, I had mentally plighted my troth.

McArdle's English classes were actually much more light-hearted and convivial than most. There was a bit of banter and a lot of clowning, largely for the benefit of Angela and Marie. But banter had never really been my forte at Eton.

Now I can clown and joke with the best of them, repartee my speciality. At Eton, however, it is difficult to shine. Boys quickly become content with their own mediocrity and then, after they've left, come to the delightful realisation that life is so much easier when they're not having to compete against more than a thousand cocksure charmers.

As I've already mentioned, that summer term we were studying Shakespeare's *Othello*. We'd read the play over the weekend, and now McArdle was taking a backseat to let the boys do the talking.

Just to recall, the story is of Othello the Moor, a senior commander in Venice who has just married the beautiful Desdemona. But Othello has a lieutenant, Iago, who at every moment is breathing bile and spite into his ear. Somehow, Iago persuades Othello that he's been cuckolded. Othello is consumed by jealousy, 'the green-eyed monster that mocks the meat it feeds upon', and, finally convinced of Desdemona's infidelity, he smothers her with a pillow.

But when we talked of the play that morning, the feeling was that the plot was unbelievable. How could this brilliant man, this leader, be duped into believing that Desdemona had had an affair?

To and fro the argument went, the scholars, or tugs, holding forth with their brilliance. Their words rolled over my head as I gazed in a trance at Angela. I could stare at her for minutes on end, feasting on her girlish loveliness.

She must have known how long I'd been gazing at her, for suddenly she tilted her head up and gave me the most perfect wink. I can still picture it exactly. Mascaraed eyelash flashing down and up. Blink and you would have missed it.

My father had once winked at me across the table during a dinner in the Officers' Mess. But it was the first time I'd ever had one from a girl, not to mention a girl I had spent so long fantasising over. Such a small thing, but it was like she had fired a broadside right at me. I could only stare at my desk as the beetroot blush suffused my cheeks.

Not that Angela and I had exchanged more than 20 words in the previous six months, but that wink had suddenly rocketed my fantasies into a whole new orbit.

I longed for her to do it again though I was too nervous to look.

While these Tectonic Plates were shifting against each other, McArdle had started to speak. He'd given us our head for 15 minutes and was now having his say.

After the shock of the wink, it took time for his words to register. "Jealousy is a strange beast – it makes you do strange things. I don't know if any of you have ever suffered from it." He was walking around now and shrugging to himself. "Maybe you have. Just like the Bard says, it eats you up. Even the most rational, sane people can't think straight."

McArdle stopped pacing and perched himself at the front of his desk. He played with the tip of his Don Juan beard, musing for a moment. "I suppose it's another of those raw emotions like love. You only truly understand jealousy once you've experienced it." He gave a little sigh and squeezed the bridge of his nose. "I know you're sceptical. But it can consume everything in its path."

He twitched, aware of the morbid tone, and flashed his palms up to us. "Guess you'll just have to take my word for it."

I was gazing at Angela again and at this moment she imperceptibly raised her eyebrows and tipped her head to me. I looked to the side and back again. But her meaning, for whatever reason, seemed quite clear to me: 'That's you.'

At the time, McArdle's words meant nothing. But how they would come back to haunt me.

For it was just as he said.

Jealousy is as powerful a motivator as love, possibly more so. It can make you do things, awful things, for which you will forever despise yourself.

And, for a short period, it can even make you believe that the sweetest orchid is nothing but a noxious weed that must be squashed underfoot.

For the rest of the week, I practised the piano as if my life depended on it. I was putting in a minimum of three hours a day, either at the Music Schools or on the piano in the house dining room, and I was just ripping through scales, chromatic scales and the rest. For the first time ever, I could play a B-flat Minor arpeggio without a wrong note. As for some of the easier scales, like D Major and G Major, I could play them with my eyes closed. I was in uncharted territory.

Non-musicians might imagine that scales are nothing but a chore, that it's the music which is the fun. Well, up until a week before, that had also been my opinion. But times had changed and I had taken to scales with a religious zeal. They are the bedrock of any good piano technique. But more than that, I believed scales were the path to India.

I'd hoped to see her again while I was practising in the Music Schools.

But instead of India, it was my *bête noir* that walked through the door.

It was Friday afternoon and I was yet again playing the First Prelude in one of the rooms. I now knew the piece so well that I could play most of it from memory. But, even on its fiftieth time of playing, the prelude made me glow, as if by playing it I was somehow in touch with India.

Suddenly there was a smart rap at the door, not a gentle knock, and in barged not my love but Savage, guitar-case under his arm. He oozed behind me and slumped into the armchair. Without a word, he stretched out his legs and placed his feet on the bottom rung of my chair.

It was unnerving. I felt like a rabbit locked into the Svengali-stare of a cobra.

At 17, a year's age difference is an ocean. But more than that, Savage was in the rowing VIII and my house captain.

And one thing more, he was a popper.

Pop, or the Eton Society as it is formally known, is the powerhouse of the school's discipline. To describe a popper as a mere prefect would be like describing the college's extraordinary tailcoats as just another school uniform.

The poppers were viewed as Gods. The society was self-electing and its members were invariably the most popular boys in the school: the sports stars, the intelligentsia, the ladies' men and the all-round good-guys.

The poppers had many perks: their own set of rooms; the right to grow a beard; the ability, just by their mere presence, to create starry-eyed awe in a junior boy.

And, most important of all, they had the world's most beautiful prefect uniform. Bar none.

Since leaving Eton, I have often thought that the only time a man can truly shine in his clothes is at a smart wedding, when he can deck himself out in tails, fancy waistcoat, button-hole and all. Well, that is what the poppers wore every day of the week, and carried it off with great style and panache.

So that day in the music room, while I was tricked out in Eton's standard black-white ensemble, this is what Savage was wearing: spit-polished black winklepickers with toes so sharp that they ended in a stiletto point, black silk socks, sponge-bag trousers with black-and-white hound's tooth check, a magnificent purple waistcoat with black trim, immaculately laundered white shirt with a starched wing-collar, or stick-ups, and a perfectly symmetrical white bowtie. The edges of his tailcoat were piped with black braid, while in his buttonhole was a gorgeous gardenia.

He was the gilded butterfly to my black-and-white moth.

He still hadn't said a word. He just sat there with his thumbs tucked into his waistcoat pockets and stared at the ceiling. His middle-fingers tapped against his hips.

"Why don't you play for me Kim?"

It was the first time he'd ever used my first name.

"What would you like me to play?"

He stared at me glassily, as if he'd suddenly been made aware of my presence. "Why don't we try that little piece that you have been practising so assiduously this past week?"

I started to play, but Savage's presence turned the prelude into a dirge.

"That's enough, thank you," Savage said, his voice silky. "Tell me Kim, do you know of a woman called India James?"

"India who?" I didn't turn a hair.

"India James. She is a new piano teacher here."

"I thought you played the guitar."

He ignored me. "All this week, Kim, I have been wondering why, at all hours, I find you practising here."

I shrugged. "I like the piano."

Savage stood up, and as he walked past he cuffed me round the ear with his guitar case.

"Jesus!"

"Sorry about that." He lingered in the doorway. "So, who is your piano teacher?"

I rubbed the back of my head, working my fingers into the scalp. "Charlie Massey."

The door slammed shut. I was left to dwell on my lack of perception. For while I had spent the past week paying homage to India at the piano keyboard, it had not occurred to me that she would also be featuring in the fantasies of hundreds of other Etonians. Idiot. There wouldn't be a boy in the school that didn't already know of her; know of her, and, like Savage, wish that they knew her better.

I've always loved dogs. They only ever live for the moment, don't give a damn about what happened an hour ago, let alone yesterday.

This is the direct opposite of me. I am perpetually wondering about the past, fingering over the details, wondering about how my life might have changed for the better – or the worse – if just one small thing had been different.

What if, for the sake of example, instead of liking dogs I'd had a distinct aversion to them? For then I might not have become a dog-walker, and might not have injured my hand, and might not have shared a piano-stool, and might not have stolen a kiss…

I would so love to have a glimpse of all those parallel universes, just to find out whether the minute occurrences really do make a difference; or whether, right from the moment we are born, our destinies are already fixed like the constellations in the night-sky.

Hopeless. Spend years fretting over it, and you'll still be none the wiser.

But as it happened, I did like dogs…

The Dame, Lucinda, had broken her leg in the spring. Her little Renault had been hit by a drunk driver and she'd been in hospital for weeks.

She had taken it in her usual stoic fashion and, instead of cursing her ill-luck, had thanked her lucky stars that she hadn't been killed outright.

She did have one regret though; she couldn't get out to exercise her King Charles Spaniel, Rufus.

So for a few months, I and a couple of other boys had been helping Lucinda with the dog-walking. Of a weekend, and sometimes during the week, I'd pop over to her private quarters and take Rufus out for an hour.

That Saturday after lunch, I went up to her suite of rooms. Her lounge was a shrine to her lost suitors – the hundreds of Etonians who had courted and attempted to beguile her for five years at a stretch, and who had then departed Eton, never to write or speak to her again. Every wall was plastered with mementoes and pictures from Lucinda's 30 years at the school. Thirty years of house photos, scores of individual boys' pictures, or leavers, and a vast selection of caps, scarves, plaques, cricket bats, oars and rugby balls.

Rufus was already raring to go, dog-lead in his mouth, tail thumping the floor. Lucinda had her crutches next to her and was easing herself into her armchair.

"It's the dog-walker-in-chief," she said. Lucinda had neat, greying hair and when her face relaxed it fell naturally into a smile. She nosed through a box of chocolates and selected a truffle before handing the box to me. "Take a couple."

"Thank you, Ma'am," I replied. Lucinda was always addressed as 'Ma'am', as if we were talking to the Queen.

I took a caramel for myself and fed a praline to Rufus.

Lucinda slipped off her shoes and put her feet up onto the leather *pouffe*.

"Much better." She sighed and wriggled into the cushions. "Do you know that until my accident, Kim, I never knew you liked dogs."

"We've always had Labs at home." I scratched Rufus under the ear. "When Mum died, Dad went off the deep end. At one stage we had five in the house."

"Five?" Lucinda was incredulous. "That might be too much even for me."

"If they saw a cat, they could tug you off your feet."

"I'm sure." Her fingers trailed over the chocolates before she plumped for a chocolate liqueur.

"Twice-a-day I had to take them out, otherwise they made the house look like a midden."

"So that's why you like dog-walking so much."

"Beats cricket." I attached Rufus's lead.

"Most things do, dear," she said, picking up her pen and cracking open her *Daily Mail* to the crossword page. "Take a few more chocolates before you go."

"Thank you."

"You're very welcome."

I took Rufus to Agar's Plough. He was yapping as if he'd spent the last six months in quarantine.

I let him off the lead and he sniffed round a bramble bush, lying flat on the ground, paws outstretched, peering intently through the leaves. There were a few games of cricket going on. How pleasant it was to be there with Rufus rather than wasting the afternoon chasing balls for other boys.

Suddenly Rufus snarled and lunged, darting into the edge of the bush. I couldn't make out what he had in his mouth but his head shook violently from side-to-side.

"Rufus! Rufus!" I looked more closely. At first I'd thought it was a rat, but then I saw it was a grey squirrel. It made a shrill, keening shriek.

Rufus champed down harder on the squirrel's neck. I grabbed the dog by his choke collar and tried to prise open his jaws, digging my fingertips into his nostrils.

Suddenly Rufus flicked his head and let go. The squirrel flailed in the air and sank its teeth into my thumb. One short, savage nip, before it was on the ground and scurrying to the nearest oak.

My thumb was thick with blood. The first thought to go through my head was, 'Christ, that's going to hurt.'

The next moment the pain kicked in, lancing through my hand – so excruciating, it couldn't have been much worse if I'd had an amputation.

I bound up the wound with my handkerchief, whimpering with the pain. I couldn't believe such a small bite could create such a seismic throb. Rufus meekly tailed behind as I stumbled back to the Timbralls.

Lucinda only needed one look. She gave me a chocolate liqueur to steady my nerves, then, her leg causing her to hobble with pain herself, drove me to the school sanatorium where they sewed me up and gave me a tetanus jab.

By the evening, my thumb had swollen to the size of a fat sausage. So long as I didn't touch it, the pain was a steady dull throb. However, the moment it was pressed in any way, it was as if a blowtorch was scorching over my knuckles.

It meant that for the next couple of days any sort of piano-playing – at least with my left hand – was out of the question.

That said, it certainly wasn't going to stop me from attending my second piano lesson.

I had been looking forward to it so much that I could hardly eat. The anticipation was so intense that it made me feel queasy – although I didn't know what I'd be able to accomplish with one hand out of action.

That Monday morning, my bathroom regime reached a new peak. I showered, shampooed, gelled, shaved, moisturised and layered on enough anti-perspirant to see me through a desert.

How I wished that I could have been a popper so I could have worn an eye-popping waistcoat and sweet-scented flower. I'd have been happy, even, just to have been a 'school officer', which would have allowed me to wear a bowtie.

But I made the best of what I had. My black lace-ups would have done justice to an army officer, my suit Bible black, and my shirt dazzling in its whiteness.

"Very nice," Jeremy said, as I prepared to leave for the Music Schools. "Shame about the thumb."

"It is." I'd applied a fresh white bandage that morning.

"How are you going to play?"

"With difficulty."

I blew him a kiss.

I leave with time to spare and as I amble down Keate's Lane I feel like a young swain on a first date. My skin is prickly, hyper-sensitive, and the blood is surging through my veins. I've never felt so excited, so alive. All at the prospect of a piano lesson.

But what a teacher.

I'm not sweating when I enter the Music Schools, but I'm as skittish as a young colt and would have jumped at my own shadow.

The walk up the stairs has all the solemnity of a pilgrimage and now I am there on the top floor, walking towards my beauty. Already I can hear her playing a prelude.

Three deep breaths, I knock on the door and I'm in. Even though I am fully prepared for the shock, the sight of her still whips the air from my lungs. She is simply that striking. My longing eyes suck her up. If anything, the last week has made her more beautiful. The scent of lily-of-the-valley has already hit me.

She looks up and for a moment pinches her lower lip as she notices my thumb. "What's happened to you then?"

"I was …" I cough. "I was bitten by a squirrel."

"A squirrel?"

"I was trying to rescue it from a dog."

"Ahh." She nods her understanding. "I once tried to break-up two dogs in a fight. You know what happened? I got bitten too. You're better off using your feet."

"I'll remember that."

"Well, I've got a present to cheer you up Kim." She stretches up to her attaché case on the piano. Even when her fingers grip the handle, she has all the grace of a ballerina.

"Thank you."

And out she brings Bach's complete *The Well-Tempered Clavier, Books I and II*, and, for a moment, it feels as if she has given me the golden key to her heart, for with this book I will court her.

"You must be note perfect with the First Prelude by now," she says. "I've heard you practising."

"I'm sorry I won't be able to play it for you today."

"Well, which one do you fancy next? Let me play you a couple."

And so she did, a prelude, a fugue, and then another prelude: Prelude 2 in C Minor.

Like many of Bach's preludes, it seems at first to be an almost mathematical exercise. It takes time to appreciate the tempestuous emotions running beneath its rock facade.

I gaze at India, dazzled by her back, her hair, her dancing fingers. And although I'd thought that I knew her face and hands so well, I notice something new.

She wears a diamond ring on the ring-finger of her right-hand. I stare at the fat solitaire and wonder what it means. Left hand, I know, would mean that she's engaged. But right-hand means what? Does she have a lover, a boyfriend? Did she buy it herself? Or maybe – hopefully – it's an heirloom.

The diamond sparkles in the sunlight as her hands ease over

the keyboard.

How it would come to torment me.

But in a moment all thoughts of the diamond are forgotten because India is standing up and patting the seat for me.

"I think you should try the Second Prelude," she says. "See how you do with the right hand."

The seat is still warm. Before playing a note, I study the piece. The key of C Minor has three flats. I play the scale; I dive in.

With just the right hand, it's not too hard. Just one note at a time and with a steady beat that puts me in mind of a ticking clock. I'm going slowly but until the last few bars there aren't many wrong notes.

"Very good," she says, and I tingle as she moves behind me. "Let's try it together."

I gape in bewilderment. In all my years of the piano, never have I done anything like this before.

She laughs at my ignorance. "Budge up."

And, as I move to the side of the piano stool, the air is being sucked from the room. India is sitting inches away from me, her white skirt in stunning contrast to my black trousers.

I can feel the warmth pulsating through her blouse and, as for her scent, it seems to engulf me. I am so aware of her proximity that my skin is on a hair-trigger. Just the slightest touch of her hair on my coat sends a pulse of electricity through my body.

"Ready?" she says. And always that smile, which I'm seeing up close for the first time.

It is all I can do to keep up with her, concentrating savagely on the music, not wanting to put a finger wrong, yet somehow trying to block off the rest of my senses, and the fact that sitting next to this woman, this Goddess, is about to short-circuit my brain.

The Second Prelude is a simile for my entire life for, despite the turbulent emotions that are raging in my heart, my fingers and my mind must always remain focused – disciplined, above all, well-tempered. The music has an uneasy tension about it, both hands mirroring each other but going in opposite directions. At the time it matched my wildly beating heart.

Then comes what will always be my favourite bar of music: the 15th bar of the Second Prelude of *The Well-Tempered Clavier.*

Not many people have an actual favourite bar.

But this, without question, is mine.

The bar's melody is pleasant enough, though for preference I think I prefer the one before it. However, the beauty of the 15th bar is that, for the briefest of notes, both right and left hand overlap.

We are already slightly turned in towards each other and the tips of our fingers touch, the flap of a butterfly's wing. An explosion wrings through my body. I've been scalded, so unexpected that my hand leaps off the keyboard. I lose my place on the sheet, grind to a halt.

India is enjoying herself. But whether it is me or the music I have no idea. "From the beginning of the line," she says, but now I am forewarned and this time I luxuriate in the gentle touch of her fingertips against my skin.

Some more missed notes, but I'm keeping up with the beat, and our hands are rattling through the ending. Although I can't believe what I'm doing – sitting on a chair with India – I rivet my eyes to the music.

We finish and she claps her hands. "Well done. Let's try it again. Give it some pedal between the phrases."

My skin has turned into one giant nerve-ending. It is as if my other senses, of taste and smell and peripheral sight, have all had to shut down for fear of overloading my poor brain.

My world is now solely made up of the sound of the Second Prelude, the sight of the notes stabbing at me in black-and-white, and the prickle of my skin as it yearns to be touched.

It happens again, another sensory explosion. But this time not where I expected. My body is turned in towards the middle of the piano, left foot on the right pedal. India has a foot on the other pedal. Our knees kiss. My body has become one vast erogenous zone. Even her lightest touch saturates my nerve-endings.

I can think of nothing else but the notes, my fingers and my left knee. I'm ready for it now; I'm willing her to dab at the soft pedal again. Towards the end, as both hands start to race against each other, she does so and, even through the fabric of my trousers and her skirt, I fancy I can feel her body heat.

My body is liquefying beside her. But I can't help myself. It is far and away the most erotic thing ever to have happened to me.

"Good technique," she says, swinging her legs away from me to stand by the window. "Somewhere along the way you've had a great teacher."

"Thank you." I blush again. Everything she does, everything she says, sparks a volcanic reaction in me. For a moment I wonder if she's aware of this – aware that her slightest touch turns me to jelly, and that just the sound of her voice sends a shiver down my spine.

However, I don't think she is conscious of it. She is so genuine, so good-natured, that not for a moment has she considered that the touch of her knee is like a cattle-prod to my senses. I don't believe she has any conception that I would do anything for her, that she only has to ask and I would happily give up my head, heart and soul.

Her bare arm rests along the windowsill. "Do you think you'll be able to keep up your phenomenal practice rate?"

I blush, but for once I am able to chuckle. I think it is the first time that I have ever laughed in her presence. "Maybe. When my thumb's healed."

"I so envy you Kim," she sighs. "I hope you never lose your passion."

"Really?"

She laughs, but it is a world-weary laugh. As if a veil has been drawn aside, I suddenly glimpse the most unimaginable pain.

"Not that I'd want to discourage you from leaving your teens, but..."

The word hangs there. Even though her tone is light, I can't say anything in reply.

She's watching the clouds as she talks again. Her voice catches in her throat. Is she choking up? "Life gets more and more complicated."

She's almost talking to herself.

"Being a teenager is much underestimated." She turns around, her eyes sparkling moist. "Shall I tell you the best thing of all about being young? It's being able to indulge your passions."

She comes over to the piano and picks up *The Well-Tempered Clavier*. "If you want to spend all day playing Bach preludes you can do just that."

I finally find my voice. "And you can't?"

"In theory, yes." She flicks through the book, staring at the notes. "But the older you get, the less time you have for your passions. And if that's the case at 23, then how's it going to be when I'm 40?"

It is the first time we've ever had a conversation that did not bear directly on music. "Is 23 so much older than 17?"

"You're probably right," she says. "But just as there are young 17s and old 17s, so there are young 23s and old 23s."

"And you are?"

She slides into the armchair. "I am most definitely an old 23." Her fingertips tap against her chin. "Unhappiness is not conducive to ageing well."

I'd like to reach out, to help her. But what she's been through I assume is so way beyond my own experience, that all I can do is nod and listen.

India seems to shrink in the chair, bowed by her memories. "My own fault. I don't know if that makes it any easier."

Her face and torso are side on, but her eyes blaze right at me.

She is on the point of telling me more, but then she catches herself, remembers that she's a piano-teacher talking to her pupil, remembers that she is paid to talk about music and nothing more.

The moment passes, and out of the face of that lost, haunted woman, re-emerges the India that I had met at our first lesson, serene and untroubled.

She looks at her watch, a silver Cartier. "You'll be late for lunch if you don't hurry."

"Thank you," I say, and what I mean is thank you for everything; thank you for coming into my life.

"A pleasure."

Outside India's room, Room 17, I have to stand against the wall. My legs are about to buckle beneath me. I lean back and wave after wave of emotion crashes over me. Never before had I realised how draining it can be to sit with the one you adore.

As I walked back to The Timbralls, I felt almost punch-drunk. Though what lingered was not what she'd told me, but the sight of her sitting there on that dirty armchair.

I'd wished I'd been more sympathetic, that I'd been capable of saying the right words.

But, I'd had not the slightest inkling of how to react. Eton had taught me so many things. Empathy was not one of them.

I tried to guess at the unhappiness that had come into her life. I wondered if India had suffered a bereavement, a set-back, or an illness. But as it turned out, I was wrong on all counts.

For in my innocence, I had forgotten the most common and the most obvious cause of all human misery.

It was heartache, pure and simple.

And soon enough I would have my own fill of it.

But there is one thing that I am still only beginning to appreciate about heartache, and it is this: that time will indeed cure it. Despite this, every so often something catches you on the raw and the pain will be as sharp as if your heart has been freshly snapped in two.

For me, it feels as if 25 years back I'd undergone a serious operation, and that somehow the scalpel was left in my guts. For although the stitches are long gone and the scar has faded to nothing but a white slash, I only have to press against my old wound and I can feel the keen knife-edge of the scalpel, just as sharp and just as unforgiving as it was all those years ago.

PRELUDE 22, B FLAT MINOR

What a year 1982 was for news.

Although perhaps I'm biased. It was the year that I started buying four newspapers a day and, if you truly immerse yourself in a subject, then you can become fascinated by almost anything.

I had become so dedicated to the Falklands that I was quite capable of reading an identical story in *The Sun, Mail, Guardian* and *Times*. But the Falklands aside, that summer term of 1982 was still an extraordinary time for news. Just off the top of my head, there was Prince William's birth, John McEnroe at his foul-mouthed best at Wimbledon, the World Cup, and the IRA blowing up the Household Cavalry in Hyde Park.

One night, I was indulging in two of my favourite pastimes: listening to the chart round-up on the radio while at the same time gobbling up the newspapers' analysis of the Falklands. It seemed that Argentina had yet to score a single hit and Britain was already gearing up for a full-scale invasion. Meanwhile, in the States, Ronald Reagan had promised support and 'Materiel'. I loved that word and liked to say it out loud: "Materiel!" It smacked of high-tech bombs, heavy-duty guns and exotic weapons of mass destruction.

The only other news was that a total exclusion zone had come into force around the Falklands.

What that meant, I did not know. But Sap was about to tell me all about it.

Sap's real name was Anthony Parrish, but he was known as Sap – short for Sapper, an army engineer.

Sap was not one of my natural friends, but we got on well enough because he was the only other boy in my year who was also apparently destined for an army career. But while I shilly-shallied, he had as good as signed up. He already carried himself like an officer, shoulders squared to attention and hair trimmed every fortnight.

Sap's face was flushed with excitement when he barged into my room. "Have you heard?" he said. "It's bloody incredible."

"We've dropped the bomb on Buenos Aires?"

"We've sunk a boat. A heavy cruiser, the General Belgrano." He was so excited that he couldn't sit down. "She was in the exclusion zone. One of our subs torpedoed her and down she went."

"Jesus!" I said. "How many on board?"

"Hundreds," Sap replied. "Two torpedoes and bang, that was it."

Before I could say any more, Frankie had come in, stinking of cigars and red wine.

He gave us a sloppy salute, a Brigadier greeting two subalterns in the mess. "Hoped I'd find you two," he said. He was still in his grey suit, stick-ups and clumping black shoes. "Well – the General Belgrano, eh? What do you make of it?"

"Fantastic hit, Sir," Sap said.

"About time too," Frankie commented. "Mind if I take a seat?"

I gestured to the sofa and Frankie sat while Sap perched on the end of the bed.

"Must be the first ship we've torpedoed since the Second World War," Frankie mused. "It's what you live for, isn't it boys? You put in years of training and then finally you get a chance to put it all into practice. Lucky sods."

"Did you ever fire a shot in anger, Sir?" Sap asked.

Frankie shrugged. "Never. Never got the chance. One quiet year in Northern Ireland, and for the rest of it just a tour of Germany and a stint in London."

"Bad luck," Sap said.

"That's what happens if you sign up for a short-term

commission. Hopefully you two will fare better."

"We can only hope," Sap replied.

I just sat at my burry, watching the pair of them. In my mind's eye I was still picturing the Belgrano as it slipped beneath the sea. The oily waves in flames, and the men freezing to death in the Atlantic before choking down that last breath of seawater.

"Did you know there's at least one Old Etonian out with the task force?" Frankie said. "Must be about 42, a year or so younger than me. I knew him very slightly when he was here. Herbert Jones was his name, though I think they just call him 'H' now. He's a Lieutenant Colonel too." He stroked the back of his hand, musing. "He stuck with it."

"Who's he with?" Sap asked.

"Two Para. Red beret and all the other trappings. Quiet chap, didn't talk much. But God he must have been tough." Frankie slapped his thighs and got up. He gave one final wistful shake of his head. "What a man. Well, good luck to the fellow."

Over the next few days, more details of the Belgrano came out. She'd been hit by two Mk 8 torpedoes, the first on the port bow and second on the stern. The ship's power and communications systems had been knocked out and over 200 men trapped inside. The Captain of the British submarine Conqueror had watched through his periscope as the Belgrano crew scrambled into the yellow life-rafts. By the time the rescue was complete, some 368 of the crew were dead.

The British newspapers were like cockerels on a dung-heap. 'Gotcha!' blared The Sun. The broadsheets called it a stunning blow to the Argentinian Navy.

But I couldn't get the picture of the drowning sailors out of my head. None of the crew had been equipped with anti-flash protection and many had been terribly burned.

This, I was beginning to see, was the true face of modern war. Not a glorious death in the face of the enemy, but being roasted alive after a sneak attack by an unseen foe.

Was it really for me? What would my father think?

The squirrel bite on my thumb got better. I still have the scar to this day, a white fleck at the base of my knuckle. I was back at the piano within five days and practising *The Well-Tempered Clavier* with all the fervour of a cult fanatic.

Divinity, English and Economics were all put on permanent hold as I devoted every spare moment to the piano. Homework was knocked out in half-an-hour, and course textbooks left untouched and unloved. And of Othello – the man whose fatal flaw I was set to so spectacularly mimic – the only times when I learned anything new were in McArdle's English classes, during the brief moments when I could drag my attention away from Angela and her mini-skirted legs.

To my delight, I mastered my first love, Prelude 17, in two weeks. If I attempted it now, it would take me months and months but, for that term, I would think nothing of putting in four hours at a stretch, practising a bar over and over again until my fingers had been drilled like army recruits.

How I came to love Johann Sebastian. All day his work danced through my head. For years, I had thought his music was starchy, but after my full-body immersion into *The Well-Tempered Clavier* I began to appreciate his diversity.

Looking back, it's possible that my reaction to Bach was almost Pavlovian – that I automatically began to associate his music with my Goddess. And it is true that the moment I heard *The Well-Tempered Clavier*, I instinctively thought of her. But does that matter? Do you have to know the why and wherefores? Do you have to analyse cause and effect? Or can you just accept that your emotions are valid without feeling the need to analyse their origins?

I enjoyed the practice. Though it was, as I've said, a means to an end, and that end was my piano lessons.

They never matched the intimacy of that second lesson, that time when our fingers had brushed against each other. But, with time, I was beginning to relax in her company; was starting, even, to revel being in her presence. Compared to that stuttering wretch of the first two weeks, I was blossoming.

I loved to look at her, of course. I could have spent hours on end just gazing at her face.

But she had a real knack with words, could make me laugh out loud. She had a delightful irony that would catch me clear in the solar plexus.

My favourite times of all were not when I was gazing at her face, nor when we talked. No, my happiest moments were when I was trying out a prelude for the first time, the two of us side-by-side on the music stool, my right hand and her left hand working together in imperfect harmony.

As we played, there might be an occasional touch – shoulder-to-shoulder, elbow-to-elbow, knee-to-knee. These moments could be guaranteed to send a shiver of excitement washing through me.

Although, what I came to like best was the magical alchemy by which the two of us created a piece of music together. Two hands and two hearts, both bringing Bach back to life. It was much more intimate than the neat virtue of playing a piece solo.

The lessons were the formal times when I was scheduled to meet with India, but I had taken to lurking around the Music Schools at all hours. I usually hoped to see her there at least twice a week. Sometimes she'd pop into my practice room, or I might catch her on the pavement as she was heading home.

I lived for those moments. For unlike my actual lessons, they were in the lap of the gods. It was their very spontaneity that made them all the more thrilling. One moment practising a prelude, focused on my music, and the next she's walking through the door. She would be pleased to see me, but I think also that she delighted in the fact she had introduced me to *The Well-Tempered Clavier*. It was the private thrill of the matchmaker who brings two lovers together.

Seeing India, even for a few seconds, could make my day, although to say that these sightings were in the lap of the gods is not strictly accurate. Like a big-game hunter, I could maximise my chances of seeing India by being in certain places at certain times. The Music Schools, for instance, were a favourite hunting ground, as was the School Hall at 11am.

But I soon learned that there was one place where, almost every morning, I could find India. As soon as I knew of it, I never once missed a chance of seeing her there.

Eton has two main chapels, one for the lower boys, which is Gothic and depressing, and the other a bigger chapel for the senior boys, which is magnificent. The upper chapel is over 500 years old, and when you walk in and stare up at the huge vaulted ceiling, it feels like you've entered a Cathedral. It is the sister chapel to Henry VI's other pet academic project, King's College, Cambridge, and it is vast – though not half as vast as Henry had wanted it. When the King had originally planned his chapel (where, naturally, the boys would send up regular prayers for his mortal soul), he had wished it to be at least 80-yards longer. But, as so often occurs with these building projects, the money ran out.

Despite this, what remains is still a spectacular school chapel, with a grand organ, old oak pews, and carved stalls for the masters. My favourite part came courtesy of the Nazis. A time-bomb landed in the schoolyard on 4 December 1940 and a day later, on the eve of Founder's Day, most of the chapel windows were destroyed. They were replaced by the most remarkable John Piper stained glass – four of the miracles on the northern side and four of the parables on the south. I have spent many hours staring up at them.

In the mornings, the junior boys had to go to the lower chapel, but the seniors had the option of going to either the upper chapel or the School Hall where some form of entertainment would be laid on – a talk, perhaps, or some music. I would do everything in my power to stay away from the chapel. I loathed it. For an entire decade, I'd been forced into various school chapels and, to this day, church services remain to me nothing but an exercise in tedium.

However, on Sundays there was no getting out of chapel and I would dutifully join the rest of the rabble and take my seat.

It was the third Sunday of term, and the upper chapel was filled to the gunnels with tailcoats. I am already going into hibernation, preparing myself for 75 minutes of torpor, when out of the corner of my eye I detect a flash of green-and-red skirt. It is India, show-stoppingly beautiful. Conversations dry up. Eyes dart. There is not a boy in the chapel who has not seen her, who is not inspecting her in the most minute detail.

She walks down the aisle like a catwalk model and, even in her innocence, she must have been aware of the reaction. She scans the oak stalls by the walls before spotting an empty seat.

Immediately after she finds her place, she leans forward to pray. She prays for a long time, and once more at the end of the service, her head still bowed as I join the merry cavalcade out of the chapel and into the sunshine.

Ever after that, I would forego the School Hall option to attend chapel instead. Most days she would be there, sliding into her seat just before the start of the service.

The chapel became my secret delight. No one, not even Jeremy, knew why I went there every morning.

On the second day she spotted me and after that she would always scan the boys for a glimpse of me and would bestow on me that impish smile. For those smiles alone, I would have endured a month of chapel services.

India was the woman to whom my thoughts would first stray. But as I've said, she was not the only woman in my dreams.

Angela had the monopoly of my English classes.

And Estelle had the pick of all my literary outpourings. We were writing to each other at least three times a week, and every one of her letters would provoke another paroxysm of delight. Always they smelled of lavender. I kept them in numerical order in my burry and sometimes at the weekend I would give myself up to an orgy of puppy love and would read every single letter from start to finish.

One Sunday, just after prayers, I was lounging with Jeremy in my room, me on my bed, polishing my shoes, while Jeremy lay on the floor with his feet vertically up against the wall.

By tilting his head back, he was just able to look at me.

"I don't spend time with you anymore," he said.

"Got a lot of work on," I smirked. Jeremy knew only too well that my sole work in progress was the piano.

"Well, I hope she's suitably appreciative."

"She'd better be." I lovingly dabbed some more polish onto the toe of my black lace-up. "If I'd met her six years ago, I'd have had a chance at a music scholarship."

"So, what do you actually do in your lessons?"

I could feel a dreamy smile wash over my face as I recalled my time with India. "I do my scales. I play her *The Well-Tempered Clavier*. She might play something back. We talk a bit and then I leave."

"That's it?"

"Just about."

"And what about Estelle and her blue lavender-scented letters?"

I spat on the heel of the shoe and worked the cloth in tight little circles. "Well, it's not as if I have to commit to one or the other, is it? All I'm doing with India is working hard at my piano practice."

"You're not just practising the piano; you're obsessed."

Before I could reply there was a thump at the door and Archie stropped in. "Evening gents." He preened himself in the mirror, scratching at a spot on his chin before turning to us. "I've just had a very interesting little chat."

"Good for you Archie," I replied.

"Very interesting," he said. He ran his finger round the inside of his greying white collar. "She spoke very highly of you Kim."

"Well, it definitely wasn't my step-mum then."

"Not your gorgeous step-mum, no. Have another guess."

"Marie wanting to borrow my English notes?" I said. "Or was it Angela?"

"None of those," Archie said. He started to kick the end of my bed. "Try again."

"All right Archie – has Brooke Shields been calling me up again from Bel Air?"

"She said such nice things about you." Archie continued toeing the bed.

"Amaze me."

"Does the name Estelle ring any bells?"

"Estelle?" I said. "You've been talking to Estelle? Estelle called here?"

"Certainly did." He was grinning now.

"Well, why didn't you tell me?"

"That's what I'm doing now."

"You mean she's still on the phone?" I was up and flying out of the door. "Archie, you are such a tosser."

I took the stairs two at a time, cursing Archie, wondering if Estelle would still be on the line. The Timbralls had just the one pay-phone for its 50 boys and there was every chance another boy had cut her off by now.

"Hello?"

"Is that you Kim?" Relief, cascading through me like cold spring water.

"Estelle! I thought you'd have hung up."

"Who was that funny boy I was talking to?"

"Don't even ask," I said, making a mental note to give Archie a hefty kick the next time I saw him. "So – how nice to hear from you! How are you? What's happening in sunny Cheltenham?"

"I'm fine," she said. "How are you?"

"All the better for hearing you."

My brain was at warp speed. We chatted about this, about that, and gradually my heart stopped convulsing every other second. I started to enjoy performing various mental gymnastics for the benefit of a girl. She said she missed me; I said I missed her.

"I wish I was with you now," she said.

"And what would you do then?"

"I might hold your hand."

"Hand-holding? That sounds nice."

"And I might kiss you on the cheek."

"Only the cheek?"

"Well, maybe both of them."

"And then?"

She giggled. "I might give you a peck on the lips."

"Just the one?"

"I'd see what sort of reaction I got."

"Maybe I could give you a peck too."

"That might be nice."

There was a tap at the window. One of the fags was mouthing at me outside the door and tapping his watch. I cheerily thumbed my nose at him.

It was then Estelle's turn to start asking the questions. "And what would you do if I were with you now?"

"Very gently, I might slip my arm round your waist."

"Only one arm?"

"Depend on your reaction. But I might try the other too."

"And?"

"I'd kiss you. But a little longer."

She sighed. "And would your lips start to open a little?"

"The tiniest fraction."

"And what about your tongue?"

"I'd use it."

"To do what?"

"To tease your lips."

"I think I'd like that. And then what?"

"I'd use it to whisper sweet-nothings into your ear."

My first-ever attempt at phone sex – or, more accurately, phone petting. I loved it. After a while we moved from possibilities to practicalities.

Our half-terms coincided and I made her an offer.

"Would...would you like to come here for parents' day?" I asked.

"And see you in your fancy little tailcoat?" she laughed. "I bet you look good in that."

"It's on the fourth of June."

Estelle was enthused. I was ecstatic.

She'd ask her parents that night; she'd get a new outfit; and on the big day – three weeks from then – she'd catch the train down to Windsor. We'd spend the day at Eton before spending the night with my parents in London. What a night it was going to be...

She blew me a kiss down the phone.

After hanging up I tore back to my room. Jeremy was still there lying on the floor with his feet up against the wall. I gave him a double thumbs-up, just like the Fonz from *Happy Days*.

"What's happened now?"

"Estelle's coming down for the Fourth."

"English students, music teachers and now pen-pals, all of them doting on young master Kim." Jeremy slowly brought his legs back over his head until his toes touched the floor. "I just hope you manage to keep them all apart."

Now as it happened, I would be able to keep my three ladies, my three loves, apart. But I was more than capable of wrecking any relationship with Estelle all by myself. And, in a small way, the abrupt end of my courtship with Estelle was to exactly mirror the catastrophic self-implosion that engulfed me with India.

By now, India and I had reached a plateau. We had had four lessons and maybe a dozen other meetings. But we maintained the formalities and kept our teacher-pupil distance. I worshipped her with my music; she was aware of my existence.

I don't know what she thought of me then. I think she must have liked me. But outside of the Music School, I don't think she gave me a thought. Why should she have? She must have had at least 20 other music pupils, all of them bright, personable, and – like me – dreaming wistful fantasies of their piano teacher.

However, it is possible that I do myself a disservice. That one term, there cannot have been a boy at Eton who put in as much music practice as me. That dedication must, I suppose, have warranted a certain admiration from India. Admiration, yes, but certainly nothing more.

And that is how things might have remained, were it not for an interlude that launched my feelings onto a whole new level – and possibly her feelings too.

For the first time, I started to see India not just as a Goddess, but as a flesh-and-blood woman with passion, emotions. Needs too.

She would still remain on her pedestal but, ever after, my dreams of India started to be sprinkled with a hint of sexuality.

And how quickly they snowballed. In my mind's eye, clothes and stockings were to start being peeled away, to reveal...well I had no idea. I had seen porno pictures of women before, though somehow I could never begin to imagine India naked. But I did know that I would like to find out.

It's a Tuesday afternoon and I have a vista of spare time to fill, and yet again I aim to fill it at the Music Schools. I'm wearing jeans and a tight t-shirt, but they are not just any old jeans and t-shirt. As I know full well, India might see me at any moment. The jeans are Levi 501s – I'd even bathed in them, just like the guy in the TV advert, to ensure a snug-fit. As for my t-shirt, it's a tight blue v-neck. About as good as I can get in Eton mufti.

All is quiet at the Music Schools. How I had come to love the sepulchral calm of that building.

I bound up the stairs hoping to snare one of the grand pianos. But just as I am about to plunge towards the practice room, I hear the soft fall of piano music. I can tell immediately that it's Bach.

I pad down the corridor, all too aware that the music is coming from Room 17. In general I hadn't liked to go too near this room on my practice days. Even then, I appreciated that it might have smacked of stalking, that less is sometimes more. But the music has me entranced. I'm drawn to it like an eel to the Sargasso Sea when the moon is full. Only later do I learn that it's Prelude 22 in B-flat Minor.

It's solemn. I can imagine it being played at Evensong. In the dark passage, I stand in silence outside India's practice room. I inhale the music. I'm so focused I'm hardly even aware that it must be India who is playing.

Abruptly it stops, halts in mid-note, and there is the sudden crash of fists slamming into the keyboard. The jarring discord clangs in my ears.

I turn to go. Standing outside her practice room feels like an intrusion, as if I have crept up to spy on her.

I start to slip away just as a fresh sound comes to my ears. Not music, but a light sob.

I can't ever recall hearing a woman cry before. Like everything else about India, it is another virgin experience.

I am turned to granite, my legs paralysed with indecision. My first instinct is to leave. Quickly flee the scene like a thief in the night, to race to the far end of the building and immerse myself in Bach.

But another part of me longs to be with her. To go into the room and...what? Help her? Offer my handkerchief?

To and fro my mind dithers, flopping between action and passivity.

I finally decide – I'll leave her to it. It would only be hideously embarrassing. She wouldn't want to be seen in this state anyway. Certainly not by me. What good could I do in any case?

But with each step away, I yearn to do something for her, although I can't think what.

I stop again, close to the stairs. The sound of her crying has changed too, almost stuttering as if she can't catch her breath. It's a cry of feral pain.

My mind changes. I'll go back. I'll knock on the door. I'll go in. Don't know what I'll do, but I'll do what I can to comfort her.

Outside the door of room 17, a room that has come to represent the epicentre of the storm in my heart, I daren't look in through the window. I formulate what I will say: "Can I help you?"

Before I can prevaricate any further, I have committed myself, knocked twice on the door.

The sobbing stops dead.

With a leaden heart, I turn the door handle.

I'm about to speak, to say what I'd planned to say. But India is hunched over the piano, elbows on the keyboard and her red tear-stained face buried into her hands. My heart goes out to her and all my rehearsed words are forgotten.

Even though she hasn't looked up, she must know it's me. I can't help being drawn towards her. I sit beside her on the piano stool and enfold her in my arms. One arm loops round her back, the other round her front, and I hold her taut to my chest. It's an instinctive act of succour that I'd offer to anyone in this amount of pain.

After the sudden heat of action, my head is spinning. It takes a few seconds for my senses to come alive again, to realise that I am holding India in my arms. My nose is buried so deep into her hair that I can smell her exotic shampoo. Her tears are running wet on my arms and her soft sobs are hot in my ear.

I don't know how long we remain locked like this, India fast in my arms, trapped in her grief. It could have been a minute, it could have been more, but all of a sudden she lowers her hands from her face and throws them round my waist before dropping her head to my shoulders. Our legs, hips, torsos are squeezed against each other, the feeling so sensuous that I didn't want to move for fear of shattering the spell.

It was the first time that I'd ever been held like this by a woman. Estelle and I had hugged and kissed. But this was more tender. It was affectionate. Almost non-sexual.

I stroke India's hair with one hand. Up to the back of her head I reach with my fingers and let them glide down to her shoulders. I've never felt hair so satin-soft. I entwine my fingers in her locks, can feel the trace of her shoulders.

She stops crying and I can sense her breath steady on my neck. Other little sensations pop into my head. The press of her breasts against my chest. For the first time I can smell her sweat, a light animal trace over the lily-of-the-valley. I lick my lips, can almost taste it.

India is talking now, barely a whisper. "Sometimes you need a hug just to remind yourself what you've been missing." Slowly she draws back from me. Our arms are still loosely round each other and for the first time I see her face. Her mascara has run a little and her lipstick is smudged, but her dewy eyes are more beautiful than I have ever seen them.

India gives a little laugh. "God, I must look a state."

All I can do is gaze at this absurdly beautiful woman in my arms.

We gaze at each other, not wanting to break the look, and then, very deliberately, she leans forward and kisses me. Soft lips pressed firm against my mouth.

The most magnificent thing ever to have happened to me. "Thank you," she says. With that, she stands up, takes her attaché case from the top of the piano and with a waft of lily-of-the-valley leaves the room.

I. Cannot. Believe it.

I draw a delicate finger across my lower lip; a trace of her scarlet lipstick lingers on my nail.

I've been pole-axed. Another experience that is so outside my remit that it will take days to make it believable.

But digest it I did, and that one kiss was enough to fire a fund of new fantasies.

It was like the dry seed of my desire had been watered and was now starting to shoot.

I had questions too. Why had she been crying alone over her music? Had she seen so much unhappiness in her life?

The answer was simple enough. She cried during the Ninth Prelude for the self-same reason that I feel tearful now when I hear Prelude 17.

Memories, that's all it was. Just a few notes can be more than enough to bring everything flooding back, as painful and as harrowing as when your heart was first broken.

PRELUDE 18, G-sharp Minor

My dreams were of India, of Estelle, of Angela, and of my coiffeured *bête noir*, Savage.

I hated him as I do hell-pains.

Sometimes I just wished that fate could teach him a lesson by breaking a limb. At others, I was not so specific. I wished that the school could somehow be shot of him – expulsion, severe illness, death.

In every way, Savage had come to be the bane of my life. The sniping was constant: unsettling jibes to his cronies whenever I was within hearing distance, little chores that he was only just within his rights to demand of me, occasional visits to my room, which were like being with a wild-cat, constantly fearful of what might happen next.

But I soaked it up like the human sponge I am – soaked it all up without complaint, just as Eton teaches its boys to do.

Life with Savage was unpleasant, but not unbearable. Besides, I'd only have another seven weeks of him and then he'd be out of my life and off to University to menace the men and charm the women there.

Only seven weeks. It didn't seem so long.

As it was, seven weeks was all Savage needed to wreak the most vile havoc. And his motive was nothing other than old-fashioned spite. I had a daily pleasure in my life that, to quote *Othello*, made him ugly.

Savage's behaviour was foul, but that's nothing strange at Eton – or any other school. Seniors will always pick on their juniors, for no other reason than that they can.

However, I was soon to realise that it was more than just petty skirmishing. It was full-out war.

Sometimes, instead of going to the Music Schools in the afternoon, I liked to go to the school library, just adjacent to the School Hall. It had a handsome dome, giving a great sense of airiness and space, as well as thousands and thousands of books, many of them real treasures; a library that would not be out of place at most British universities.

It also had more than just books, it had hundreds of records. Tuck yourself away in one of the little booths, put on your headphones, and you could be a million miles from Eton.

That particular day I was listening, unsurprisingly, to *The Well-Tempered Clavier*. The more I heard of it, the more I came to love it. The Fugues, in particular, were an acquired taste. I liked to get a couple of Bach biographies, so that I could learn about the man as I listened to his music. I can still remember all his details: born 1685, died 1750; two marriages; 200 cantatas, 350 chorales, the Brandenburgs, the Partitas, the English Suites, and a whole lot more. But most extraordinary of all was that Bach had 20 children, of which half died before adulthood. Some men might have been destroyed by these infant deaths, but they only seemed to make Bach stronger. Week in, week out, he kept relentlessly churning out his music, the notes pouring out in a never-ending spring.

Along with the biographies, I – of course – had my newspapers. Every day I had to have my Falklands fix.

Argentina had struck their first major blow. HMS Sheffield, a Type 42 Destroyer, had been hit amidships by an Exocet. The missile's 363-pound warhead had detonated eight feet above the waterline and the blast had ripped open the watertight doors from their bulkheads. Twenty-one men had died, most of them trapped in the galley or the computer room.

I inspected the grainy black-and-white newspaper pictures. Thick grey smoke was pouring out of the jagged hole in the side of the ship. One moment the crew had been sitting down for a cup of tea at 10am in the Sheffield galley, the next they were blown into oblivion. It was revelatory – that a multi-million pound ship had been knocked out by a 'cheap' £300,000 missile. It gave me the first inklings of the fallibility of modern technology.

Was this what I wanted to be doing for the next 20 years? Putting my life on the line at the dubious say-so of the army's political masters? How would I fare, I wondered, if I were ordered to war? And what if I didn't believe it was a just cause?

It's much easier for a soldier if he never asks questions. If he can just receive his orders and, without a thought, act upon them. But I questioned everything.

I worried at my thumbnail, chewing at the skin, barely even aware of the music. I was listening to the Prelude 18 in G-sharp Minor. It came to an end. My finger automatically drifted to the record arm for the play-back.

I then leaned back on my chair, hands behind my head, and stared up through the skylights. My thoughts drifted effortlessly from the Falklands to India.

I savoured the memory of how she'd yoked herself to me in that practice room. Her moist eyes, the smudged mascara and... that kiss.

I closed my eyes, wrapped up in my music and the magic of the memory, trying to recall the exact texture of her lips.

I blew her a kiss through the skylight.

I was not even aware that Savage was in the room – that for the past five minutes he had been sizing me up, waiting for his moment.

I didn't hear him creep up behind me, or see him as he caught a foot round the front legs of my chair.

He gave it the smallest flick and my chair arced over backwards.

The headphones were wrenched from their socket in a shriek of noise. My stomach heaved and I smacked onto the floor. It was brutal: the one moment dreaming of my love, the next flat on my back, legs in the air and staring up at Savage's sour face.

He settled himself in a chair in the adjacent booth. "Very painful," he said. "Shouldn't have been leaning back, should you?"

All I could do was stare at him like a fish on the slab. I was winded and my head throbbed. I could feel the saliva dripping out of the side of my mouth.

Savage rubbed his hands. Even though it was a half-day, he was still dolled up in all of his popper gaudiness – green silk waistcoat set off by a white rose in the lapel of his tailcoat. "What have you been listening to?" He flicked off the record arm and picked up the disc. "What a surprise. *The Well-Tempered Clavier*? I would never have guessed."

I didn't get up, but lay there on my back, mentally hurling every form of abuse that I could think of.

"I wonder who you were blowing kisses to? Or should that be 'To whom you were blowing kisses?'" Savage stared at me, his eyes boring through to the back of my skull. "It wouldn't by any chance be your music teacher, India James?"

I closed my eyes. It was easier to think without looking at Savage. I had forgotten my little lie.

Savage had crossed his legs. He was idly kicking my foot.

"The pulchritudinous India James, whom you claim never to have heard of."

"India James? Is that my music teacher?"

"You are such a dickhead." He kicked me again, harder. "So, now we know why you've taken to practising the piano at all hours."

I unhitched my legs from the chair, rolled over onto all-fours and pulled myself up. "What are you talking about?"

"Must be very pleasant to have piano lessons with Miss James. Such a lovely woman." He tapped the record with his fingers, and all of a sudden hurled it at me like a Frisbee.

I ducked but too late. It shattered as it caught me under the ear.

Pain ballooned through my head. I dabbed at the side of my face and looked at the smear of blood on my fingers.

Savage was still talking. "Breaking school property? They'll have you barred from the library." He was on the balls of his feet now. He pulled out another disc from the record-rack, juggled it in his hand, and slung it at me with all his strength. It ripped past and smashed into the oak panelling at the end of the room.

Savage had this blithe insouciance as he selected the next record. He surveyed the cover, slipped it from its sleeve, and drilled it at me. "Smash up three records and that might warrant a fortnight's rustication."

A fourth record caught me on the hip and a mad, crazy flush of anger washed through me. It was the first time in my life that I had ever been out of control. I rushed at him, arms swinging, teeth bared, demented with rage.

It was my first proper fight. At prep school, I'd wrestled and grappled, but nothing like this. The truth was that I loathed fighting. I would have far preferred to have jousted with words than go through the loutish business of inflicting pain. But I was incensed.

He was quick, so light on his feet that he was dancing like a featherweight. I'd gone from 0 to 60 in under three seconds, and was throwing a flurry of blows to his face, to his body, though he batted them away.

But mixed with my rage was a certain animal cunning and I struck the low blow that he'd never dreamed of. I hit him in the crotch as hard as I could, driving my fist home, and, when he doubled up, my knee exploded into his face. It caught him on the forehead. He was stricken, a mewling ball of animal agony on the floor, his immaculate tailcoat rucked up around his back.

I was panting, sweat dripping off my face, blood trickling from under my ear. I pulled out a handkerchief to dab at the wound on my neck, then circumspectly picked up my books. Without a backward glance, I marched out of the library.

My heart was drumming with excitement and abject terror. I'd just bested one of Eton's most senior boys.

I thought I was going to get expelled – was certain of it. Savage's word against my own? Who would they believe?

I went back to my room, cleaned myself up, and spent the rest of the afternoon expecting at any moment the heavy thump of my tutor's tread on the stairs.

I tortured myself. I could not envisage any other outcome than having the full weight of Eton's disciplinary system unleashed upon me.

For two or three days, I was a twitching bundle of anxiety. At every turn I imagined that I'd be put on the Bill and called up to see the Headman. But ever so gradually it dawned on me that nothing had happened. That nothing was going to happen. That, for some unfathomable reason, I had got away with striking a popper.

I do not know what Savage did afterwards in the library. I can only presume that he cleaned up the debris, for I never heard a word about the smashed records.

And, in the short-term, my mad fight with Savage did make for a more pleasant life at Eton. I no longer had to put up with Savage's little social calls to my room. The sniping was less overt. I was still aware that he was often denigrating me to the other boys. But he knew now that I was a wild one; that I might just be capable of hurling myself at him again in a wild flurry of fists.

In all my innocence, I actually imagined that Savage had found other fish to fry, that there were easier boys in the school to pick on.

How unlikely is that?

Now, of course, I can see that, like every other bully before him, Savage was saving up his revenge for a time when he could inflict maximum damage. Merely biding his time before delivering the knock-out blow.

Soon enough I was back in my well-regulated schedule of divisions and rushed homework and, hour-upon-hour, in the Music Schools.

How I adored her. If I had one single picture of her, I would include it in this book – but, as it is, I never thought to take a photo of India. When it finally happened, when we started courting, I thought we would last forever. I believed there would always be plenty of time for pictures. I could not have conceived there might be a time in my life when I would be without her.

But then again I could never have conceived that our relationship would be snuffed out with such shocking abruptness.

It is a Saturday afternoon, dreamily hot, and my shrine is one of the Music School's grand pianos.

I must be the only person who's mad enough to feel the need to be in the schools to practise two bars of music. Two bars of music, 21 notes with the right hand and a similar number for the left.

I had found that the way to learn a difficult piece was to repeat the same bar over and over again until my fingers knew where to go, finding their place on the piano like well-trained pups. Sometimes, I would play a bar a hundred times over to master a tough piece of finger-work.

This particular afternoon, I have set myself the task of learning just two bars from the G-sharp Minor Prelude – the same one that Savage had destroyed in the library. The G-minor key has five sharps, but on the plus side the prelude is slow.

The right hand already knows what it's doing and even the left hand is competent. But when I put the two together the difficulty factor grows exponentially. It's like a complex version of that challenge of patting your head and rubbing your stomach at the same time. My brain issues different orders for both left and right hand and somewhere along the way the commands get mangled in my nerve endings. Time and again my fingers can do nothing more than stutter over the notes, trembling with indecision.

It is a seemingly endless round of repeating the right hand notes, the left hand notes, and then trying – and failing – to put them together.

Any other time, it might have been dispiriting. But I am at prayer and, when you are truly at worship, you are not even aware of the minutes and hours as they tick by.

My eyes are screwed up, a deep furrow on my brow as I try to make the fingering work better. Always with Bach it's down to the fingering. If you don't get that right from the start, you don't stand a chance.

I'm concentrating so hard that I don't even notice the knock at the door. I look up and India is already in the practice room, is walking towards me with that knowing smile, and in her hands are two steaming mugs of coffee. I was in awe – as if the Virgin Mary had suddenly appeared in person from behind the altar.

"Thought you could do with a break." India skirts round the side of the grand piano and hands me a mug. "Are you white without?"

"Thank you." That is all I can say.

"Cheers." She slides light as gossamer into the armchair next to the piano.

Her eyes lock onto mine and all I can do is drink. It is a taste explosion. In four years at Eton I had never drunk anything but powdered coffee straight from the jar. This was the real thing.

"What have I been missing?" I say.

It seems as if her face is forever on the verge of breaking into laughter. "Freshly ground coffee," she says. "I made up a thermos."

I took another sip. "Fantastic."

"Do you know the best part?" She cups the mug between her manicured fingers. "It's making the coffee in the morning. Pouring in the beans, grinding them up. The smell's better than the taste. Try it some time."

"I will."

After the first rush, I am starting to come down. I take in India's clothes. A long, white cotton dress, brown leather sandals, and hair that gleams in the afternoon light. Simple, devastating beauty, and all I can do is gawk and nurse my coffee.

"Have you tried it black?"

I wrinkle my nose in distaste.

India leans over and stretches out her mug. For the most fleeting of moments I have a glimpse of her cleavage. Down my eyes dart and the image of pert breasts, tanned and cupped snug in a white lace bra, is freeze-framed in my memory.

"Thank you." I accept her mug. As I bring it to my mouth, I can see the slight trace of her lipstick on the rim. I place my own lips on the same spot and sip. The taste of the black coffee is a kick to the roof of my mouth – tart and acrid, like a shot of raw spirit.

"I don't think I'll ever have it any other way again."

"Don't go overboard like you did with *The Well-Tempered Clavier*."

All I can do is smile, for I am so smitten with this woman that my brain has stalled.

I return her coffee cup. The electric thrill of her fingers. But something more than that – the dull throb of a warning bell. I look over to the door.

"Somebody there?" she asks.

"Don't know."

But I do know. For an instant I have seen Savage standing at the window, glowering in impotent rage as he watched us drink coffee together.

How he would come to hate me for it.

"It wasn't that tall popper?"

"Don't think so." I try to sound smooth, easy.

"Sometimes it feels like he's stalking me."

India leans back, looking at me over the rim of her mug. There is nothing but silence, each of us alone with our thoughts, I wondering what's on her mind, and she reading me like an open book.

"I wanted to thank you," she says. "You were very kind the other day." She nods to herself, musing. "Brave, too."

"The least I could do." I'm on autopilot, incapable of proper thought. On the surface, I appear to be having a normal conversation with the world's most beautiful woman.

India is still looking at me, but her eyes are far away. "I don't know why I play that piece any more. It always makes me cry."

"I loved it."

She sweeps back her hair over her shoulder and for a moment she looks far older than her years, as if just the memory of the music has aged her.

"Bitter-sweet memories," she says. "My music is an album of my past. Every piece comes with its own memory." India stands up, opens a window and also the one next to it. For a few seconds, the room is filled with the sound of another Jumbo flying to Heathrow on the Eton flight-path. It's a deafening roar, matching the rush of blood to my cheeks as India sweeps over to sit next to me at the piano.

"Move over," she says. "Let's see what you're at."

She hums the music as she scans it. My mind is descending into the abyss of total meltdown. It has become a mental reflex whenever India comes within a yard of me.

But there's something different too. A new scent, not lily-of-the-valley but something more sharp, lemon and limey. I hesitate to go there. Could it be a man's perfume?

My eyes sweep down to India's fingers. She's still wearing that diamond solitaire on her right hand. Does she have a boyfriend? Of course she has a boyfriend, or a lover, or someone at least to keep her warm in the cool of the night. How could it be possible that she has not been snapped up years ago?

But to that question, I don't think I will ever know the answer.

I lick up the honey and ask no questions.

India starts to play the piece, both hands, a little slower than I remember it from the record, but note perfect. I can only sit with hands in my lap and marvel at the bounty that she bestows on me.

Very softly, she starts to talk. But it's strange because, although her fingers are focused on the prelude, her mind is on something else altogether.

"I've never been surrounded by so many people before," she says. "And, at the same time, I've never been so lonely."

I stare at the music. If only I could think of something sympathetic to say. But Eton is not the place to learn soft words for when someone bares their soul.

Her fingers continue to trip through the music. The rigid beat of the prelude has become the one fixed point in our firmament while all about us everything falls to pieces.

"I don't know what I expected when I came to Eton. But I never expected anything like this."

I can't breathe for fear of breaking the flow. I stare at my faded blue jeans. A piece of dried egg crusting on my knee; grease marks at the ankle.

"Sometimes I imagine I'm a zoo animal." For a second she turns from the music to stare at me, though still she keeps playing. "All by myself in a cage, with food and water and various ways

81

of passing the time. Every day a thousand outlandish visitors come to inspect me. They look and they talk, but none of them are allowed to touch."

"I thought it was the boys who were the zoo animals."

The spell is broken. She looks again at the music. "What am I complaining about? I can check out any time I want – but you can never leave."

"Nice line for a song."

She sniggers, the first time I've seen her laugh like a schoolgirl. "I've been listening to *Hotel California* too much." She plays the final bar, holding the last notes with the pedal. "I wonder what Bach would make of The Eagles."

"I wonder what The Eagles would make of Bach."

"Good." She's laughing now, leaning forward, head in her hands. It is infectious. For me, it's like a dam-burst. Five, six weeks of keeping everything in, holding it together, trying to stop myself from falling at India's feet.

At first I allow myself a little sly grin, pleased with my feeble witticism, then it's a chuckle, a laugh, and then I catch sight of India. She's shaking, shaking with laughter. I don't ever recall seeing anyone like this before. Red in the face and her lips peeled back to reveal every one of her white teeth, and, for the first time in my life, I am howling with laughter – laughing at her, at Bach, at Eton, at the whole ridiculousness of it all, and the tears are streaming down my cheeks. But where once I might have been mortified, it now feels natural to be crying in front of India.

She rocks backwards and forwards, catches a glimpse of my scarlet face and wet cheeks, and lets out a shriek of release, and our laughter is so loud that the room is awash with yelping noise. But I don't have a care; I'm hardly aware that our knees are touching, that she's holding my hands, and that every time we catch each other's eye we both break into a fresh peel of laughter.

I don't know how long it goes on for. Anything could set us off. My stomach muscles ache from laughter, ache as if they'd been physically pummelled, and, when we are finally spent, we are still tittering at the memory.

The most incredible release – better, I think, than sex. That kind of wild infectious laughter can never be planned, can only come naturally. I've had many memorable love-making sessions, but the number of times that I have laughed like that, laughed till my throat was hoarse and my muscles ached? I can count them on the fingers of one hand.

India's face is flushed and she's still giggling as she wipes away the last of her tears. "The nicest thing to happen to me all year." She retrieves the coffee mugs. "I'll never forget it."

Nor I.

And that is how I will always remember India, with tears in her eyes and a laugh so exuberant that it could draw the birds from the trees. Not for me the memories of the dog days when India was beset by the past and trying to cope with my rabid jealousy, or even those flickered moments of sexual ecstasy on her face.

For me, the way that I would always like to remember India is of her on that lazy summer afternoon, next to me at the grand piano, and with that bewitching laugh that defied even the Gods to blight her happiness.

PRELUDE 3, C-sharp Major

I was fiddling with my bowtie. But it was finicky – like tying a knot behind your back.

In theory I knew exactly what to do. But the practice of tying a white bowtie with my neck corseted into a starched wing-collar was tortuous. It was like my hands were in mittens, my grubby fingers tweaking and poking until I was left with nothing but a limp rag round my neck. Ten minutes, 15 minutes, and I was still nowhere. The once pristine bowtie was sweat-grey at the edges.

I was going to be late, I knew it. I charged to Jeremy's room where he was pinning a dyed-blue carnation to his tailcoat.

He raised his eyebrows. "Very fetching."

"You couldn't finish this damn thing?"

"Of course."

I sat on the bed as he tugged the knot free and started afresh. "She'll eat you up the moment she sets eyes on you."

"We'll see."

Jeremy cinched the last piece of the tie home and squared it off. "I suppose you might as well make the most of being allowed to wear a bowtie on the Fourth." He cupped my cheeks in his hands and kissed me on the forehead. "You'll blow her out of the water."

"I can only hope." I was rushing out of the room now, straining like a greyhound in the traps.

"And what of Angela? And what of India?"

I laughed cheerily. "Those fantasy girls are just going to have to fend for themselves for a few days."

Yes, indeed they would.

For I was going to Windsor Station to meet the girl who could make my dreams a reality: Estelle.

I know that it makes me sound capricious, that I could so easily switch my allegiances without a second thought. But that is the way of schoolboy fantasies. I still dreamed of India. I still gazed in adoration at Angela in English classes. But it was Estelle who wrote me love letters, Estelle who was available, Estelle who called me up, Estelle who wanted to kiss me, and Estelle who had alluded to doing a lot more besides.

In just under a month of letters and phone calls, our infant relationship had reached a critical mass. When I think of it now, it all seems so quaint, so old-fashioned, that it makes me laugh out loud. For the fact is, through letters alone, I appeared to have acquired myself a girlfriend. Nothing had been consummated, no love had been declared, but, as I walked to the station, I did feel like I was on a promise.

I'd been looking forward to it for days. I didn't quite know what I was going to do when I saw her on the platform, but I knew that I was definitely going to do something. A hug, certainly. A kiss on the cheek? On the lips? I was not sure of the correct etiquette.

The build-up had been intense. I was like a submariner in the week before he returns home to his loved ones. Testosterone was blazing through my system. My beard growth had doubled. I was in a perpetual blue swirl of pheromones.

How I ran.

Flying down the High Street, past Hills and Saunders the photographers, and the various school outfitters, Welsh and Jeffries, New & Lingwood and Tom Brown, then over the Thames bridge and a jink down to the station, my coat streaming behind me like Struwwelpeter's great, long, red-legged scissor-man.

Eton to Windsor station is about a mile and you can run it in eight minutes if you are in good trim.

But just try it on a summer's day. Try doing it in waistcoat and thick black tails with a tight, white collar round your neck.

I made it just as Estelle was walking past the ticket collector.

I must have looked like the wild man of the woods, my coiffed hair matted with sweat, tie askew and face like a fat strawberry. Estelle's jaw just dropped.

The sweat was steaming off me and I could feel it dripping down my face and seeping into my collar.

I cupped my hand round her waist and gave her a damp kiss on the cheek. She didn't recoil. But she didn't respond either – it was like her system had shut down at the shock of seeing me.

"Hi," I said.

"Hi." She took a step back to inspect me. "Been for a swim?"

"Sauna."

"I thought you had to take your clothes off beforehand."

"A minor detail that may just have slipped my mind." I mopped at my forehead, but it made no difference. I was bathed in sweat.

"You look like you could do with a drink."

"I'd love that."

How thoughtful Estelle was.

She was a very considerate woman, would have made somebody a wonderful wife. I would love to know what happened to her. But the horrid truth is that, within the day, our little ship would already have foundered on the rocks of my jealous rage.

We went to the station café, where I had lemonade and she had tea. I'd taken off my tailcoat and unbuttoned my waistcoat, and gradually I could feel the breeze start to dry my sodden shirt. And gradually, too, I started to take in the wonder of Estelle, who, after a month of letters, was finally sitting in front of me. She was the perfect epitome of girlhood, with skin as ripe as a downy peach. She just had a trace of lipstick; she didn't need any makeup to highlight her cheekbones or her lustrous eyes. She just glowed. Sun-kissed hair oozing down her shoulders, a beige two-piece suit, creamy stockings and brown court shoes. A dream.

And the wonder of her was that I could touch her. For the first time in my life, I could do more than just feast my eyes on a girl. I could stretch out my hand and stroke her fingers, or her knee, or her face. I could play with her hair and nuzzle her neck; I could even lean over and kiss those pink lips.

And I did just that. Leaned over and kissed her, my mouth slightly open, hoping for a hint of a reaction. But there was none – no responding pressure, no parting of her lips. We stayed like that for a second before she pulled back.

And the unsettling thing was that Estelle didn't even allude to it. She carried on with the conversation as if I'd dabbed a piece of lint off her shoulder.

"So tell me about this June the Fourth," she said. "My mum told me it's up there with Ascot and Henley."

"News to me." I stared at the bottom of my glass, fiddled for the slice of lemon.

"But it's more than just a school parents' day..."

"I suppose it used to be. Fifty years ago it was a huge Society event. All the blue-bloods would descend on Eton *en masse* to inspect their sons at play."

"But why's it on the fourth of June?" Estelle persisted. "What are we celebrating?"

"George III's birthday."

"Was he the founder?"

"No," I replied. "He just liked the school. He was mad. Apparently he'd walk up and down the High Street chatting to the boys. If he didn't recognise one, he'd go up and ask them, 'What's your name? Who's your tutor? Who's your Dame?' And then, whatever their reply, he would always say, 'Very good tutor, very good Dame'."

"And the school liked him so much, they celebrate his birthday every year?"

"He's also the reason why we all look like apprentice undertakers."

"Undertakers?" she said. "I was just thinking that you look quite…dishy."

It was then her turn to surprise me. She leaned over and kissed me. For a split second her lips parted and I felt the tip of her tongue dart against my lips.

Satisfied, she leaned back in her chair.

"I'd been hoping you'd do that," I said.

"Good." And she did it again, arms snaking round my neck and lips locking to mine, her head tilted to the side as she dabbed her tongue against my teeth.

Extremely erotic. In full public display, with the crowds milling around the station.

I spent a couple of minutes in the toilets, trying to slick down my hair and adjust my uniform, then we walked back to the Timbralls. I carried her overnight bag and every step of the way I had a silly grin plastered to my face, for clutching onto my arm was a prize above all others: a *bona fide* girlfriend. I basked in Estelle's reflected glory. It was the first time I'd walked down the High Street holding hands with a girl. My girl. There was not a boy, not a master, who could have walked past us and not registered that fact. You can forget stick-ups, bowties, sponge-bag trousers and fancy silk waistcoats. The only status symbol worth having on June the Fourth was a girl on your arm.

The plan was that at noon we'd meet my father and stepmother before they went downstairs for drinks with Frankie. While they tucked into the sherry, Estelle and I would entertain ourselves as best we could.

We'd then all meet up for a picnic and a stroll round the playing fields. After a final Absence at 5.30pm, my father would whisk us all back home to Chelsea. Estelle was to be spending the night, and I could only dream of what might happen when my parents were in bed and we had the chance to get better acquainted.

But I tried not to jump the gun.

Estelle and I were ambling back to the Timbralls. I gabbled. My hand, damp as an oily flannel, clutched tightly onto Estelle's fingers.

I pointed out the boys' houses, the upper chapel, the tuck shop, and Tap, the school pub.

"And there's the Burning Bush," she said.

"That's right," I said. "How did you know that?"

"Oh, you know…" She trailed off.

"You've been doing your homework!" I was irrepressible.

She made a smooth recovery. "Hours of it."

We moved onto other things. But, later, I did recall that conversation. Had she really done her homework? Or had someone told her about the Burning Bush?

Or had she, just by chance, been to Eton before?

When we arrived at my room, I carried Estelle over the threshold as if we were newlyweds. I only wished I'd had a camera to record the exact moment when a woman bounced on my bed for the first time.

"I think I'm going to like it here," she said.

"Are you going to be a regular fixture?" I sat beside her, arm snug round her waist.

"Might be," she laughed. "Though you could do something about those posters."

"If only I had a picture of you."

"What's with the Labrador poster?"

"Oh that?" I kissed Estelle's neck. "Haven't I mentioned Labradors before?"

"And I'd always taken you for a poodle man."

"A poodle for pleasure." I gave her a tickle and she squealed. "But a Labrador for ecstasy."

She snorted with laughter, and was still snorting when there was a brisk rat-a-tat at the door.

I leapt off the bed and was brushing down my clothes before the door-handle had even turned. Immediately, I could feel my vocal chords constricting, as if my chest were being bound with wrought iron bands.

My parents seemed to fill the room.

My father was in a tweed Savile Row suit, which immaculately disguised the slight paunch he'd acquired since leaving the army. He carried himself as if he were about to be presented to the Queen, back ramrod straight and shoulders squared. Around his mouth and eyes were scores of tell-tale smokers' wrinkles.

My stepmother was still the svelte society beauty that she'd been ever since I'd first met her ten years ago. She wore a Chanel outfit that must have cost a term's school fees. Her face was a stunning contrast with my father's, for, where his skin was corrugated with lines, she had hardly a wrinkle. I never found out if it was down to her daily beauty regime or if she'd been off to Brazil for a nip-and-tuck.

She did have a name – Edie – but I never used it; to me she was never anything other than my stepmother. She offered me a moist cheek to kiss.

"Kim." Her gaze lingered over the trainers that had been kicked under the bed and the mound of papers strewn by the window. "You shouldn't have gone to all this bother."

"Hello boy," my father said. He cuffed me a light blow on the shoulder. "Nice to see you again, Estelle."

"And you too Sir," she said. She bobbed.

My stepmother had been staring out of the window, but turned to inspect Estelle. Glacial.

"Much been happening boy?" my father asked.

"Beavering away," I said. "You know me."

"Glad your school fees aren't being entirely wasted."

I smiled. There was an awkward silence. I registered that he was wearing a black tie. "You're in mourning?" I asked.

"Colonel H. Jones." He turned to Estelle. "Did you hear about it last week?"

"No Sir," Estelle replied.

"Shot down as he stormed a machine-gun post." My father's yellowing fingertips twitched for his cigarettes. "Man should get a VC."

"No smoking in the rooms," my stepmother said.

"Quite right," he replied, returning his silver cigarette case to his coat pocket. "No pulling out now though. Not after what they've done to the Coventry and the Antelope. You see the pictures of the Sheffield?"

I nodded.

He sighed, looked almost maudlin. "What I'd give to be seventeen and with my whole army career ahead of me. Best career in the world."

"Is it?"

His eyes narrowed and for a moment fell on the newspapers by the window. "Are you reading the bloody *Sun*?"

"Sometimes."

"I hope I'm not paying for that rag."

"Borrowed it from Jeremy."

And it was just like it had always been, all my life. I've never seen anyone do instant rage quite like my father.

"It's an unspeakable, unreadable piece of shit!" He looked at me, defying me to challenge him. "Surprised they allow it in the school."

My heart drummed. At that moment I wasn't even aware of Estelle or my stepmother in the room. All I could see was my father, white with rage, and yet again I reverted to a seven-year-old stripling, pissing my pants with fright in my father's study as he hauled off his thick Sam Brown belt.

The blood pulsed in my ears as I stared at the floor.

My stepmother broke the moment. "I think we should see Kim's tutor, darling."

My father twitched and the red mist lifted. "We should." The creased lines relaxed round his mouth and eyes.

I was shell-shocked, like a lone survivor after an earthquake.

I shrugged, kicked the floor after they'd gone. "Sorry about that," I said.

"Forget it," Estelle said.

"It's not always that bad."

Estelle stood in front of me. "You haven't even met my parents."

"You're not saying they're in the same league?" I slipped my hand round her waist. "They couldn't be?"

Our lips locked against each other, tongues exploring. We broke off to gaze at each other. My eyes were drawn to her lips and it occurred to me that actually I'd much rather be kissing Estelle than looking at her. So that's what we did for half-an-hour, without a break. What a carefree time in my life – when I could be sated by a kiss.

In sedate silence, my father drove us to Dutchman's, one of Eton's immense playing fields. Once he'd selected a spot under a horse chestnut, the picnic was laid out on the rug. Every piece of food had to be unwrapped before anything was allowed to pass our lips.

My father eased himself into a deckchair and surveyed the spread of gravad lax, thick white rolls, chutneys, cheeses and punnets of fresh-picked strawberries. "Very good," he said. We were allowed to begin.

He poured me a glass of Bollinger. My hands shook as I drained it in one. It was like having dinner on the edge of a steaming volcano, always aware that an explosion might be just minutes away.

I forked up some salmon. My mouth was so dry I could hardly swallow. The fish stuck to the top of my palate. I coughed and helped myself to more champagne.

"Offer some to the ladies first," my father reprimanded.

I would have done, but I was still coughing. I tried to swallow but the salmon was tight in my throat. I heaved, and plate, glass and cutlery tumbled to the ground.

"Watch out!" my father said. "For God's sake!"

I clutched my hands to my throat, trying to catch a breath. My stepmother was behind me, thumping at my shoulder blades. A cough, another cough and a belch as a gobbet of pink flesh shot out of my mouth. It landed among the bread rolls.

"Jesus boy, can't you control yourself?"

My stepmother stroked the back of my neck. Estelle offered a handkerchief.

"Don't they teach you any manners here?"

I wiped the spittle from my mouth.

"Disgusting." My father picked up the bread rolls and tossed them all, every single one, into the bin-bag. "What a shame."

Oh, what a sad little picnic we were. All around us was good-natured hilarity, scores of Etonians soaking up the sun with their parents, and then the four of us, united by our edgy silence.

The strawberries lay untouched on my lap. I strived to make polite conversation. "So how are the boys?" I asked my father.

"Both of them boarding now," my father said. "Tears before

bedtime, all that sort of thing."

My stepmother looked up. "Darling."

"Best thing for them." My father shrugged, indifferent. "Learn more about life in one year at a boarding school than you would in ten at a Comprehensive." He looked at me, eyes crinkling at the side. "Isn't that right boy?"

"How should I know?" I pushed the strawberries round the plate. "I can't remember a time when I haven't been at boarding school."

My father sniffed. "Thought about which regiment you're going to join yet?"

My hands twitched. "Possibly the Green Jackets."

"The Green Jackets?" he blasted. "Is that the best you can come up with?"

"Maybe the Lifeguards?"

"Better. A bit." He flicked out his cigarette case and mechanically tapped out a cigarette before flicking his Dunhill lighter. He leaned back in his deckchair and exhaled. "That Colonel Jones. God, I'd have been proud to have known him."

I was shrivelling up inside. But I had never known anything else with my father. With his sons and with his underlings, he adopted a scorched earth policy. I glanced at Estelle. She, in her turn, was being interrogated by my stepmother.

My father looked at me again, the smoke streaming out of his nostrils in twinjets. He sucked once more, greedily, before stubbing the cigarette out under his feet. "Damn proud."

We packed up and meandered over to the Thames to watch one of Eton's grandest spectacles, the Procession of Boats.

What an extraordinary relief it was to watch my parents march off to see some army friends. I had Estelle all to myself.

But I didn't enjoy it for long, for there was another clunky note, as if I had been playing Bach's First Prelude and botched the final chord.

And this was because Estelle knew ALL about the Procession. Knew exactly how all Eton's rowers would be dressed up in their finery. Knew how the crews would row past the galleries and stand up till all nine of them were at attention with their oars vertically in front. And she knew too how the rowers would doff their boaters and wave to the crowds.

Oh yes, she knew everything.

We found a place next to the elite enclosure for the Headman and his selected guests. The riverbank was lined with hundreds of spectators, and it is regrettable but true that the vast majority of us were praying for the crews to get the wobbles so they'd be pitched headlong into the river.

How we longed for it. We were like a baying mob at the Roman circus, on the edge of our seats as we waited for the Christians to get butchered.

About five or six of the crews had already rowed past. They made a splendid sight, sweeping round the bend before getting to their feet. They'd laced their boaters with flowers and, when the hats came off, the garlands would be strewn across the water.

We were watching the ten-oared Monarch, packed with Eton's most prestigious boys, and there in the middle of the boat was Savage. Even from a hundred yards away, I could recognise him. They wore white trousers, navy blue monkey jackets and floral boaters. The cox, minute in comparison to the rowers, was in a full admiral's uniform with a fore and aft hat.

The Monarch gave one final hard pull and from the middle they started to stand up. Savage and the number five lifted their oars clear out of the water and hoisted them vertically into the air. Then, hand-over-hand, they crept up their oars until each was standing as erect as a guard's officer.

The two rowers on either side of Savage then crept to their feet, the next two and the next.

There was an eerie hush as the boat meandered down the river. The stroke and bow lifted their oars from the water. The pair of them, along with the cox, tried to stand up.

Now was the time of maximum vulnerability. Nothing to stabilise the boat and with over half-a-ton of crew above the waterline.

The stroke, bow and cox had doubtless practised the manoeuvre scores of times. But the stakes are so much higher when you're performing in front of more than a thousand spectators and every one of them hoping in their dark hearts that you will fail.

The cox was slightly beyond a crouch when the boat started to rock. You could see it first in the oars as they tilted like poplars in the wind.

Estelle clutched tight onto my hand. An expectant murmur thrilled through the crowd as we realised that the cream of Eton's rowers were in trouble. The boat was rocking wildly. We could see the heavyweights twitching from side-to-side, over-correcting as they tried to keep her steady.

They might have held it but they must have sensed the animal hum from the bank. A cacophony of shrill cat-calls started up.

A magical moment as the Monarch teetered onto its edge. The oars now pointing this way and that.

Estelle let out a visceral moan. I was keening like a Zulu warrior at the charge.

And the boat was gone. A great shriek of delight went up from the bank. It heeled over to the side, and crew, cox, oars and all plunged into the river. Savage, I'll say this for him, looked elegant to the end. He was the last to go and managed a farewell wave of his boater before he too thrashed into the water.

Bedlam. I have never heard a sound like it, have never experienced such universal happiness at other humans' misfortune. There was something almost dirty about the noise, the air of deep satisfaction that there might have been after the execution of Charles I.

The river was a mass of oars and paddling rowers and lost boaters and, in the middle of it all, the capsized Monarch sailed serenely on.

Animal excitement was etched into Estelle's face. She was panting with exhilaration. And when she caught my eye, she hugged me for the sheer mayhem of it all. Hugged me, laughed and kissed me once, twice, three times.

I screeched out a great wolf-howl of delight. I was effervescing with joy. For being there with Estelle and for having witnessed this age-old ritual go so spectacularly wrong.

Then Estelle whispered something in my ear.

I couldn't hear her for the shouting, but the hairs on the back of my neck instinctively started to bristle when I finally made her words out.

She said it once more, this time louder: "I love it when that happens."

It took but a moment to pick up the inference – that not only had she been to Eton before, but that she'd been to the Fourth. It was unavoidable. No one could miss it.

On the outside I was still letting out great whoops of delight. But on the inside, my guts turned to ice.

Now it seems so petty, to be getting so uptight about a girlfriend's possible dalliances in the past. Now it seems as if everyone comes with history, has had a dozen lovers at the very minimum.

However, this was the first time that I had ever been on the verge of falling in love and this was the first time I had ever experienced the raw stab of jealousy. What an emotion it was. Instantly I had pieced the story together, could envisage Estelle attending the previous year's Fourth of June. Could see her exactly as she clung onto the arm of some other louche Etonian. She'd probably been wearing the same outfit.

Jealousy can cast such a horrible shadow over your life. Even in the happiest times, it can still come up and bite you. And, in my case, I was cruelly mesmerised by pictures of Estelle kissing another Etonian. I could picture it all. It almost made me feel sick.

I put on a brave face, of course I did, pretended that we were having the most fantastic time on this most fantastic of days. But, inside, it was turmoil. Estelle sensed it immediately, could feel the way that I no longer wanted to hold her hand. Even to this day I'm still not sure if she knew exactly why, though part of me thinks that she wouldn't have dropped such a loaded comment into the conversation unless she had deliberately wanted me to find out.

We mooched back to the house. I made Estelle and my parents

some tea and toast. I was still putting on a good front; even then I was quite the expert at putting on a veneer of imperturbability. No one could have guessed the dark thoughts that were scuttling through my imagination.

I left them all in my room for 15 minutes while I went off to the School Yard for Absence. Almost the whole school congregates for one final roll-call before they are officially freed for half-term, and never in your life have you seen such an array of black tailcoats. Hundreds and hundreds of them, all flocking in little colonies around the green statue of Henry VI.

I barely gave the boys a thought as my mind was being put through the mill. On the one side, longing to kiss Estelle again, to feel the touch of her hand; on the other, consumed by the most raging jealousy. And the most wretched thing of all about this jealousy was that it felt like a righteous emotion, as if it was me on the moral high ground, as if I had a perfect right to feel angry at Estelle. It felt as if that very afternoon she had cuckolded me.

I was so far away it took a few moments to realise that India was standing in front of me.

She was by herself, wearing a silk floral dress and cream cardigan, a rug tucked under her arm, and a little leather satchel on her back.

"Hello Kim." As she spoke, she wiped the fringe of brown hair from her forehead and swept it over her shoulders.

"Hello." I beamed with pleasure. All thought of my other love evaporated from my mind.

"Thought I'd come and see one of Eton's most venerable customs."

I don't know whether the champagne had belatedly given me a second wind, but I felt suddenly playful. I no longer had this awful weight over my head as if my every word with India was being monitored and evaluated. "You ought to try taking part – now that really is fun."

"Do you think they might be able to hold an Absence for the teachers?"

"I think that could be arranged, Miss James." I was dancing, a cherry blossom on the wind.

"Shall I stay and watch you do your thing?"

"Churlish not to."

I made my way over to Lupton's Tower for my roll-call and India followed.

As the names were read out, the boys would raise a finger and cry out, "Here". But with India behind me, I of course had to do something different. "Here Sir," I said, abasing myself with a grand theatrical bow as if I had just been introduced to the Queen.

India laughed all the way back to the Long Walk. "You do amuse me, Kim," she said.

"Your pleasure is my purpose."

I don't know if she'd also had a drink at lunch, but she let out a peel of laughter.

"I'll miss seeing you at the Music Schools," she said. So pretty. So very vulnerable. She was clutching the rug in front of her, and looked more like a teenager than a teacher.

"And I you."

And with that I gave a wave and turned on my heel. Even at 17, I knew that sometimes it is best to quit while the going is good.

India. After Estelle, she was so pure, so refreshing.

I went back to my room, ripped off my tail-suit and raced to join my parents and Estelle in the Merc. Suddenly I was a cheery, irrepressible swain. All it had needed was five minutes with India and every trace of jealousy had been excised out of my system. So Estelle might have been to the Fourth of June before, and might have kissed another Etonian, and…so what?

Home was in Chelsea and I guess it was quite a pile – five storeys and a great clutter of accumulated brown furniture. Though I'm sorry to say that, for me, it was just 'home' – nothing more, nothing less – just as Eton was simply 'school'. Still, it certainly impressed Estelle. As I carried her bag upstairs to the third-floor spare room, she gasped at the garden and the pictures.

"This is just beautiful," she said, as we walked into the guestroom. There was a posy of flowers on the bedside table and the last of the evening sun was glinting through the window.

"Not half as beautiful as you."

I took her in my arms and kissed her. Not passionately but with affection.

"I think I'm falling a little in love with you," she said.

"Well hold onto your seat."

She pecked my lips and let out a contented sigh as she nestled her head onto my shoulder. After the madness of Eton and the stifling pressure of my father, it was so pleasant to stand there and hug. My mind was a whirl of half-digested thoughts but, almost without thinking, my hands were slipping underneath her shirt and finning over her back.

It was the first time I'd ever touched anyone's skin like that. Warm and supple.

"Not now," she whispered. "But maybe later?"

"Maybe later?"

"Maybe after your parents have gone to bed?"

"Maybe a very good idea."

"Definitely a very good idea."

As we went down to supper, she gave my bottom a light pat. How much it seemed to promise.

Neither of my two brothers were at home so it was just the four of us for dinner.

We all drank red wine and it was the only thing that I could touch all evening. The cook had left out bread, cheese and a light salad for dinner, but I couldn't swallow a mouthful. No – already I was far away in the spare room, gently undressing Estelle.

The music with which I attempted to seduce her was, naturally enough, *The Well-Tempered Clavier.*

The Third Prelude, in C-sharp Major, evokes such mixed memories for me. It is a jolly, ebullient prelude. But now I cannot listen to the piece without remembering the wreckage of my relationship with Estelle, for the Third Prelude is a constant reminder of the destructive power of my jealous rage.

Snug on the Chesterfield, we'd already listened to the first and second preludes and fugues. She was melting in my arms. Deep kisses, my hands already up the back of her shirt.

Then that Third Prelude started, and I decide to move things on.

I was only seconds from disaster.

My right hand had wormed up to the back of Estelle's bra-strap and I was trying to undo it.

I knew what I was supposed to do, knew that I was meant to unfasten the clip, but nothing was happening.

Estelle gave me a delicious smile and leaned back. She took off her shirt and undid her bra – unclipped it at the front where the catch was. And there she was in front of me, naked from the waist up, basking in the firelight. It was so unexpected. I'd thought there might be resistance, but instead it was her who was taking the fight to me.

She was the very image of a girl on the brink of womanhood. The swell of young breasts, the firelight flickering shadows over her downy skin.

I had dreamed of this moment for so long. And now that it was upon me, all I could do was gaze.

But just as I was finally moving forward to touch her, she said something.

Words that I will never forget.

Words that were like a vat of cold seawater on my burning desire.

She smiled. "You Etonians are all the same."

That's all she said.

My jaw dropped in bewilderment. From every recess of my brain, alarm bells were jangling.

My hideous, primeval jealousy was back, far, far worse than before and this time baying for blood. There was nothing I could do to stop it. Trying to prevent the words coming out would have physically choked me.

I moved back from her. The expectant smile dissolved from her face.

"You mean there've been others?"

"Well…" She gave me a coquettish smile. "You don't want to know."

I was bristling now, bristling with outraged hurt. "Why don't you just tell me?"

"Ask no questions and get no lies."

How I was on the rack. On the one hand, I was on fire to know all the details – when, where, with whom, and for how long. Explicit details too; I wanted to know everything, every single thing, so that I could be disgusted at what she'd done – and disgusted also with myself. And on the other, I could still hear the quiet insistent voice saying, 'Don't go there; don't go there.'

But how could I not go there? I had to go there. My jealousy was a ravening monster that had to be fed. I even moved back towards Estelle and cupped her hand, looked into her eyes, told her she could trust me, insisted that it wouldn't make any difference.

As it turned out, all my hunches had been correct. She had been to Eton before, had come along to the Fourth of June the previous year to see a boy whom I didn't even know. It had been his last term.

I. Was. Outraged.

I sat there, posing like a father confessor, but all the while feeling like a cuckolded husband. I insisted – yes, insisted – on knowing every last detail. They, too, had kissed in his room, had watched the Procession of Boats.

It had all fizzled to nothing and so Estelle's story came to an end – she had tears in her eyes. And all I could think of was not forgiveness, or warmth, or sympathy, but cold, unremitting vengeance.

God, I was repellent.

I couldn't begin to get my head round the fact that Estelle had been doing all this before with another boy. Not just any other boy, but another Etonian.

She tried to hug me, but I had none of it, had withdrawn to the end of the sofa and sat there huddled in a festering bundle of jealous rage.

And you know the worst of it, the very worst of it?

She actually pandered to me. She went along with the idea that it was her – yes, her – who was at fault.

Oh, if only she'd slapped me hard across the face and told me to grow up. Or walked out and left me alone.

But no, she did none of that.

"Can you forgive me?" She tried to hug me.

In my vileness I twisted away.

"I'm tired," I said. "I think I'm going to bed."

She quickly put on her top and watched as I left.

Over breakfast, we barely said a dozen words. Even at the station I rebuffed her.

I would never see her again.

PRELUDE 9, E Major

Just a few days later, on 14th June, the Falklands War came to an end at a cost of 255 British lives and 777 wounded. Among the Argentinians, 652 men were dead or missing.

The stories had been shocking, quite different from any other war that I'd ever read about. The 33 Welsh Guardsmen who were killed on the Galahad, the 20 SAS commandoes who were drowned when their Sea King helicopter struck an albatross, the taciturn Old Etonian, Lieutenant-Colonel Jones, dying the hero's death as he stormed a machine-gun nest.

But far more moving for me than the stories were the pictures in my newspapers. The submarine HMS Conqueror returning to Faslane with a jaunty Jolly Roger on its conning tower to mark the sinking of the General Belgrano. The Sheffield, with smoke and flames pouring out of its guts. The Antelope, still gushing oily smoke as its prow slipped into the Atlantic. And a photo of a rifle, a paratrooper's helmet and a jam-jar of daffodils, marking the spot where the Falklands' second VC, Sergeant Ian McKay, fell on Mt Longdon.

Frankie ran a Union Jack up the house flagpole. Sap was so gung-ho that given half a chance he'd have quit his A-levels and joined up.

But all I could do was stare at that tragic picture of the rifle and Sergeant McKay's helmet, and wonder if the military was for me. Was that what I wanted out of life? Another decade or two in the sole company of men? More rules, more regulations?

There was a plus side, I was aware of that. I would be

maintaining over a century's worth of family tradition. For the first time, my father might be proud of something I'd done. The truth was, I had no idea what I wanted to do after I left school. But if not the army, then what else could I turn my hand to?

I was equally in two minds over Estelle. For days, I imagined myself the wronged victim. I believed that I was 100 per cent in the right, that it was me who was in need of succour, and that it was within my remit to offer forgiveness.

Every night as I went to bed, I would torture myself with vivid images of Estelle at the Fourth of June, not kissing me but another Etonian. Truly, it felt as if she had done the deed right in front of my very eyes.

Occasionally, I would relent. I would leaf through her letters, putting them to my nose and smelling her perfume. I could recall every one of our kisses and how I had stroked her back; ah yes, and that image of her topless, sitting in front of me – that was another memory that was forever playing in my mind.

But every time Estelle called on the house pay-phone, all these happy memories were snuffed out by my jealousy, which was like a tank steam-rollering everything in its path. When we spoke, I was clipped, formal, like an upstanding Victorian father dealing with a disobedient child. I made light of her coming to Eton the previous year. I said it didn't matter, I said I forgave her – and she was grateful that I did.

It was all supposed to be behind us. But everything was different. It kept cropping up in conversations. I believed I had a perfect right to bring the matter up as and when I felt like it. My daily letters had become curt and precise.

For although I'd said I'd forgiven Estelle, I could never forget.

Now I can only shake my head at that foolish, foolish boy.

For in this life, there are so many things that it is possible to feel aggrieved about. But jealousy over your loved one's past should never be one of them.

Things might – possibly – have been different if I had been able to work through my feelings. Though how laughable the very thought of that is at a school like Eton. I didn't even feel able to confide in my best friend Jeremy.

The truth was that I was not even able to come clean to myself.

The letters and the phone calls, they fizzled, they sparked, and, after a short period, I had stamped it out. Killed it.

And my primary and foolish feeling at the time was that Estelle had received her just desserts.

Shortly after half-term, I was in an English class. I remember it well, for it was the first time that Shakespeare had ever really resonated.

In previous years I had studied *Romeo and Juliet, Titus Andronicus, Macbeth, King Lear, Julius Caesar*. All of them had left me cold. Stories of flawed men and conniving women. Not one of them had meant a thing to me.

But Othello, the dark, charismatic, trusting Moor…

I got it.

I could understand the madness, the cold logic with which his clinical mind had appraised the situation, the seething impotent rage, and the final red raw explosion of anger as his unbridled jealousy was given its head.

Angela and I still liked to look at each other during the lesson. We would gaze at each other across the room, and probably both imagine all manner of fond and libidinous encounters.

She was still looking at me as she raised her hand to ask a question.

"Do you have to be in love to feel jealous?" Her hand came down and for a moment I thought her accusing finger was pointing dead at me.

Her eyes never left mine.

The question stopped McArdle in his tracks. He was intrigued, had never thought of the question before. He perched himself on the edge of his desk.

"Interesting." He temporized and tugged at the point of his beard. "Never thought about that before."

For a while he stared at the ceiling. "If you're truly in love, then you won't suffer from the grosser excesses of jealousy. You might still feel the odd pang, but you could work it through. True love can dilute almost anything."

McArdle was up now, strutting around the front of the room, hands behind his back. "The problem arises when you're in love for the first time and you experience jealousy for the first time. Like, for instance, Othello.

"He's been so used to being in control of everything about him. Then out of nowhere comes this powerful new emotion and he has no idea how to deal with it. Yes – the first time it hits you, it can be as powerful as love itself."

My eyes were on Angela but I was taking it all in. It all made perfect sense.

McArdle had paused in mid-stride as if struck by a new thought. "The first time you experience them together, the two are like yin and yang, black and white, each as strong as the other.

"It takes practice to learn to deal with jealousy, to control it."

He shrugged and smiled. "It takes practice to learn to cherish the one you love."

Wise words indeed, and, as he said them, Angela unfolded her hands and proffered her palms towards me, as if to say that this was me, a yin-yang mixture of love and jealousy.

I blushed to the roots of my hair, for it was as if she had found out my darkest secret.

Since half-term, India and I had had only one music class together. Although she'd seemed pleased to see me, the lesson had been formal – as if the coffee and crying, and, yes, that kiss, had never occurred. I didn't know what it was about. But then I had never truly expected anything to happen with India. I was grateful to gather up whatever scraps fell from her table.

And then everything changed. And I mean everything.

I can recall each moment.

My life has never been the same since.

It's a half-day, a Thursday, and, yet again, it's another scorching afternoon.

I'd been practising *The Well-Tempered Clavier* at the Music

Schools. But this relentless diet of Bach could pall for even a devotee like me and after a couple of hours I was taking a break to go for a dip in Eton's outdoor pool. I remember it distinctly – I was wearing faded jeans, a white t-shirt and some Green Flash plimsolls. Under my arm, my sheet music, towel and trunks.

I was taking a different route from my usual one, going via Judy's Passage, one of Eton's main walkways.

I've just crossed the Eton Wick Road and was just about to turn into the high-walled gloom of the passage.

And suddenly from the other direction appears India.

"Hello you," she says. She looks exquisite in another of her white cotton dresses, a rug under her arm and leather knapsack on her back. India's beauty in the flesh was always far superior to any of my memories.

"Good afternoon."

We stand opposite each other at the end of Judy's Passage and India takes in my towel, my music book.

"You're right," she says.

"I am?"

"On a day like this, swimming is definitely better than Bach."

All I can do is smile. "And where are you off to?"

"Oh, you know – any leafy bower…" She kicks at a dandelion, about to say more. Then her eyes dart down the passage. The smile trails from her face. "God, it's him."

"Who?" I squint into the shadows, making out a silhouette. I can recognise the figure only too well.

India is already one step ahead of me. "Come with me." She takes my hand and we are dashing over the Eton Wick Road. We dive into the elderberry bushes by the Master's Field, and, like scrumping schoolchildren, drop to our knees. It's crazy, it's madness, but India and I are hiding in a bush because neither of us wants to be seen by Savage.

We watch him as he emerges from Judy's Passage. He's wearing his full pop regalia and sunglasses. For a heart-stopping moment, he stares directly at the elderberry bush, looks straight at me. I'm sure he's spotted us, must have spotted us.

Then he looks to the left, to the right, and lopes off down the Eton Wick Road.

For the past minute, I've been holding my breath. I let out a huge sigh. And I realise with surprise that India is still holding my hand. She gives it a squeeze.

Yes – she gives my hand a squeeze.

"Can't stand that boy," she says. "I see him almost every day."

"I'm stuck in the same house with him."

"Did you see him when the Monarch capsized?"

"Did I see him?" I laughed. "I only wish I'd got it on film."

We're resting back on our heels, easy, comfortable, squatting amid the roots and dry old leaves of an elderberry bush. Over the green tang of the tree, I can smell her lily-of-the-valley.

I wish I could have bottled up the moment – that time when we seemed possibly on the brink, my guts churning with a mixture of terror and expectation.

An elderberry bush on the Eton Wick Road, with dead leaves scrunched beneath us and dappled sunlight filtering through the branches. It is not the first place that springs to mind for the beginning of a romance. But that, nonetheless, is where it all started.

"I can feel your pulse." India is lightly holding my hand, two fingers of her other hand against my wrist.

I gaze at her, our heads only a foot apart. "Yes?"

She presses her fingers and counts. "Fast."

"It is?"

She counts off the seconds. "150 beats a minute. At rest."

She had found me out. For two months I had done my best to mask my ardour, to hide my feelings, to be nothing more than the model pupil who was devoted to Bach and his preludes. But now...

All had been revealed. There was nothing more to hide. "I'm sitting next to you," I whisper. "You're holding my hand."

"I am?" She looks at my hand as if for the first time realising it is attached to my body. "I am." She brings my hand close to her face and looks at my fingers, my nails, glances at my palm. "A kind hand."

And with that, India, my 23-year-old music teacher, the most beautiful woman I have ever seen, the vision whose very presence makes me go weak at the knees, raises my hand to her lips and kisses the inside of my wrist.

It is the most mesmerising thing I have ever seen or felt. India's eyes are still locked on mine, but slowly she is planting kisses on my wrist.

Inch-by-inch she is working her way up the bare flesh of my arm.

My body is in a vice. I couldn't move if I wanted to. Couldn't speak even if I had words to say.

I'm in freefall, have finally been swept off the precipice and have no idea how or when it will all end.

India isn't moving her head. Instead she is drawing my arm towards her, reeling me in. She's at my elbow and I can feel her hair trailing on my hand. Her kisses are the lightest of touches, the delicate stroke of a humming-bird's feather.

My arm may be still, but the rest of my body has started to shake. Cramps in my legs, fire in my belly, and the hairs on my neck prickle like a pin-cushion. I am fascinated. Ensnared. Even in my most outrageous dreams, I had never thought to imagine she would be staring into my eyes and kissing my arm.

She kisses the sleeve of my shirt. I dare myself to think how it may end. For now her unblinking eyes are just inches from mine, drawing me in. I can't see her lips, but I can feel them. Pecking at my shirt. Her breath is warm on my neck, her chin light on my shoulder.

That lily-of-the-valley – how can I ever forget it? For me the scent could never be anything other than India.

I am a statue, not moving an arm, a leg, a finger, even an eyelid.

But underneath, I am a raging, pulsating cauldron of emotion and desire. Total turmoil masked by a stoic veneer.

A car goes past, a sigh of wind. Ever more slowly, India kisses my neck, her lips lingering longer. A kiss on my jaw. On my cheek. The silk caress of her cheek against mine. I haven't moved, can't move, but I am quivering at the hope, the desire, of what might happen next. My thumping heart feels as if it will shatter with the strain.

A kiss on my cheek, just an inch from my lips. She pulls back ever so slightly, looks me in the eyes, so close that I can feel her long black eyelashes.

India.

Kisses.

Me.

And nothing will ever be the same again.

The lightest touch of an angel's wing.

I have been touched by God.

India draws back once more, smiling as she gazes at me. Her fingers lock through mine, holding my hand tight. My hip rests lightly against her thigh.

A slight lean forward, she kisses me again, not on my lips, but on the other side of my mouth. All the while, those eyes, those black tarns, never leave my gaze for a moment.

And then she kisses me on the lips once more, still so soft, but India holds it a fraction longer.

She brings her other hand up, and with her long pianist's fingers strokes my cheek. I move my head to the rhythm of her hand.

It is as if her kiss has released me, for it is my turn. As delicately as India herself, I kiss the inside of her wrist. Draw back.

And kiss her on the lips. No open mouths, no darting tongues. A reverential kiss and for the first time her eyes close, as if she has come home.

Without a word needing to be said, we break off and enfold our arms round each other. Not knotted, but firm enough for trust. I stroke her hair.

I am bound in the moment. Not marvelling at what has occurred, not amazed at my luck that India is still in my arms.

No, I had given myself up to my senses – to the cocoon of scent that surrounded us, the warmth of India's chest pressed against mine, the texture of her hair at my fingertips, and the tenderness with which she strokes my neck.

Still holding me fast, she kisses me on the ear, whispers,

"Thank you."

I rub my cheek against hers. My voice is hoarse with excitement. "It is I who should thank you."

India strokes my cheek, little soft dabs on my skin. There are so many things to say, the whys and wherefores, and how longs and how manys, but there is nothing that cannot wait, because now she has kissed me again and, for the first time in my life, it is a kiss that feels natural. Right. In the correct order of things. Just perfect.

One kiss, another and another, harder, more urgent, more insistent, and I can feel her lips start to melt beneath my own, parting fraction by fraction. She leads the way, but is doing everything at such a leisurely pace that it feels as if we have all day to pleasure each other. There is no coarse stab of a tongue, just this total awareness that her lips are pressed open against mine.

I am in her hands, am taking my cue from her.

We are both holding back, both waiting to see who will be the first to break, to move from lips to tongue.

Heady desire. I am alive for the sense of her lips.

How brutish those past kisses with Estelle seem – gross, open-mouthed snogging, when all I had wanted to do was bury my tongue into a girl's mouth.

For now I am receiving my first proper lesson in how to kiss, learning that kisses, like every other act of love, are always sweeter when savoured slowly.

My eyes are closed; I have given myself up to India's kisses. Nose-to-nose, lip-to-lip, then, with all the delicacy of a mouse emerging from its hole, I can feel the light touch of tongue.

As delicately as if I were coaxing a butterfly onto my finger, I dab my tongue. The lightest of touches.

Her tongue glides against mine, almost lazy, not a full charge, but with artful patience.

Wherever India goes, I follow. She touches my teeth, lets her tongue slip between my lips and I don't know how long it's taken, how many minutes have ticked by, but she's now kissing me with wanton abandon, her lips moving firm against my own, working her mouth against mine.

What a kiss; what a woman; what a day.

I lose track of time. That first kiss lasted so long that even my mind stops. My life is India's lips and India's mouth.

I never want it to end, aware that if it did stop India might come to her senses and realise she was kissing a 17-year-old schoolboy.

But when she does eventually stop, she crushes me to her breast, and slowly my senses return. To realise that I was sitting in the brush of an elderflower tree, that the shadows were lengthening, and that in my arms was my beautiful piano teacher.

One more time I look at her face and gaze into her eyes, just to confirm that the unthinkable, the unbelievable, has happened. But yes, yes, it really is her, it is India in my arms.

"Hello," she says, and it is as if she has spoken to me for the first time, as if our relationship has started afresh. Which in a way it had. For we were no longer teacher and pupil; it felt like we were lovers embarking on our maiden voyage, with the wind set fair and not a smut of cloud on the horizon.

"Hello." I hugged her again. I had never known a hug to feel so good. I saw those lips once more and could not stop myself from kissing them. I still could not bring myself to believe such things were permissible.

"Happy?"

I laugh at the thought. "Right here, right now, with you underneath this elderberry?" I say. "I have never been so happy in my entire life. You?"

"I think I'm happy too." She traced her fingers along my jaw-line. "Shall we go somewhere else?"

"Some leafy bower?" I echo her earlier words.

I'm rewarded with a peck on my lips. "You leave first."

As I stood up, I had a last regretful look at our den and at India, still sitting on the leaves and gazing at me like a beautiful nymph.

After the shade of the bush, the sunlight was dazzling. I squinted in both directions and the road was clear. I called India out and she emerged like a delicate fawn. In the Master's Field, she brushed off the worst of the twigs and leaves, and we walked

– walked, but did not touch, walked with a gap of three or four feet between us. If we had been more sensible and more alert to Eton's thousand eyes, we would not have been seen within a hundred yards of each other. At the time though, we were feckless and so dazed with love that we didn't recognise the need for discretion, had not even contemplated the thought that the mere sight of the pair of us walking together would be enough to launch a score of rumours and a flurry of speculation. No – we were oblivious to it all, incapable of thinking about anything but our doughty ship that we had just launched onto the high seas.

But although we couldn't touch as we walked, we could still talk. There were so many things that I longed to ask her. When had it all started? Why me? Why now? Would it last? Could it last? When could I see her again? Could I see her again? Could she kiss me again? Please? Hundreds and hundreds of questions, but, even then, even with my first true love, I knew that some things were left best unasked; that sometimes there is not the need to have every question answered in full; and that, more often than not in life, ignorance is bliss.

Wise beyond my years. It showed an awareness of the delicacies and the pulse of a relationship. Sometimes, I was quite capable of being sage and practical. If only I could have been like that all of the time.

But of course I was still a schoolboy – and schoolboy emotions are nothing if not volatile, the one moment climbing the dizzy peaks of love and the next terrified at how far you have to fall.

Well as it happened, I did fall – and am quite possibly still falling.

However, don't think for a moment that I would have missed that climb. India took me to the extremes of love and rage, and jealousy and sorrow, and they were in every respect the emotional high-points of my life.

We found a weeping ash tree far from Eton's playing fields. India slipped off her knapsack, sat down and patted the rug next to her in invitation.

I sat and, not daring to believe my luck would hold, I slipped my arm round her waist.

It had been twenty minutes since we'd kissed and I longed for more. I leaned over; she leaned up to kiss me. And she kissed me – again. And once more, as powerfully as the first time, I was overwhelmed by India's beauty.

Without a word, India started rummaging in her knapsack, and as she did so she was humming to herself, humming the courtly Ninth Prelude in E-Major.

She was wooing me with Bach, her head gliding to the beat as she found her thermos. Her movements, like everything else in her life, spoke of controlled efficiency. She was as relaxed as if she were at the keyboard. She unscrewed the thermos top, poured and passed me the glass.

"Here's to us," she said. Ice-cold lemonade, homemade, astringent and razoring the back of my throat.

I sipped three times and passed the glass back to India. "And here's to you."

She drank and lay back on the rug, stretching out her arm to take my hand. I had never seen her looking so beautiful. Her white dress stark against the tartan rug, her hair in a billowing brown halo about her head, and her face lit by shafts of dying sunlight.

We could have talked, but instead we gazed unblinking into each other's eyes. I leaned over and kissed her.

I hate to admit it now, but I think that the time under the weeping ash was the high-water mark of our relationship – when everything was new and fresh, when our potential was limitless, and when my heart and mind had not yet been soured by demons.

We kissed and hugged, and the sun was now low on the horizon, peeking through the treetops. I checked my watch. My heart lurched.

We had been together for three hours. I'd missed Absence.

"I've got to go." I climbed to my knees.

She just smiled. "It's been a wonderful afternoon."

"I want to…" I didn't know what to say. "Thank you for everything. Thank you for the lemonade. Thank you for you." I was standing up now, though still holding her hand.

"It is I who should be thanking you."

She was using my words on me.

"Do you want to come too?"

"I'll stay a while."

I knelt and kissed her fingers. As I left, I looked round one last time. She was still sitting there, in black silhouette against the sky, and, as she waved, her diamond ring glinted in the dying embers of the day.

BOOK 2, PRELUDE 3, C-sharp Major

A blissful moment the next morning when I was aware that something incredible had happened, but could not remember precisely what. It filled me with an expectant glow, as if something extraordinary was right around the corner.

Then it came to me, the whole flood of memories washing through my system, over and over again, and they all boiled down to the fact that I was in love with India, had spent the whole of the previous afternoon kissing her. I had kissed India. We had kissed for three hours, and hugged each other, and held each other's hands. She'd stroked my face, caressed my hair, kissed my arm, my hand, my face, my lips.

I could not keep it to myself.

At Eton, it had become second-nature to keep my feelings hidden, my secrets hugged tight. But this was different, it wasn't a weakness, this was something I wanted to bellow to the world: I was in love.

I found Jeremy in his room after breakfast.

He was at his burry reading *The Times* and continued reading even after I'd sat in his armchair.

"Doesn't look you'll be fighting in the Falklands," he said.

"Plenty of other battles." I gazed at the ceiling, dreaming of my love.

"Indeed there will be. Plenty of other places to die your hero's death." Eventually he looked up and examined me curiously for a few seconds. "Something's happened to you. You don't even want to talk about the end of the war."

"Something has." I was still staring up at the ceiling. "I'm in love."

"Anyone I know?"

"My music teacher."

"India James." Even the sound of her name caused my stomach to spasm. "I thought you'd been in love with her for weeks."

"I have. But now I'm not just in love; now I really love her."

Jeremy's eyes were still on the paper. He turned another page and, as casually as only he knew how, asked: "What's new?"

I steeled myself. But I had to tell him, had to share my joy with someone. "No loose tongues, you promise?"

"Of course."

He pushed his glasses back up his nose and for the first time gave me his full attention.

"I'm going to trust you on this one," I said. "Do you know why I was late for Absence yesterday?"

"Yet more piano practice?"

"No," I said. "India kissed me."

He took it well. The only indication Jeremy gave that he'd heard me was that his elbows were now on the desktop and his hands clasped underneath his chin.

"And what I want to know is – was it a one-off, or will there be more?" I was suddenly enthusiastic, longing to voice my hopes and fears. I leaned forward, hitching up my trousers. "We were kissing for hours – hours and hours. But will she wake up this morning and be wondering what the hell she was doing, or will she be as smitten as me?"

Jeremy nodded, encouraging me to tell all.

"It just came out of nowhere. I met her in the street. One moment we were talking in Judy's Passage, the next we were hiding from Savage in a bush, and…" I broke off. The astonishing memory of what had happened was still not even close to sinking in yet. "…she kissed me."

Finally he spoke. "You and India James?" he said. "*Fouquet in Le Touquet!*"

"For yesterday, yes. But what about today, tomorrow, next

week?"

Jeremy shrugged. "Send her flowers? Write her a letter?

"I don't know. I don't know." I was dry-washing my hands. "I don't know if it would be too pushy. I don't want to force the pace."

"So you sit back and wait for India to call the shots?"

I gnawed at a dag on my thumbnail, trying to work out the best plan. "But I don't want to be too passive either."

"Maybe she'll be as nervous as you. Maybe she's sitting there at the breakfast table right now, also wondering if it was a flash in the pan."

"Maybe."

It was possible, but it didn't sound very likely. It was hard to imagine India as anything other than my unobtainable piano-teacher. She certainly couldn't be in this swamp of indecision, or so I thought.

"You could always write her a letter, an affectionate letter that says, in an easy, roundabout way, that you're not averse to seeing her again."

"Yes!" I would write her a letter – not over the top, not risqué. But affectionate and leaving the door wide open for more. "Brilliant."

I was already up, raring to put pen to paper.

Jeremy shook his head from side to side. "You and India James? That's the weirdest thing I've heard in a long time."

"That's exactly what I thought." I now had my hand at the door.

"You're not going to blab this to anyone else, are you?" he asked.

"Oh no."

"Because some people are not nearly as discreet as me…"

How right he was.

I returned to my room and immediately started writing. It wasn't more than three sentences long, but it needed seven drafts before I felt that every word and every nuance struck the right tone. Cheery, loving, affectionate; telling her that if she wanted more I was available. But not over-eager, not cloying, not suffocatingly close.

I found her address from the Fixtures and decorated the envelope with a picture of a stave of music. The first prelude in C-Major, the first piece that I had ever learned for her.

I was still not sure whether it was the right thing to do; I thought I was being far too forward.

In hindsight maybe it was exactly what was needed.

Maybe it was just what she was hoping for.

Back and forth, back and forth, torn by indecision, and, before I could torture myself any more, I'd dashed the 150 yards down the road and popped it in the postbox.

The very moment that I heard the envelope fall to the bottom, I regretted it. It was being far too pushy. What could she see in me? I was a 17-year-old schoolboy. For God's sake, I was one of her pupils.

Further agony, not knowing if I had done the right thing. For the rest of the day, I was at turns jubilant and cringing that I had been so forward as to write to her.

It was lunacy. The more I thought of it, the more I'd convinced myself. With an angel like India, you needed to be cool, take it slow, give her enough space and freedom to find her own way.

By the afternoon, I had all but persuaded myself that through that letter alone I had blown it.

It makes me laugh to think of it now, but I had even started writing India a second letter in which I asked her to kindly disregard my first note.

I didn't send it, but I came very close to going to the Music Schools, not to kiss her, or to touch her, but to talk and to know that it had not all been some fantastic chimera of my imagination.

Luckily I restrained myself.

I had sent her one warm, courteous letter and that would have to suffice. If it didn't hit the mark, then our fledgling romance was never destined to get off the ground in the first place.

Or so I thought when I was not torturing myself over my own stupidity. A letter? How could I have been so ignorant, so obtuse, as to send her a letter?

If it was bad that night, it was even worse the next day.

When would I see her again? Would I have to wait till our next lesson on Monday? Would India pretend nothing had happened?

Would she ignore my letter? Greet me with a cool "Hello", and say not a word of our kisses?

Of course, I allowed myself to dream too, to hope that it might come to something, that we had embarked on the most extraordinary romance and that there would be more kisses and more caresses.

But these were the occasional breaths of fresh air that kept me going as I swam through a sea of despondency.

The bulk of my imaginings were that India was in the very act of terminating our relationship; that she'd already applied for a transfer within the Music Schools. Oh – to have kissed her, to have had this glimpse of paradise, and then to have had it snatched away.

I couldn't eat, couldn't think straight, couldn't concentrate for one single minute on any class or any conversation.

Saturday rolled on, and still I had not heard a word.

I decided that very afternoon I would scour the Music Schools and hunt her down. If only to call her bluff, because even knowing the worst would be better than being in this terrible limbo. Or so I convinced myself for a couple of minutes. And then I would shy away from the very thought of going to the Schools; no, I would go swimming, read, let India dictate the run of play.

I then decided that I'd wait till the Monday, would turn up to my piano lesson and, unless India alluded to our kiss and our Thursday afternoon, the subject would never pass my lips. A clinical, practical solution.

But sometimes you've got to go with your heart.

And that – praise God and all his angels – is what India did.

We don't have it anymore in Britain but, 25 years back, there was the great luxury of a second post. Two bites of the cherry, one at breakfast and one at lunch, just to find out if anyone thought enough of you to write.

And she had.

I have India's letter here in front of me now, matching cream paper and envelope, black pen, and handwriting so elegant that it is almost copperplate. The moment I first saw it sitting in my pigeonhole, I knew it was from her.

And my favourite thing of all about it is not the letter itself, but a little drawing on the back of the envelope of two people sitting underneath a tree. Because when I saw that picture I knew instantly that it was all going to be ok – that, far from being finished, we were a 'Go'.

That picture meant that I didn't have to tear the letter open then and there; I allowed myself the luxury of reading it in my room.

And this is what she wrote:

Dear Kim,
I'm still having to pinch myself.
I was wondering if you might like to come over for tea on Sunday. Any time after three.
Much love, I xxxxx

Five kisses, I counted them, and after I had read and re-read her letter, I hugged it tight to my heart and felt this enormous explosion of relief, total and utter relief. She wanted me. She wanted me.

The next day after lunch, I contented myself with a wash, a shave, and the smartest clothes in my wardrobe. A shower might have prompted unnecessary questions.

For already I was getting canny, had realised that a spray of aftershave might have piqued the other boys' interests.

I left the Timbralls at 2.45pm wearing my standard garb for a hot weekend afternoon, just jeans, t-shirt and music book. Your regulation Etonian off for a normal practice session at the Music Schools.

Only this time, instead of turning right at Keate's Lane, I continued straight down the High Street, past the last of the boy's houses, until gradually the college had stopped and I had entered Eton's civilian world. Instead of school shops, I was walking past pubs, cornershops and tearooms. Dreaming of greeting India at her door, of her warm in my arms.

I was all but on her doorstep when I realised that I had no gift. I jogged back to the florists for flowers. Roses, red, red roses. Roses for my love. A cliché, I know, but, apart from being made to buy flowers for my stepmother, I had never bought flowers for anyone before.

Within 50 yards I'd realised my foolishness. I was horrified at myself. A schoolboy with red roses in his hand? Could I have made it any more obvious? Even the most ignorant dullard could not have missed the inference.

That first time I was relatively lucky. A few cars passed me by, but there was hardly a boy in sight. Over the next few weeks though, when I was to make an almost daily pilgrimage to India's door, I was to be much more circumspect.

But that was because, over the next few weeks, I was to have much, much more to lose.

I hurried on down the street, trying to mask the flowers with my arms while I checked left and right for boys.

India lived in one of the little cul-de-sacs off the High Street, not far from the Windsor Bridge. Many times I'd walked past her road but had never realised that this was the home of my love.

Gravel scrunching underfoot. Flowers in precise herbaceous borders. And there at the end was number 16, with a clear varnished oak door and a brass knocker. Parsley, thyme and sage growing in pots by the porch.

Before I knocked, I stared at the house. I still remember it so well that I can describe it precisely – for this has always been my house of love.

Since my Eton days, I have honeymooned in style in Paris, have stayed at some of the world's finest five-star hotels, have whisked girlfriends to spas in Thailand, and have found love and passion in the most luxurious of resorts, with silken sheets, champagne on ice, oysters for breakfast and every other kind of aphrodisiac for lunch, tea and supper.

But none of it, not a single five-star hotel, not a resort, not a spa, can even compare in my heart to number 16, with its Spartan lines, cotton sheets and baby grand piano.

I loved it from the first moment I saw it – but then, I would have loved even the shabbiest bungalow if India had lived there.

It was Edwardian, peeling white paint on the walls and

windows, a bit tatty at the edges. Ivy grew up the sides, chimney perched on the end. I stared up at the roof, soaking it all up. So this was it; this was the home of my love.

My eyes were still on the roof when I caught her, caught her staring at me from an upstairs room. So motionless that I'd almost missed her. She had her finger pressed to her lips, as if cautioning me to keep a secret. She waved and was gone, gone almost as quickly as she was eventually to disappear from my life.

I can hear her coming down the stairs. My heart is drilling with excitement. The door opens, and she stands before me – welcoming me, yes me, into her home. Of all the boys and all the men that could have been invited into her home, she has chosen me.

Just at the mere sight of her my heart convulses. Should I kiss her? Should I touch her? What would she like?

"These are for you."

"Thank you, Kim." She takes the roses and inhales. So stylish. I could almost have believed it was the first time she'd been given a bunch of flowers. "Why, they're lovely." And with that, she cups her hand round my waist and kisses me on the cheek. Kisses me as if it's the most normal thing in the world, as if it's a girlfriend just saying thanks to her guy, as if we are already an item.

We're in the communal hall that she shares with the flat downstairs, handsome flagstones, a table for the post. I recognise her coat hanging on one of the pegs and her boots lined up underneath.

"Let's go up." She carries the roses in both hands and I follow just a few steps behind. Her light-blue cotton skirt swaying in front of my eyes. I have to hold myself back from stretching out to touch her. Another thick oak door at the top of the stairs, and then we step into the one place which, more than anywhere else on earth, I have come to associate with love.

"Welcome," she gestures with her hand, as if to say that what's hers is mine.

I still remember every inch of the flat, even down to the exact pictures that she had on the piano.

And the predominant feeling about it was that it wasn't meant for a woman, that it was more of a bachelor lair, with heavy oak panelling on the walls and high raftered ceilings.

From the stairs, you stepped straight into the main room. It was beautiful in its simplicity. A lofty gracious ceiling, three windows, a creamy sofa with two matching armchairs and, in the corner, the baby grand piano. Underneath the piano was an old wooden trunk and, on top of it, three stacks of sheet music. Nothing more – no television, no side-tables, no clutter of any kind.

India goes to the kitchen to put the flowers in a vase and, when she returns, she laughs as she sees me wallowing in her atmosphere. The noteboard beside the door has photos, letters, notes, mementoes. Three pictures on the wall, one of New York, one of Sydney, and one of Johann Sebastian.

I walk to the piano, a Steinway with a light brown patina. I play a chord and stare at the pictures above. Two photos, one of India between her parents and one of a beach, a sunset and a silhouette in the surf.

"Like it?"

"I love it."

"Do you want the guided tour?"

"Very much."

And with that she came over, slipped her hand into mine, and showed me her home. Off from the main living room there were three doors: a spare room-cum-office with a desk, a double-bed and shelves thick with books; a galley kitchen with a small café table and two chairs; and a grand old-style bathroom with a sink and bath that would not have looked out of place in a baronial hall.

I took it all in, staring wide-eyed at her books, her shampoos, her moisturisers, her herbs on the shelves. I wanted to see everything.

"Ready for the highlight?" She led me to the oak spiral staircase in the corner of the living room.

The stairs were steep, so steep that as I held her hand I was offered the most tantalising of glimpses up her skirt. I was hot, sweating, my chest taut with nerves.

At the top, India's bedroom.

It was the most elegant room I'd ever seen. Viewed even with the most unforgivingly objective eye, it was still breathtaking. And this is what it contained: a double bed with nothing but two plumped pillows and a plain white duvet, a small wooden side-table, on it a lamp and a book of Walt Whitman poetry; off to the side, a shower-room and toilet, and, at the foot of the bed, a wrap-around window that took up an entire wall, with a view so stunning that all I could do was goggle in amazement. The Thames was but a stone's throw away and behind it, looming high above us, was Windsor Castle. I had never seen the castle looking so beautiful, the river so alluring.

But it was far more than just a window. It was a vast sliding door, with a patio that stretched over the length of the living room.

As we stepped outside, she discreetly let go of my hand. For India, far more than I, already knew that Eton was nothing but a goldfish bowl.

She stood at the door and watched while I prowled round the edge of the patio, my hand trailing over the clematis and the black wrought-iron railings; I was a dog marking its new territory, a lover discovering the confines of his nest.

I looked at her, framed in the patio door. Even weeks later, even years after, I still found it difficult to believe that she was mine. Mine to kiss, mine to hold, mine to love.

For on that patio, I didn't feel like a swain, but like a gangly schoolboy who had been invited for tea by his teacher.

We gazed at each other, India in the doorway, me leaning against the railings on the far side of the patio, holding tight for fear that the ground might swallow me up.

Without a word, she beckoned to me. The smallest of gestures, just a wag with the crook of her little finger.

I went over.

"I think we should go inside," she said.

"Why's that?" I followed her in.

She stopped by the side of her bed and turned to me. "So I can kiss you."

Possibly the most beautiful words I have ever heard. I beamed with delight. For although now it seems obvious that India was interested in me, then I'd still been tormented by doubts. Perhaps I'd been reading it all wrong; perhaps she was just being the good teacher taking an interest in her boys; hell, I didn't know, perhaps she just felt sorry for me?

Yes, even when something like India was in the very palm of my hand, I could still find reason to doubt. And I did this right to the very end. Could not allow myself to truly relax and believe that India loved me and only me, that she accepted me in all my lumpen teenage entirety, and that all she wanted in return was my love. No, I could never just simply accept that.

"You want to kiss me?" I said. In that instant I had become cocksure. From being craven and nervous, she had empowered me.

"Very much." She took a step towards me, lightly clasping my elbow.

"And why is that?"

"You do it so well."

"I do?"

"Beautifully." She tilted her chin up and kissed me on the lips. Languorous. Long.

"Like that?" I breathed into her ear.

"Yes," she said. "Just as good as I remember it."

"Another?"

"Please." She looked up at me, pouted and closed her eyes.

I traced my fingertips lightly on her cheek, kissed her on one side of her lips, the other side. Then drew back.

India's eyes were still closed as she clasped my fingers. "I want more," she whispered.

"Like this?" I kissed her on the mouth. It was even sweeter than that first time under the weeping ash, because now there was the added knowledge, the expectation, of what might happen next.

"Like that." Her arms snaked up round my shoulders, braced round my neck, and, just as before, her moist lips began to open.

But this time she was pressing against me as well as kissing, pressing hard, leaning into me until I was falling backwards onto the bed and she was lying fully on top of me; once there, her lips showering my face with kisses, teasing me with her tongue.

And what I remember more than anything is not her lips, her mouth, or her hands, but that mane of brown hair that surrounded us like a curtain. Just our two faces, locked together in a sweet-smelling cave, her hair so dark, so thick, that all I could make out were her eyes burning in front of me. I abandoned myself to her kisses.

But it wasn't just her hair, her mouth, her double bed that made it all so memorable. My eyes are shut, one hand solid round her back, the other soft against her chin. We kissed, and we kissed, and we kissed – but nothing more. There were no hands slipping up shirts; no fingers fumbling at bra-straps; we were locked into each other's mouths.

Of course I was aroused. How could I not be? It was now by far the most erotic experience of my life. But our erogenous zones seemed taboo. Lips and mouths were one thing, but breasts and buttocks were out of bounds. I wouldn't have dared to go there, would not have let my hand stray. She might have thought it too forward. Might have thought I was pushing too fast.

But besides all that, I was content. Just to be allowed to kiss India, my Goddess, left me replete. I could have kissed her for days, weeks, on end. Thoughts of sex, in all its many mysterious ways, may have crossed my mind in the abstract, but the actual reality of making love with India and other such intimacies had not yet entered my head. Truly.

Until that afternoon developed.

For as we kissed, eyes shut, my senses wrapped in the smell of her hair, the taste of her mouth, the texture of her lips, I felt a delicate quiver. At first, I did not know if it was deliberate, if it was really meant for me. But then it came again, a soft pressure against my belt as she pressed her hips against mine. I knew what it meant in an instant – that now anything was possible. That together we might scale the sexual peaks.

I responded in kind. I pulsed back and, when she did it again, I stretched my arm down and, as tentative as any first-time lover that ever walked this earth, I stretched and stroked her upper leg. She purred.

Holding me fast, she rolled over. For the first time I was on top, her legs parted just a little. I leaned on my elbows and gazed down at her. As gorgeous a woman as I have ever seen.

India then writhed against me, parting her legs a little more until we were comfortable. "That feels good," she said.

"It's beautiful." I kissed her. "You're beautiful."

She traced her index finger along my jaw-line, my cheek, over my eyelashes and up to my hairline. "And to think that I haven't even offered you a cup of tea."

"Shocking."

"Shall I put the kettle on?"

"How will I be able to kiss you?"

She then idly kissed me before whispering, "Sate me."

"I'll try."

We kissed for five minutes, or maybe longer, only this time her hand slipped up my shirt and was stroking my back.

"I could come down to the kitchen with you," I said.

"I'd like that."

I followed her down, my hands not wanting to leave her for a moment, forever pawing at her shoulders, her hair, and, when we made it into the kitchen, we had to kiss again. The kisses seemed like oxygen that we needed for our very survival.

We had Earl Grey with lemon and then she played for me. *The Well-Tempered Clavier*, of course – it was becoming our music. The music that would always come to remind us of how much we loved each other.

She was playing not from Bach's first book but from the second – he'd finished it in 1742, some 20 years after the first.

I sat on the piano-stool beside her. "Book Two?" I asked.

She was concentrating on the Third Prelude in C-sharp Major, a true behemoth with seven sharps, so difficult that I would never have dreamed to touch it.

"Got to keep raising the bar."

"Is there much difference between the books?"

She paused, fingers poised above the keyboard, weighing up Bach's two heavyweights. "The second book might be a bit more mature. But you can hardly tell the difference. Although I've always felt the First Book is just that little bit looser. A bit freer, not quite as tight." She wrinkled her nose and shrugged. "I think we're all like that when we start out."

She started to play again, picking up from where she'd left off.

"I love it when you play for me," I said. "I always have."

"Thank you." She leant over and kissed me on the cheek without missing a beat. "I know you do."

She loved *The Well-Tempered Clavier*, she truly did. The music touched her soul, and, through her, it touched mine too.

From sight, she played preludes, fugues, the whole gamut, and there was not a note that I did not treasure.

I never realised at the time that India was such an accomplished pianist. She must have been close to concert class. To me she was only ever my piano teacher, my love, and the beauty who played me Bach.

We sat with our legs pressed easily together, knee-to-knee, thigh-to-thigh.

But already, only hours into romance, before even we had consummated our love, I was rocking the boat and conjuring up storm clouds from out of nowhere on the horizon.

That picture of India on the piano, tanned and wearing a sarong as she stood barefoot in the surf; did she look like she was in love? Who'd taken the picture? Was it the man who'd given her the diamond ring?

And when I took my leave, even at the very moment that I was kissing India goodbye, my eyes were raking over the noticeboard, staring at the notes and letters. In the corner, there was a photo of India with a man. I was ghoulishly riveted. He was tall, had his arm slung round India's waist. A rival? An ex? I couldn't bare to think, didn't even want to go there.

Oh, but I would, I would.

Somehow, I could contrive to spoil almost anything.

So as I walked down the stairs, I was not dwelling on my

memories, was not rejoicing in the fact I'd be seeing India for a piano lesson the next day. No, I was not thinking of what was to come. I was thinking of the past, her past, and what had happened in the days before she even knew of my existence.

Pitiful. Only hours into our relationship, I was ripping away at India's private veils.

So many couples these days believe they should keep nothing from their partners. They want to know everything about each other. Demand to know every secret. Accept nothing but total candour.

But I, I who have learned from bitter experience, believe that you should know just what your partner wants to tell you, for many secrets are best left unsaid.

PRELUDE 5, D Major

That Sunday evening, I didn't try to read or work. After supper, all I had been able to do was flop on my bed and stare at the ceiling.

Little memories would occasionally come back to me, things that I hadn't perhaps caught the first time round. The way that my guts had been so tangled in knots that I couldn't swallow a mouthful of shortbread. The trace of her tongue along my neck, her saliva growing cold on my skin. The warmth of her lips on my ear before she nipped my lobe. And the caress of my cheek as we said goodbye, her fingers rasping as they went against the grain of my short stubble. Those were the things that I was savouring. And as for my incipient jealousy, what of that? It had, for the moment, been tucked back into its box. I hadn't even begun to come down from the high of my afternoon with India at her home.

Then, a knock at the door and Frankie walked in, still wearing stick-ups and a white bowtie.

"Evening Kim," he said. "Can I take a seat?"

"Be my guest." I gestured to the sofa. I was already standing up, moving to my burry. I never liked to talk to him while I was lying on my bed. It left me at a disadvantage.

"Almost a shame about the war, isn't it?" he said.

"We'll be getting withdrawal symptoms, Sir."

"I hope not." He forced a chuckle. "So what have you been up to Kim?" He was good-natured, avuncular; deadly. You could never tell whether his questions were genuine or whether he was fencing for information. Maybe it was just my guilty conscience.

"Bit of music, Sir."

"Still on *The Well-Tempered Clavier*?" He cocked an ankle over his knee. "My grandmother used to play it for us. It's charming."

"Yes." My antennae were quivering, could scent danger.

"Must say your piano teacher must be very impressed. All that practice you're putting in." He'd leaned back now, hands clasped round his knee.

"I suppose so, Sir."

"It's Miss James, isn't it?"

Then I knew he was shamming.

"That's right."

"Good for you." A very slight raise of his left eyebrow, which could have meant whatever I took it to mean. "Yes, very good for you."

I could have said something anodyne. But I didn't. I stared at the cuticles on my fingers, careful not to display even a tremor of emotion.

The lull stretched on and on before Frankie spoke again. "I'm more than happy, Kim, to turn a blind eye to almost any of my boys' extra-curricular activities. Just so long as they are not actively thrust in my face."

"Yes Sir?"

"So, I wish you well with your piano practice. But in future I would recommend a little more discretion if you're going to get into the habit of buying bouquets of red roses."

"Yes Sir?" Not even a trace of inflexion in my voice. By God he had me though. Already, in under three days, we had been found out. I had to press my nails tight into the palms of my hands to stop my knees from shaking.

"I saw you when I was driving down the High Street. You looked so guilty I thought you'd stolen the school's Gutenberg Bible."

"Oh, yes Sir." My brain was humming with excuses, denials, anything to mask the truth. "Bought them for a classmate."

"And whom might that be?"

"Angela Evans."

"Her birthday, I presume."

"Nothing like that," I replied. "I just fancy her." In a way this was true. For a moment Frankie was floored. But then he was back, grinding away.

"And where does Angela live?"

"I don't know. I met her in a café."

Not a bad recovery. Almost plausible.

But Frankie revealed nothing. Not a thing. All I could feel was this minute appraisal as he studied my face. Again, that deadly raised eyebrow.

He levered himself out of the low-slung sofa. "Well, the best of luck Kim," he said. "You're going to need it."

A warning shot. I could hear the whistle as it whipped over my bows.

The next day, Monday, I was due for a piano lesson at noon. Just the thought of it had me skittering with anticipation. Every division was a wash-out.

Time seemed to arbitrarily expand and contract. In the hour before I was due to see her, every second was an aeon.

But for the last ten minutes, when I was set and on my way, I was on autopilot. It was as if one moment I'd left the Timbralls and the very next I'd arrived at the Music Schools, with my entire journey boiled down to one solitary second.

As I walked up the staircase in the Schools, I was still uncertain about my reception. I couldn't believe that my luck would hold, that India wouldn't have snapped out of her enchantment and that I wouldn't be cast back into the wilderness. That is how I was before every one of my meetings with India, even if we'd just spoken on the phone five minutes earlier. Always with heart in mouth, half-expecting to be shown the door. I perpetually felt unworthy of her love; I could never understand what she saw in me.

Having said that, even if she'd explained it to the last detail, it would never have been enough. Even though she would come to love me, she never explained why. I flatter myself that I may indeed have had certain unique qualities, but there at Eton, among more than a thousand boys, many of them far more prepossessing than myself?

I could never work it out.

Though perhaps I do myself a disservice. I had certainly shown her compassion and tenderness, as well as a total and utter dedication to my piano practice. Who knows? Maybe it really was all down to *The Well-Tempered Clavier*, which made me stand out from the other boys like a shining beacon.

Lick up the honey stranger, and ask no questions.

I licked it up.

In the end, though, I could not refrain from asking the questions. They were the scabs in my life that had to be picked.

When I knocked on the door of room 17 at noon, India was playing the piano. The smile on her face was of a woman in love.

She stretched and clasped my hand, and before I had said a word was pulling me down to kiss her.

"I've been like the *Princess and the Pea*," she said, throwing her arm round my neck.

"Tossing and turning?"

"Did you put something in my bed?"

"Did I?" I scratched the side of my mouth, pretended to think. "Maybe I did. I think I might have had it too, though."

We sat on the piano stool, clutching at each other as if we hadn't been together in weeks.

"I'm so happy when I'm with you." She hugged me tight, kissed me again, then sighed and broke away to sit on that shabby old armchair. She leaned forward, suddenly earnest. "We're going to have to take care."

"I know."

"People are looking into this practice room all the time." She swept back her hair. All I wanted to do in that moment was kiss her again.

"So…" She paused, as if readying herself for a pre-prepared speech. "So I think that when we're here in the Music Schools, I should teach you music."

I nodded and wondered if this was it.

But instead of a bullet, she offered up a rosebud.

"That isn't to say that I wouldn't love to be holding you, but…"

"We can't be caught."

"Yes." She was relieved, as if she'd been expecting a stand-up row.

I was already up to speed. If we were spotted, if word got out, India would have been dismissed. I would almost certainly be expelled. And our little craft would be holed beneath the waterline.

"Something more subtle than red roses?" I said.

India nodded. "They were beautiful though."

"Meeting away from your home?"

"I'm so glad you understand." She clicked her tongue, smiling with relief. "I thought this conversation might be difficult. But of course it isn't. Everything's easy when I'm with you."

"It is?"

She grinned in acknowledgement – and, you know, maybe that was why she fell in love with me. I didn't have the emotional baggage that comes with age and experience. I was just a schoolboy, eager to take her hand, willing to learn.

So, for the next 45 minutes, we reverted back to our old relationship, I the pupil and she my teacher. Once she stood behind me to point out a bar of the notes and I could feel her legs pressed against my back. But we were both models of restraint, did not kiss, did not paw, and, although my fingers itched to touch her, they remained glued to the keyboard.

Even the conversation was seemly, straightforward. I was there to learn the piano, and, since we could not kiss, we did what we always did. She taught me how to love *The Well-Tempered Clavier.*

"I think we're done," India said at length. She was standing by the window. My Goddess. I came to love those last piano lessons. For India's beauty – like everything else in my life – was always more beguiling when it was off limits.

"Thank you," I said. I stood up, not sure whether to risk a kiss.

"I was wondering…" She played with the hem of her skirt. "If you might be free tomorrow afternoon?"

"For you, anything."

"Shall we go for a walk?"

"I'd love to."

"Maybe outside Eton?"

"Windsor Park?"

She came over from the window, kissed me. "There's nothing I'd like more."

We arranged to meet by Windsor Castle at 2.30pm, and the next day after lunch I was flying upstairs the very moment that Frankie had left the dining room.

It was the first really wet day that I remember that summer. The cricket matches, tennis and athletics meets were off, and it was raining too hard even for the sculls to get out on the Thames.

But nothing short of a monsoon would have prevented me from seeing India.

In those days, it's now hard to believe, Etonians had to dress up even to go into Windsor. If they weren't in tails, they had to wear half-change of jacket and tie, just to ensure they stood out like Belisha beacons from the local town boys.

I wore a thick black donkey jacket and kept off the worst of the rain with my black Eton-issue umbrella. The rain slanted in hard, spraying the bottom of my coat. I stopped off at Rowland's, the school tuck shop, to buy India a box of chocolates.

There was not a boy or a master to be seen.

I'd thought she might not be there, that it might have been too wet for her, or too cold, and there was always the possibility that overnight she might have fallen out of love with me.

But there she was, standing underneath her umbrella, a lone figure next to Queen Victoria's slick-wet statue at the Castle entrance.

She was well-wrapped, with jumper, boots, her creamy Mac and a cashmere hat that was snug around her head, and, as she saw me toiling up the hill towards her, the smile on her face just grew bigger and bigger. When I finally threw my arms round her, she was openly laughing. We kissed, we hugged, and, at that moment, if any wretched Etonians had been out there in the rain to see us then they could have watched and be damned.

"Let me take that rug," I said.

As our fingers touched, we could not resist ourselves; there in the rain we clung to each other in open-mouthed ecstasy.

"I wondered if you'd come," she said.

"How could I not?"

She sighed contentedly. We had our arms set round each other as we strolled down the hill to the George IV gateway. "I hope you'll always think so well of me."

"Don't ever doubt it."

"I won't."

She looked up and kissed me. But did I detect something in her eye? That she'd been hurt, that she knew only too well how such promises are cheap, and that, above all, love is only for the moment, for who knows what tomorrow will bring?

We walked to the park and onto the Long Walk, which is straight as a die and undulates from Windsor Castle. At the other end is the Copper Horse, or Copper Cow as it is known at Eton, a vast copper horse with a paunchy George III atop. We had the whole three-mile walk to ourselves.

Although, we could not walk even 30 yards without stopping to kiss each other. We might say a few words, but then there would be that slight tug at the waist, we would catch each other's hungry eyes, and the next moment we were swept up in a tide of kisses.

No matter how far we walked, it seemed that we were never any closer to the Copper Cow. We'd been out an hour and George III on his granite plinth was still nothing but a black blip on the slate-grey horizon.

Again we stopped, kissed.

"Is it time for tea?" she said.

"Chocolates too."

Without another word, we stepped off the tarmac and over to the nearby horse chestnuts, where the grass was long and the wet branches hung heavy over the ground. We found a tree that was dense with leaves, the grass oiled but not wet, and, like two lovers preparing for bed, we spread out the rug and smoothed its edges.

India took off her knapsack and slid into the warm folds of my coat to lie on top of me. Underneath that chestnut tree, the sky grey with rain, every cell of my body was vibrating with love. I longed to declare it. But I didn't, for fear that she might think me too pushy, too young, too inexperienced.

She had her elbows tucked in underneath my arms, her head inches above mine.

"You seem too good to be true," She gazed into my eyes. "Sometimes I thought I'd never find happiness again."

It was like the last string had been cut, as if the door to her heart was now wide open, for suddenly we were kissing crazily, madly, and I'd rolled on top of her. Her hands were soft against my skin, slipping under my shirt, her ankles locked round my knees, and when we broke off she was panting, her face flushed and wet with perspiration.

"I want you," she said.

I kissed her, felt her hips rise up to meet me.

"I want to make love with you," she said.

I gazed at her, quizzical, not daring to believe.

"Please?" she asked.

How incredible it all now seems, that India, my first love, should so politely have asked for me, as if, even for a moment, I could ever have had a doubt.

But I had none, knew that to make love then and there, beside the rain-spattered Long Walk, was what I wanted more than anything else in the world.

How it all comes back to me. Kissing as if our lives depended on it, feasting my eyes on her face, her lips, and all the while thinking that this was it, my time had come, that for the first time in my life everything was on offer. Oh – to have the prospect of making love with India. I can hardly begin to describe it.

Some of my peers were in such a tearing hurry to lose their virginities that they would have been happy with any girl on earth. Would probably have paid for the pleasure.

I had not gone down that route. But still…the very idea that I should be about to make love with India, the Queen of all my fantasies, that she should want it, should be urging me on, should desire it as much as I did myself?

Beyond my wildest, wildest dreams.

We were a writhing mass of wet boots, steaming jumpers and slippery coats, her hands all over my back, my chest, curling up round my neck, and, from nowhere, I don't know how, her bra is unclipped and her shirt is open over her taut stomach. I stop kissing her and lift my head back to gaze at the wonder that lies beneath me. Her breasts smooth and perfectly contoured, her skirt riding up almost to her waist to reveal tanned legs and a hint of white lace underwear.

I look; I devour her with my eyes. She is so beautiful that I am choking with desire, can barely swallow. It is still raining, the thunder crackles overhead, but now India, my love, my sweet, is sitting up, and, as I pull off her jumper, her blouse, she is unbuttoning my shirt, lips roving over my chest. For a moment we kiss, her mouth hungry against mine, and then she is tugging at my belt. It's frenzied, delirious passion; we are desperate for each other. One by one the rivet buttons on my trousers are unpopped and along with my boxers are pulled to my knees. From this wild, reckless abandon, there is a breathless pause. She looks me in the eye, so beautiful, and moves down, touches me with those long, manicured fingers. The most exquisite sensation of my life. Happening in front of my very eyes.

"Stop," I say quickly, my fingers entwining in her hair.

She does. I am on the very brink. I rock back on my knees trying to steady myself.

As we kneel we kiss, and I unbuckle her belt, letting my fingers work their way round the top of her skirt. Buttons are magically released, zippers undone, and, with a last kiss, she stands up. Her skirt glides in a shimmer of white to the ground.

There, underneath a dripping chestnut tree, with the rain raging all about us, India stands all but naked before me. I kneel at her feet, a pilgrim at prayer, while in front of me is my golden Goddess.

Still wearing her boots, her bare skin is almost brown in the weak afternoon light. In stunning contrast to her skin is the almost luminous whiteness of her knickers, and through the lace a tantalising glimpse of what lies beneath.

My eyes are soaking up everything, her breasts above me, her dreamy face that is awash with desire.

I remember the texture of her skin, fever hot, yet flecked with splashes of cool rain from the leaves overhead. It was the first time that I had ever really touched, kneaded, clasped the skin of another. To those in a relationship, this matter might seem so mundane as to be barely worthy of mention. But how I marvelled at its softness, its downy curves, its rich scent of animal musk. Stroking her skin with the tips of my fingers, pressing more firmly with the heels of my hand, and then grasping her tight about the waist, her skin going white between my fingers. Delicately I tip my tongue to taste salty sweat.

"Stop," she says. "Stop. Please stop."

With a rueful kiss, I rock back on my heels, gaze up. Her eyes roll and her eyelids flutter as she comes back to earth.

"God, I am so close."

She kneels beside me and we kiss, more leisurely, not quite the crazy passion of before, and with deft fingers she unties my boots, tugs at my socks, eases off my trousers. Hands on my shoulders, her eyes caress my naked body.

"Beautiful," she says, lying back, and in a moment I have unzipped her boots. My fingertips curl round the trim of her knickers, and India lifts up as I peel them down her legs and over her stockinged feet. Everything is happening slower and slower, for now that we are naked, both time and possibilities seem limitless.

I'm kneeling between her legs, gazing with dumbstruck awe at India's naked beauty, at this divine woman who appears to be offering herself to me.

As I write this now, my hands still tremble at the very thought of it. Her hair in a brown halo, her skin aglow with desire, and the raindrops flickering through the trees, tart and cool against the heat.

The most perfect blend of love and passion.

She stretches out, takes my hand and pulls me on top of her. She kisses me. Is it a tear on her cheek or a drop of rain? I have never seen such a look in a woman's eyes.

But even then, even in the very heat of the moment, I am still able to take a step back.

"What about protection?"

She smiles up at me, grateful. "It's all right."

That's all she says. I stroke her cheek and feel her strain up against me, her back arching off the rug.

Then the moment that I would never, ever, have dreamed possible, the moment when we start to make love, gazing all the while deep into each other's eyes.

That very instant, a rip-tide of ecstasy washes over me. I can do no more than hold her close to my chest. Well, what else would you expect of a 17-year-old virgin?

We look and we smile, with pleasure, with relief, with gratitude.

"Incredible," I say. "Just incredible."

And so began the most intense, the most dramatic three weeks of my life. Tuesday, 22 June 1982, I can remember it to the very day, for it was the day after Prince William was born and the newspapers were awash with the good news.

I tug the coats on top of us, wrap over the folds of the blanket and we lay there revelling in our love, smiling at the knowledge that I am still inside her.

We are immune to any sensation other than that to be found under our chestnut tree. The Queen and all her cavalry could have marched past on the Long Walk and we would not have heard a thing.

India licks my ear, her hands straying to my buttocks, and starts to rock against me. Seamlessly, without even being aware of it, we have moved from stroking and caressing to making love again, and I begin to pulse against her.

"So good," she says, arms rigid round my neck, and slowly she is turning me so that it's her on top this time, arms straight, locked onto my shoulders. Her head arches backwards. I watch, I learn, I marvel.

I am minded of that first time in her flat, when she'd tumbled me onto her bed, and how her hair had fallen round my face to cut out everything else in the world but her kisses. This time there are so many other sensations; I can feel the entire length of her naked body, from feet to lips, pressed directly on top of me.

Locked into a welter of new sensations, tastes and smells, I want it to go on forever. But just as the symphony is about to reach its dizzying peak, India reads my mind, can feel my thoughts from every twitch and pulse of my body.

A moment to cool, then India, that most adoring of lovers, my houri and my fantasy girl, arcs back and lets out a stuttered cry that is both a howl of pleasure and a plea for mercy, as if she can't cope with the glut of signals that are detonating from her every cell.

This time there was no doubt about it, she is crying, the tears falling freely from her eyes and dropping onto my face, my chest, and, as she leans forward to kiss me, she is also chuckling with laughter. "Better and better," she says.

India poured us tea, strong and milky, and we fed each other chocolates, holding them between our lips and accepting a kiss in thanks.

All I wanted to do was to kneel beside her and gaze at her glorious nakedness. She smiled – and that is how she is in all of my memories, forever smiling – and, artfully, took a sip of tea. Then, with her mouth still hot, peppered me with kisses until I was burning up with lust. Without a word she lay back, her hands on my hips, the better to guide me.

That third time we made love was slower, softer, a steady rolling river that picks up speed, going faster and faster until it empties itself into the ocean. This time, as her legs locked round mine, she did not scream, did not yelp, but whispered, "I want you." Over and over she said it, even as her fingernails sank into my back, even as her neck muscles turned to spun-steel and her breath was reduced to nothing but a hoarse pant. Without our even realising it the rain had stopped, and as we peeked through the wet branches we could see a rainbow starting to tip against the Copper Cow.

PRELUDE 15, G Major

I ran and ran back to the Timbralls but still missed Absence and, when I later checked in with Frankie, he put me on Tardy Book, which meant a week of early rises.

However, he could have had me flogged in front of the entire school and I would not have minded. That night, the next day and the next, you could not have wiped the dazed smile off my face.

Many times since, I have been in love. But at Eton I was in the throes of love's first careless rapture. A time when I was ever-optimistic and also a time when I had yet to be burned.

I had horded up every moment of our time in Windsor Park and guarded those memories like a rapacious miser. Over and over again, I replayed that most magical of moments when she'd first asked to make love. The sex, the lust, the passion, I dwelt on them too.

But, now I may as well confess, there was one niggle. Just a momentary glitch, a small grey cloud on a perfect day.

It was nothing much to worry about.

All the same it vexed me and that vexation would grow and grow until it was a huge, blistered sore.

It was the moment, just before we'd made love for the first time, when I had asked India about protection. She had replied that it was "all right".

I knew full well what she meant – she was either on the pill or using some other method – but what it chiefly meant was that, before she even knew my state of mind, India had already taken care of contraception.

These days, I suppose, it is probably the norm for women to be on the pill when they're not in a steady relationship. But back then, it was not something I'd even thought about.

There were any number of possibilities. However, the one that mocked me the most was that India had been on the pill for months, even years, just on the off-chance that she might want to have sex with any guy who took her fancy.

I know this must come across as tacky, sleazy, downright demented, for page after page I have been setting up India as my Goddess. I've been raving about her looks, her compassion, how much I adored her. And yet, just at the very time that I felt I had fallen in love with her, I'd already started to think the worst of her. Already I had her pinned down as a slattern who would hop into bed with the first stripling that took her fancy. After all, why else had she come to Eton?

It makes me sound as if I were completely deranged. I will endeavour to explain as best I can.

India was my first great love. But it was as if within my heart there were a malignant sewer-rat forever chewing away at this perfect love, chewing and chewing until everything had started to rot and fester.

And why, why did I allow this to happen? Why did I allow my jealousy to get so out of control? Why didn't I ever talk it through with India? Why did I do nothing but feed the rat until it had cankered everything inside me?

But, jealous souls will not be answered so; they are not ever jealous for the cause, but jealous for they are jealous.

There were any number of possible explanations; you can take your pick. That I never felt worthy of India's love, that I wanted to destroy her before I got hurt. In fact – let's get it out there right now – that I was a sick jerk who wilfully destroyed the best thing ever to come into my life.

I can only hang my head in shame. I accept it all, deserve all recriminations, for none of these accusations can be any worse than what I believe to be the truth. And that, as Oscar Wilde so tragically summed up, is that each man kills the thing he loves.

And I did that; I killed it. Killed it stone dead, with a cold eye and a cruel heart.

And the shame of it still makes me weep.

I couldn't see India on Wednesday, but on Thursday afternoon I was with her, with love in my heart and freshly-picked dandelions in my hand. We met on the Thames towpath and, after we had hidden ourselves, made sweet love to the accompaniment of the shrill coxes on the river and the bawling coaches on the bank. What I remember of that blazing afternoon is not so much the sex as lying there afterwards gazing at India as she slept, perfect in her nakedness. I felt not like a lover, but like a truant schoolboy that had come across her unawares. I still could not credit that I could look, stare – even touch. Although I did just that, trailing a blade of grass across her stomach and up to her breasts. Up and across her shoulders, along her arms, her fingers, and back down her stomach.

She still had her eyes closed. "I like that," she said.

"And that?" I dabbed at her midriff with my tongue.

"Very much."

Her hand came up, stroked my hair. Her legs twitched imperceptibly and, even before I'd heard her moan, I knew that India was again looking for love. We made love three times.

Three times? Hah! I can only laugh at the supreme ignorance of that 17-year-old Etonian. For then, I honestly thought that three times was the norm – that it was the standard two-hour sex session.

I didn't know I was born.

India draped her arm round my hips and pressed herself close. "Tell me about yourself," she said.

"Me?" I said. "Where do you want me to start?"

"Your family?"

"My family?" I never thought about my family much. Family was just family like school was just school.

"My family?" I said again.

I tried to visit a place where I had not been for many years.

I took a deep breath. "Nothing much to tell. My mother died

when I was six." I stared at the sky, imagined myself scudding through the clouds. "I have the pictures, but I don't have the memories."

"What do you remember?"

"Not much. Not much at all."

"You must remember something."

I toyed with India's nipple, stroking it taut. My mind was a blank. I could remember nothing.

Then, just a glimpse of a memory, a thin beam of light waving in the distance on a dark night.

"I'd forgotten all about it," I said. "But we used to bake bread together in the morning. I remember kneading dough on the kitchen table. The smell of bread filling the house and the blast of hot air as we opened the oven door. It's strange. I hadn't really thought about it in over a decade."

"I'm so sorry."

"No need to be. It was cancer. Just something that happens, and it happened to us.

"She was a fantastic cook too. I remember that whenever I came home, the house always smelled of food."

I shrugged, impervious to the memory, impervious to any sort of mental pain.

"Within two years, father had married again. They had a couple of boys."

"And how's that for you?"

Up until then, I'd never thought about it. It was just the set of circumstances that was my life – neither good, nor bad, perfectly endurable though not necessarily enjoyable.

"We all just do our own thing," I said. "My father goes to his club, Tom and Ali go to prep school. My stepmother keeps the house immaculate."

India kissed me.

"You get on with things as best you can." I closed one eye, squinted at the sky. It was easier if I didn't look at India. "One thing I remember clearly was the day my father came to my pre-prep. I'd just started boarding."

"At six?"

"That was the way of it," I said. "I'd spotted him drive up. He was by himself. I sensed immediately that something was wrong. I saw him walk into the private entrance and I had to wait 30 minutes before I was called in to see the headmaster.

"I knocked on the study door and the headmaster let me in. He told me that my father had some news, and he left us to it. My father was sitting in an armchair in the corner. I've never since seen anyone look so grey – ash grey, with black whorls under his eyes.

"I didn't know what to do. He beckoned me over and hugged me. It was probably the last time he ever held onto me like that. He was holding me tighter than I'd ever been held before."

India blew her nose, wiped a tear from her cheek.

"Eventually he spoke to me. 'You're all I've got left now,' is what he said, before telling me that mother had died. But I didn't cry. Even then I knew that big boys don't cry.

"I had ten days off. Stiff upper lip at the funeral and the wake, and when I returned to school everyone was on best behaviour. For a while, everyone treated me with kid gloves. I was quite special. The kid with the dead mother."

I played with India's hair, twirling a tress between my fingers, studying each individual hair.

"And life continued. My father continued in the Army, found a nanny for me for the holidays and soon had found a step-mum to look after me for free." I was hoarse and sipped some lemonade. "She did the best she could. But it must be hard to love your step-son as much as you love your own sons."

I kissed India on the lips, dabbing with my tongue. "So that's my story. Not the best of childhoods, but there must have been many worse."

India smiled as she cuffed away another tear. "Thank you for that," she said. "Sometimes you need to be reminded of what you've got."

"And what have you got?"

"Both my parents are still alive, still together." She tapped a finger on her cheek, as if in thought. "Oh yes, and a very affectionate boyfriend."

"I've heard about him. What's he like?"

"You'd like him," she said, nails raking over my chest. "He's a bit younger than me, tall, ever so handsome."

"Sounds like quite a catch."

"An expert in the art of love," she continued.

"Daresay he had a good teacher."

"A useful pianist." She ticked the points off on her fingers. "Polished manners, considerate, obedient, witty, and, best of all, he appears to have no baggage."

"No baggage?"

"Yes." She kissed me. "One of the many reasons why I love him."

"Oh, you love him now, do you?"

"Without doubt."

"And is it mutual?"

"It would be such a terrible tragedy if it weren't." She was giggling. "What do you think?"

"As tragedies go, it would have to be up there with *Hamlet*." I replied. "But I think he probably loves you too."

"Even with all my baggage?"

"It makes you what you are," I said. "Besides, how much baggage can a piano teacher have?"

"How long have you got?" she nibbled at my lip. "There was my short-lived spell at Bristol University. Should have read music. In a moment of madness I opted for medicine."

"Doesn't sound like excess baggage to me."

"And the overly-attentive uncle who blighted three years of my childhood?"

"Unpleasant, but still portable."

"And the broken heart that I thought would never be healed?"

"I'm sure your boyfriend is doing his best."

She kissed me, pressing the length of her body against mine. "I love you so much."

"Me?" I kissed her back. "What about that boyfriend of yours?"

"What do you think he'd say?" Her hands fumbled and teased.

I broke off from those magical lips. "I think he'd say that he loves you too."

"He would?"

"Very much."

Our final bout of love-making reached new peaks of intimacy. A crew rowed past not ten yards away from our makeshift bed. She was on the verge of crying out when suddenly she pinned me back and drilled her tongue into my mouth. I could feel her silent scream of ecstasy thrilling through my bones.

It was wonderful. It was always wonderful.

And I could rake over our love-making for page after page, could fill the entire book with it. But that would be self-indulgence.

Because my story is not just about love and sex, but also how I sowed the seeds of my own self-destruction and how I created such a fertile breeding ground for my incipient jealousy.

That Friday I couldn't see India because she was tied up with lessons. As a poor second-best, Jeremy and I went to Tap, the school pub. Tap was a revered Eton institution, where boys aged 16 and up could learn to handle their drink. We were only allowed a couple of pints, but that was more than enough to set most of us well on our way.

Some people, when I've told them of Tap, express amazement that Eton should be encouraging its boys to drink. But it is better by far for boys to learn about getting drunk in a controlled environment than to do it on the sly and end up soused and vomit-stained in a gutter.

Tap was a strange mix, as if a northern bar had been transported from Yorkshire and dumped onto the Eton High Street. It had dark panelling and low ceilings, while on the walls were a few school photos plus a couple of oars and some cricket bats. There was also the Long Glass, which held a quart of ale, and over the years had humiliated countless Etonians. Unless you knew the correct angle to hold the glass, it was guaranteed to dump a pint or so of beer in your face.

As usual the bar was heaving so Jeremy and I were sitting in the beer-garden. We were nursing pints of lager – we had both yet to acquire a taste for bitter – and, for a moment there in the sun, you could almost have believed you were having a quiet pint in your local.

Jeremy had not spoken for a couple of minutes. I had just told him that India and I had made love. Not, I hope, in a boastful way, but because he was a friend and an ally, and because, even then, I realised he needed to be kept abreast of events.

In total silence he heard me out, pursed his lips, nodded, templed his fingers, and when he could think of nothing else to distract him, pursed his lips again and continued to nod.

"*Fouquet*," he muttered. For a few seconds he was speechless. "You lucky, lucky bastard."

I could only shrug, the cat with the cream. I was indulgently embarrassed at my good fortune.

I might have told Jeremy more, but I was silenced by the loud, crowing voice of Savage who had walked into the beer-garden with two of his cronies. He sneered at me but didn't say a word, returning to the bar while his friends sat down at a table. We knew their names, but they would not have been aware of our existence. One of them, Howells, was also a popper, dressed in sponge-bag trousers and a garish orange waistcoat, while the other, Buck, wore stick-ups and a silver-buttoned black waistcoat, the badge of office for another elite Eton society, Sixth-Form Select.

It's hard to describe how oppressive it was sitting just a few yards from these senior boys. They may have been only a year older than us, but they were Eton's cream and didn't we just know it. Both Jeremy and I found we were unable to say a word. We played with our pints. We stared at the sky. We attempted to look as if we were sharing an amicable, contemplative silence.

Savage, King of all he surveyed, came out with a tray of drinks and peanuts. Immediately the braying Hooray Henry behaviour started – the sort of thing that most people expect of public school boys at play. We were about to skulk from the beer-garden, leaving our half-drunk pints, when Jeremy stayed my hand.

Buck had asked Savage a question. "How's it going with you

and India James?"

Howells laughed and clapped Savage on the back. "Yes – how is the wonder that is India?"

Savage took a long sip from his pint, and this stupid 'Aw shucks' grin appeared on his face, as if he'd have loved to have told them all about it, but it just wouldn't be right.

"Come on," persisted Buck. "Don't keep us in suspense."

Savage helped himself to some peanuts, milking the moment. He tipped his head back and trickled them into his mouth one by one. "Saw her this morning," he said. "Gagging for it."

Goosebumps on my wrists. It was like the air was being wrung out of my lungs. But with a studied, manic intensity, I picked up my glass and drank.

Buck, the stooge of the group, giggled. "But you've done more than kiss her?"

Savage, his coiffed black hair nestling into his collar, dribbled more peanuts into his mouth. "What do you think Bucky, old boy? Do you think we've just spent our time necking, or do you think that just possibly we might have got a stage further than that?"

I looked at Jeremy. He mechanically lifted his glass to his lips, his face an inscrutable mask.

Howells chortled. "Surely not another notch on the Savage bed-post?"

Savage shrugged and kissed the tips of his fingers.

"Tell us. Tell us," Buck exclaimed. "We want details."

"A gentlemen couldn't possibly comment," Savage said, adding underneath his breath, "Insatiable."

I could hear the blood thumping in my ears as ice-cold anger swept through my veins. It couldn't be possible. Could not be possible. Savage was just being the braggart he always was.

By then Jeremy had me by the elbow and was dragging me out of my seat but, even as we left, I could hear another shriek of laughter from Buck. I looked back to see Savage grotesquely thrusting his groin at the table-leg.

It made my stomach heave. Was it possible? Could he? Could she? I didn't know what to think.

Jeremy was the first to speak. "He's a bag of piss and wind."

"Yeah."

"He's a bullshitter; you know he is."

"Yeah."

But it was as if that gnawing sewer-rat had done a back flip in my belly, twisting and turning through my guts. Of course I knew it wasn't possible that India and Savage could have been together. She'd said she loved me. We'd been making love only the previous afternoon.

And yet, and yet...

It was like hot coals being pressed to the soles of my feet. Because, of course, a little piece of me not only believed Savage, but actively wanted to believe him.

So, as we walked back, I went along with whatever Jeremy said. I agreed with him and pretended I was mollified. But underneath I was incandescent with anger. I needed to know, had to know and, if I had been able, I would have gone round to India's house that very moment.

But I couldn't do that. There wasn't time and she wasn't due home for another hour yet. I spent the time in my room. Pulsating with rage. Cursing Savage as a liar. Wondering how to pose my questions. Whether to be upfront, to just tell her what had happened, or whether to be circuitous?

I know it seems ridiculous now. Of course India loved me and only me, and Savage was nothing but a lying, boasting hellhound who had not even come close to laying a finger on India.

But, at the time, things were not so simple. India had said she loved me, but I had no idea why. And, if me, then why not somebody like Savage, who I knew was more sporty, more funny, a hundred times better-looking? Besides, had she said she loved me exclusively and above all others?

Give me enough time and I would be able to conjure up every conceivable worst-case scenario.

Although my calm, rational side was yelling at me to get a grip, there was always this insistent sniping, this little whisper of violence in my heart that said, 'What if he's right?'

I called India at 7pm, a bristling mountain of indignant rage.

And you know what happened?

The very moment that I heard her voice and heard her say "I love you", the heat of my anger was doused, as if a burning match had been dropped into an ocean. For that was all my jealousy was: barely a spent match compared to the sea of her love.

She loved me. Of course she loved me, and only me, and, as for that shit Savage, he was beneath contempt.

India and I chatted for a few minutes. We swapped endearments. But instead of mentioning what had happened in Tap with Savage, I still vaguely alluded to him. I was casting a fly on the water, just to check for any reaction. Not that I didn't trust her, but...

"Got supper in a few minutes," I said. "In the delightful company of your old friend Savage."

She laughed. It was so open, so natural. Not even the slightest bit forced. Her and Savage? It was unthinkable, impossible.

"Well, enjoy yourself," she said.

But still I gave it one more tweak. I had to make sure. "But you must fancy him just a little bit?" I laughed as I said it though maybe it did sound a bit hollow. It might have given India the first hint of the monster that she was dating.

"Kim!" She shrieked with laughter. "I do hope you're joking. He's beyond awful!"

How happy I was to hear her say that. But you know, in this life, whatever you look for you will find – and that even goes for when you're searching for a speck of malice in the most honest and the most caring heart that was ever to fall in love.

Al fresco love-making – is there any finer way on God's earth to have sex?

You can keep your linen sheets, your king-size beds, your cosy central heating, your room service, your mini-bars and your five-star hotels.

For me, sex is always better when it's outside, with your toes grinding into the grass and your back bared to the wind. Rain, shine, clouds, snow, hail and thunder, embrace them all.

Bedrooms speak of middle-age spread and pedestrian love lives.

But sex outside? Raw and naked, with the sun seeping through the trees? With a blanket, a bar of chocolate and a thermos of ice-cold lemonade? This was how I was first introduced to the joys of love-making, and it was as if, after four grinding years at Eton, I had come to realise that I was living in paradise.

I may as well admit it though. There is one other ingredient that always adds piquancy to sex *au naturel*: the very real prospect of being caught.

For although there are thousands of acres around Eton that are just perfect for discreet love-making, there are also many hundreds of boys and masters, their heads filled with bile and boredom, who would delight in catching two lovers in the act.

The first time it happened was that Saturday afternoon.

By now, India and I were so meticulous about our trysts that we were like a couple of veteran World War II spies. I had started to view Eton through fresh eyes, for I was ever on the search for out-of-the-way meeting spots, and soft, secluded nooks.

We would meet in the hidden spinneys of Eton and Windsor and only when we were far from prying eyes would we kiss and cling to each other as if our lives depended on it.

We were out in the fields past Eton's nine-hole golf course. I had discovered a thicket of brambles, right in the very centre of which was a luxuriant bed of grass. If you jumped up high into the air from outside the thicket, you could just spot this hidden bower behind the thorns.

Getting in there had been a test. We'd crawled on our stomachs, hauling our way through on our elbows like buffed commandoes. But get through we did, and the nicks and cuts to our hands and arms only added to our pleasure. We were so in love, so besotted, that everything life hurled at us, even the inconveniences, were nothing more than spice for our passion.

India pulled a thorn from the palm of my hand and kissed the wound. It reminded me of that first time she had kissed my wrist underneath that elderberry bush near the Master's Field. How my life had changed in barely nine days.

With all the ease of lovers who have the night ahead of them, we peeled off each other's clothes, kissing and caressing every part of each other's bodies until we were husky with lust and aching to make love.

India had taught me well and already I felt I was becoming quite the veteran lover. I had come to understand the monumental power of delayed gratification.

I was teasing India, teasing her with my fingers, with my hands, and with my tongue. We were both naked now, surrounded by our wall of thorns with only the sun peeping in on our bodies. India was on her back, her eyes closed, her fingers knotted tight in my hair as she tried to guide me.

But I was having none of it.

I trailed my fingers up the side of her thigh, and nuzzled at the side of her neck, my tongue light against her ear. I drew back and blew lightly on her lips as my hands glided down across her stomach. I paused again, just beneath her tummy button, so close that she thought this time, this time…

Her breath was short, staccato. "Please." She was begging me. For a moment she grasped my teasing fingers, her knuckles white.

"Please," she whispered. "Kim, you're killing me."

I was spinning her out as long as I dared.

Then suddenly an alien sound fell on our ears. It was one of the Eton beaks. I couldn't see him but I recognised the voice of that dry old stick Malcolm Singleton, another of the school's die-hard bachelors. "Hi Sultan! Sultan come here!"

Singleton was not four yards away from us, standing on the other side of the bushes. India's body froze, every muscle locked.

There was nothing we could do. Either he found us or he went on his merry way. So I did one of the most swinish things that I have ever done as a lover.

I started to kiss India again as my hand worked down to her inner thigh. Her fingers were taut in my hair. Then, to the sound of Singleton's Labrador rampaging through the bramble bushes, I gave India the soft touch that she had been craving. Her mouth was rigid against my lips and I could sense the breath about to shriek from her throat.

The dog had worked its way through to the centre of the thicket and was now sniffing around us. Its tail wagged against my leg. India was trembling, and I could see the ripple of her stomach muscles. With the Labrador, and Singleton shouting on the other side of the brambles, she'd got the giggles. Suddenly she was stuffing her top into her mouth. She made no sound, but I could feel the laughter detonate through her body.

"Sultan! Sultan, come here!" It was Singleton again, only his voice was lower now. He was squinting through the brambles.

As for me, I was methodically going about my business of bringing India to the most shuddering orgasm of her life. Whether Singleton saw anything or not, I will never know. I do think that most of Eton's masters are gentlemen who, more often than not, prefer to ignore their pupils' myriad of misdemeanours. After a slight grunt of surprise, he was marching off and calling over his shoulder for his Labrador. We were left with the sunshine and the sound of the skylarks.

"Kim." India choked, her voice tight. "You are a monster. But God, how I love you."

And with that, her spine arched, her arms laced round my neck, and she clung to my head as if she were drowning. She was so shattered that for a minute, two minutes, she was too weak to move. I wormed my way around her cheek to kiss her.

"I love you," I said.

"I love you," she replied. Her smile started to tip the sides of her mouth. We rolled to and fro on the blanket until India was astride me, her knees secure round my chest.

"I love you so very much." She drummed a tattoo on my chest. "But I'm going to have to make you pay for that."

And so she did, stoking me until it felt as if there was a furnace raging in the pit of my stomach and until it was now my turn to beg for release. It makes me smile just to think of that. Not quite the dominatrix, but without doubt the mistress of all she surveyed. At that moment, India could have asked me anything in the world and I would have given it her.

We cuddled, we made love, she sipped her homemade lemonade and trickled it from her lips into mine. Finally, we were spent and lay in each other's arms, staring up at the sky and the Heathrow planes that forever drone over Eton.

"I think I ought to tell you something," India said with a kiss. "To avoid any embarrassment."

Instantly my heart was yammering, claxon bells were ringing. Was this it? Was this the bullet? Was she about to reveal some ghastly skeleton from her early life?

But I could relax.

It was none of that.

"It's my birthday tomorrow," she said. "I thought it better to tell you now than to spring it on you on the day."

"Brilliant!" I said. "What present would you like?"

"Only you," she said. "Just you and nothing more."

"That can be arranged."

I kissed her. My heart was filled with rapturous love. A most devilish idea was forming in my mind.

"How old will you be?"

"Twenty-four."

"Twenty-four?" I'd never really thought about her age before. India was just India, my first great love, and her age was an irrelevance. "Maybe I ought to be there to bring it in?"

"Kim, you are mad."

"I mean it." I was bubbling with glee at the thought of it.

"I mean it too."

"It'll be great," I said. "Wait till after lights out and I could be with you in five minutes."

"You're mad." She kissed me again, and that dreamy look had come into her eyes that meant she wanted more than just a kiss. Her fingers wandered down my chest. "You're mad but I love you."

We talked as we made love. She gasped, she purred, and she asked me, "Are you serious?"

"Of course." Up until then, I had not thought about the sheer enormity of what I'd promised to do. But love and teenage bravado had given me wings. The more I thought about it, the better it sounded. Despite my love of the outdoors, a whole night of love with India, with soft sheets and feathered pillows, and that blissful moment when I awoke with her in my arms.

She writhed against me, her fingers deep into my back. "You know I'd love that more than anything." She panted. "But you will take care?"

We didn't need to utter another word. We bucked, we churned and braced against each other, our lips locked.

"Trust me," I said.

And she did.

As I walked back to the Timbralls, my mind ticked over all the various options.

I'd never broken out of the house before and when I came to consider the practicalities, it did seem a most foolhardy venture.

But my love was expecting me and I could not let her down.

My first problem was how to get out of the house. I tried the downstairs lavatory window. At a push, I could have squeezed out. But when I went upstairs, I discovered a far more expedient option: the fire-escape.

I asked Jeremy if I could borrow his bike.

"Jesus." He shook his head as he handed me the bike lights. "If they catch you, you're toast."

As I knew only too well. Just being caught outside the house after dark would have warranted instant expulsion. But I thought that so long as I covered my head, I wouldn't be recognised. And if it ever came to a chase, I would work my way home on Eton's hidden paths and shortcuts.

What an idiot, to risk everything for a night with India. And I would do it again for even a single kiss.

That evening I was a bundle of nerves, like a sprinter in the run-up to a big race. I did my best to stick to my normal routine, washing and brushing my teeth.

Jeremy was in the washroom too. All he could do was shake his head before pointing his cocked fingers to his temple and pulling the trigger. But nothing he could say was going to stop me.

In the passageway, I chatted to Frankie. I was fortunate that he didn't come into my room, for his acute antennae couldn't have missed that something was up.

With the radio low, I started to lay out the things I'd need. Jeans, t-shirt, dark jumper, trainers and a snug hat to pull low over my brow. Some gaffer tape for the fire-door. Fresh batteries for Jeremy's bike lights. I bit at my thumbnail, wondering if I'd missed anything.

I had.

I had no present.

I scanned the room for anything that might service. A few crinkled novels and some dog-eared books of poetry, some shabby schoolboy clothes, posters. Useless, all useless.

I had a nose through my box of trinkets. There were a few collar studs and five cufflinks; nothing remotely worthy for my love.

But as I raked through the little plastic box, I saw the one thing that would be a fitting present for India.

I would give her my watch.

It was the most expensive thing I owned, a classic Heuer, with a thick crocodile skin strap and a handsome face that almost covered my wrist. My father had given it to me for my 16th birthday. It was my most treasured possession.

Without a second thought, I decided to give it to India.

But perhaps you can already tell that this Heuer is not just some light detail that I have tossed into the mix? Before my tale is done, we will return to it.

With the lights off, I dressed and peeled off some strips of gaffer tape, sticking them lightly to my arm. At 11.30, I stole out of my room. Every door pulsated with menace. There were at least 15 other boys' rooms on the corridor, with the most dangerous of all, Savage's, adjacent to the fire-escape.

The passage was lit by the dim pink glow of the night-lights. I tiptoed along, feet next to the walls, testing every step.

Earlier that evening, I had already tried the fire door. It had seemed simple enough. You pressed the horizontal bar down and the two bolts at the top and bottom clunked back. But when I tried it in the still of the night, the crack of the bar seemed to sound like a rifle shot.

I was champing on my lip with nerves. I hung there motionless, my hand on the bar and the door three inches ajar.

Somehow the house stayed fast asleep. I gave it a minute and peeled off some strips of gaffer tape, slapping them on the top and bottom bolts to secure my route back in. Outside, I closed the door behind me, not shut tight, but enough to prevent a casual glance noticing anything amiss.

I felt a huge surge of exhilaration. I was out – out and on the road to my love.

For a while I stood on that black cast-iron balcony, leaning against the wall and staring at the stars.

To schoolboys everywhere, I could not recommend the experience more highly. It was one of the most exciting things I've ever done.

I crept down the fire-escape stairs, scrabbled onto one of the Timbralls' bins and jumped over the outer wall. Only as I looked back at the smooth bricks did I realise that breaking back into the house was going to be a teaser. The wall had to be a full ten-feet high.

Still, I'd deal with that when I came to it.

Jeremy's bike was where I'd hidden it, tucked away behind a van in a corner of New Schools Yard. A last look at the Timbralls, a brooding black block against the starry skyline, and off I rode, slapping the black Sebastopol cannon on the way and whistling a jaunty tune to myself.

I wasn't heading direct for India's home, which would have meant riding past any number of beaks' houses on the High Street. Instead, I made a wide detour that took me past the Music Schools and the lower chapel before heading cross-country over the South Meadow playing fields.

It was one of those times in my life when it felt so good to be alive, with the wind in my face, the air tart on my lips and cold in my throat. I was on a mission and that night I felt I could not possibly fail for the Gods were with me.

On the far side of South Meadow, I turned the bike lights on and rejoined Meadow Lane. In another minute I was by Windsor Bridge.

It would have been too conspicuous to leave the bike outside India's flat, so instead I locked it up near Rafts, where Eton's scores of boats were stored, and skipped over to her cul-de-sac. I was grinning every step of the way. I'd done it! We'd bring in her birthday together.

I gave the bell a short ring and in moments she was tripping down the stairs. She wore silk pyjamas, a white cotton dressing-gown, leather slippers on her feet and, as she stood there in the doorway, her hands clasped her cheeks in amazement.

"You made it." She was still shaking her head.

"Did you think I wouldn't?"

"I'd better make it worth your while," and with that, she took my hand and we were tearing up the stairs, up through the living room, and up the oak stairs to the heaven of her bedroom. And, of course, she'd been expecting me. The patio window was open, and the table, the walls and the windows were lined with scores of dainty, round, tea-light candles. By the bed, a bottle of Bollinger on ice. For my first introduction to indoor sex, it couldn't have been any better.

Windsor Castle was a blaze of light above us and a zephyr of wind was seeping in off the river, bubbling at the blinds. We held each other by the window, India's eyes sparkling bright as she gazed at me. "You came," she said. "You're here for my birthday."

"Ask of me anything you will."

Her hand slipped underneath my shirt. "Well…"

We made love on the bed. We timed it to perfection, tapering our finish to the exact stroke of midnight.

For the last time, I looked at the Heuer on my wrist.

"Happy birthday, India." I kissed her. "I have another present for you too – not much, but a very small token of my esteem." And with that, I took off my Heuer and gave it to her.

"You can't give me that!" She gaped. "It's your watch! It's far too expensive!"

"Seriously, I want you to have it."

"Really?"

"Really."

"But it's beautiful." She examined the Heuer before strapping it to her wrist. It was a perfect fit. In fact, even though it was a man's watch, the Heuer looked sensational, more than just a watch but a piece of jewellery.

"I love it." She lifted her arm up and the watch glinted in the candlelight. "And you know what I love about it best of all? That it's yours, that you used to wear it. Now I'll always have a part of you next to me." She kissed me. "Do you really want me to keep it?"

"Of course; that's why I gave it to you."

She gazed at the watch one more time before catching sight of my empty wrist. "But what about you? What are you going to wear?"

I shrugged. "I'll be fine."

"I can't have that." She leaned across me, her breast touching my arm as she stretched to the bedside table. "You must have this."

She gave me her watch, a silver Cartier with black leather strap, a little larger than your typical petite ladies' watch, but not as big as the Heuer.

"But it's your birthday, not mine!"

"I want you to have it."

I tried it on. "Are you sure?"

"Of course," she said. "Every time you look at it, you can think of me."

And India was right about that, for as I write these words now, I have that same Cartier watch on my wrist. A little battered, a little knocked at the edges, but every time I look at it, I do indeed think of India.

I popped the champagne and we nestled down to the luxury of a mattress, cotton sheets and soft pillows. While sex outdoors is an incredible experience, oh the simple pleasures of a bedroom.

Neither of us slept that night. We made love, we kissed,

we caressed.

And we talked.

"What were your other girlfriends like," India asked.

"Other girlfriends?" I said. "Are you joking?"

"Someone like you, Kim?" India said. "I thought you must have been snapped up long ago."

I laughed at the thought of it. Me with legions of girlfriends? "You flatter me India." I poured her more Bollinger. "I was keeping myself chaste for you."

"Chaste rather than pursued," she laughed, swirling the champagne as she stared at the rainbow of colours in her cut-crystal glass. "I wish…I wish I could say the same."

And the silence stretched and stretched till it was at breaking point. After asking me about my past loves, India was undoubtedly waiting for me to volley back the same question.

I knew she wanted me to ask her. But I couldn't. Wouldn't. I didn't want to know. The thought of learning about India's exes was too awful.

She spoke again, quickly. "There's something you should…"

"I don't want to know."

"But-"

"Don't tell me." I was too fast for her, far too fast for her. I knew what she was going to start describing and I shut her up by tickling her armpits and her tummy. I'd known that finally she was about to embark on tales of boyfriends past – and I knew at that moment too that it was a place I never wished to visit.

To have started unearthing India's past would have been like spitting on a sublime work of art. I felt my perception of India would never have been the same again.

I tickled her until she was squealing for mercy, red in the face, ribs aching with laughter. And just as I'd hoped, the moment of terrible confession passed by. Everything that India had wanted to say had diffused into that great ether of thoughts that are left unspoken and unheard.

From that night on, I think India sensed my jealousy. She never once brought up the subject of her ex-boyfriends again.

However, I was nothing if not contrary.

For although I did not wish to hear a sentence, a single word, of India's sexual past, another, darker, side of me was burning to know it all. I wanted to know how many lovers there had been, when she'd lost her virginity and with whom. I wanted to know about the snapshot downstairs of the guy that she'd been holding, and the story behind that picture of her piano when she was looking so beautiful in the surf. And why certain *Well-Tempered* preludes made her cry. Exactly how long she'd been on the pill before she'd met me, and – one other thing besides.

The diamond ring.

That night she had it on the ring-finger of her right hand and, as I lay in the crook of her arm, it was winking in the candlelight, daring me, goading me on.

I didn't ask her outright.

But I brought the subject up. Even though I knew it would torture me, I had to ask. I couldn't help myself.

"Nice ring," I said. Sly. Devious. Probing.

She stared at the diamond, splaying her fingers out to catch the light. She was on the very cusp of telling me.

I willed her on.

I urged her to stop.

"I don't know why I still wear it." She sighed. "Sometimes it's hard to let go."

The blood was draining from my cheeks. Was this it? Was she going to tell me everything? Was I about to learn that my golden Goddess had feet of clay?

"Do you like it?" she said, but then she answered her own question. "No, I know you don't want to know."

I cocked my head. I said nothing although I hated it, of course I did, because it would become a daily reminder that India had once loved a man other than myself.

She knew all this without a word being said. "You're right," she continued. "It's time to move on."

She worked the diamond off her finger and tossed it onto the bedside table.

"Look," she said, and held up her long, bare fingers. "A fresh start."

We kissed and I gazed at her hands.

All I could see was not bare fingers, but the indent from where her diamond ring had once been.

I couldn't even rejoice that the ring was off and that I wouldn't have it thrust in my face every day because, jealous twisted teenager that I was, every time I looked at India's manicured fingers, all I could think was that once that diamond had been there.

And here is a tip if you ever have the misfortune to bring a jealous lover into your life.

Don't ever pander to them, because all you will be doing is stoking the fires. Cave in once, twice, and they begin to believe that they're in the right, that they're being reasonable.

So India had thoughtfully caved in on this one. She had taken off her diamond ring because she thought it might make me happy.

It did nothing of the sort.

For a few hours, I had a guilty glow. I knew I had won a very minor battle. But, before the cock had even crowed thrice in the morning, I was thirsting for more information. I wanted to know who had given her the diamond, why she had worn it so long.

Another side of me was horrified at my petty victory. For I had walked into the stagnant swamp of my own jealousy and, the more I floundered, the more it sucked me down.

PRELUDE 17, A-flat Major

Breaking back into the Timbralls was just as formidable as I had feared.

At 4.30am, I had given India a final birthday kiss and, as the first glimmers of sunlight were pinking in the east, I was racing back over South Meadow and onto Keate's Lane. I should have felt uplifted, exhilarated. But I was disgusted with myself. I felt soiled by that whole repugnant business with the diamond ring.

I loved India and only India, and somehow I would have to learn to embrace her past because that was what had turned her into the joy of my life.

I made a vow there and then.

Whatever the provocation, whatever the circumstances, I was never going to quiz India about her past loves.

If she wanted to tell me about them, then I would listen quietly and with sympathy. She had been hurt, I knew that. If talking was going to help her get over the past, then I would hear her out.

But as for doing any of my own digging and as for grilling India about those photos, from that time forth, I would never speak a word.

In a way, I managed to keep that vow.

But, like a weasel-tongued lawyer, I was to stick to the words of my promise but not its spirit.

I left the bike tucked by a pillar in Cannon Yard and gave General Peel's cannon another slap for luck.

Some puffs of smoke were trailing out of the Timbralls'

chimneys as the boilers fired up, but the house was still asleep.

I examined the smooth brick wall that separates the Timbralls from New Schools Yard. There was not even a hint of a handhold.

I decided to do what I had seen the Eton Rifles do when they were out practising on the assault course; I ran at the wall full-tilt, kicked my foot into the bricks and stretched up to get a hand over the coping stone.

Not even close.

Worse, the sound of my kick against the wall echoed across the yard in a dull, flat boom.

I tried it again. I ran faster, strained to kick higher.

I was still nowhere near and, to my fevered ears, the sound of the kick was like a discharge from that old Sebastopol cannon.

All thought of India had melted from my mind. Trapped outside my own house? How I could I have been so stupid?

I was petrified.

It was now past 5am and cars were already out on the Slough Road, which runs directly next to the Timbralls.

I walked to the back of the house and onto Sixpenny. But the walls there were, if anything, more insuperable, higher and topped with razor-wire. And there was worse to come. Already there were a couple of lights on in the Timbralls. The house was rousing for the start of a new day.

I tore back to New Schools Yard and sat down by the railings to take stock. I just had to think. How could this be happening to me?

I studied the wall. It seemed insurmountable. But then, when I looked to the side, I felt a thrill of joy as I realised the main gate might serve as a stepladder.

How I would come to love that hefty black gate, with its steel bars so conveniently placed for a boy in desperate need of a ladder.

I was up the gate in under 20 seconds. My earlier gloom dissolved in a surge of adrenalin. Of course it was going to work out all right. The result had never been in doubt.

I trotted along the top of the wall, as carefree as a tightrope walker, and was soon darting up the fire-escape and into the house. I was meticulous in covering my tracks, clearing off all the gaffer tape before slotting the fire-door back home.

I was hauling off my clothes even before I was back in my room. I sat on my bed grinning to myself.

I'd spent the night with my love and had got clean away with it, and, as I slipped between the sheets, I knew that my night-times at Eton would never be the same again. For, if India was in her home and willing to see me, then every night I would go to her. I would not get sloppy, but would be every bit as vigilant and wary as I had been that first night.

Sometimes, though, it doesn't matter how vigilant you are. For it's not your mistakes or blunders that find you out, just the natural order of events. Things happen; inconceivable things that would have seemed so unlikely that they would never even have raised a blip on your radar.

So that Sunday, I saw India after lunch and hand-in-hand we walked the fields. I gazed admiringly at my Heuer that was on her wrist. I think I almost preferred it to seeing her Cartier on mine, for it was my mark and stamp and signified that she was mine.

I took my leave of her at 6.30pm in time for Absence, but the birthday celebrations continued that night when again I crept to her door. We would eventually learn to sleep with each other but, in those early days, when everything was so fresh, we would spend our time making love, talking and playing the piano. For night after night after night.

I would try to steal a cat-nap when I could, but I was having to get by on barely three hours sleep a day. Worse, I was still on Tardy Book and was having to report into the School Office at 6.30am every morning.

Did I ever want to have an early night instead? Just skip an evening with India and curl up in my Timbralls bed for a refreshing 12-hours?

It would have been like choosing a Big Mac over Lobster Thermidor – opting for the safe and the pedestrian over the wild, mesmerising passion that I shared with India. Nothing, least of all lack of sleep, was going to stop me from seeing her.

But even by the middle of the week, those long, long nights of love-making were starting to take their toll. My skin had the lusty glow that comes from sex outside, but my eyes were red-rimmed with haggard bags that sagged to my cheekbones. I was bone-shatteringly tired, and it was all too obvious both to my peers and to my teachers.

I was in an English division, still gazing at Angela, staring at her but looking right through her, and the tide of words was rolling over me in a never-ending stream. My ears were as impermeable as rock, not a word could register.

At first I was just thinking of India, revelling in my memories of her. Soon enough though, my reveries had turned to dreams, and I was far away from that dry-as-dust Caxton classroom. We were flying over Eton, free as larks and buoyed by our love. We were naked, holding hands, and were swooping through the school buildings with all the elegance of swifts – up, up, skirting round Lupton's twin towers and the chapel turrets.

I didn't know how we were flying, but instinctively I knew that the moment I looked down, the moment I started to doubt, I would plummet out of the sky.

We were swooping over Chambers now, watching the black morass of penguined-boys outside the School Hall, stuck in their privileged rut. And I, with my soul-mate, was free of them all.

One by one the boys started to look up. A wall of noise came up to us, but not the 'oohs' and 'aahs' of circus-crowd amazement, but a wave of laughter. They were laughing at us, laughing at our nakedness, and our love. India and I were so very different from them that all they could think to do was mock us.

I stared and I began to doubt. Maybe our love couldn't keep us up; maybe we did look ridiculous without our clothes; maybe it would be much easier just to don my black suit and blend back into the Eton morass.

And out of the sky I tumbled, heel-over-head, seeing first the upturned mouths of the braying boys and then a last glimpse of my love. India was still gliding above me but her face was a picture of spectral horror, her mouth locked into a never-ending scream.

I finally hurtled headfirst into a wall of manic, savage, laughter – and that, as you may have realised, was the sound of my classmates laughing at me in my English division.

I came to with a start, my head jerking back and my eyes wide open. Instantly, I knew I was the butt of a classroom joke. Every boy in the room was jabbering, even McArdle was smirking. Although when I glanced at Angela – and for this I will always be grateful – she had a gentle smile on her face, not of mockery, but of tender sympathy.

I was lambasted.

"Ah Kim," McArdle said, strutting round his desk like a well-heeled barrister at court. "Sorry to have disturbed your nap."

And you know what? Something snapped. For four years, I'd been soaking it all up, accepting the abuse was all part of the Eton turf. Suddenly I didn't feel like playing this craven game any more.

"That's all right," I replied, like the churl I was.

McArdle paused mid-stride, turned to look at me. "Care to tell us what you were dreaming about?"

"Not especially, Sir."

The laughter died. The boys scented a tussle.

"Or is it so very tedious to hear us talk about *Othello*?"

"It's nothing personal, Sir."

The tide had turned and the class was on my side now, tittering for me.

"You mean your tiredness is a general malaise?" McArdle tugged at his beard. "Well, you'd better have a ticket then. Talk it through with your tutors, just to see if there's anything they can do to help."

"Fair enough."

Inside, my heart sank. A ticket to be signed by both my housemaster and my personal tutor – yet another means by which Eton stamps its heel on her unruly charges.

At the end of the division, McArdle filled out the yellow slip. He wrote my name and under it, 'Falling asleep in class'.

"Have it back by tomorrow."

"My pleasure."

He scrutinised me for a moment from behind his desk, before adding one more word to the ticket: 'Insolence'.

The ticket dangled from McArdle's fingers. Again that surge of bravado. "I think I prefer the word 'Cheek'."

McArdle handed me the ticket in silence. Just as I was supposed to be, I was numb as I left the room.

It made the surprise that was awaiting me outside all the more disarming. For there standing on the pavement was Angela in her tartan mini-skirt and skin-tight navy jumper.

I rolled my eyes and raised my arm. Angela, fly as anything, high-fived me and we laughed at the crazy school we inhabited.

My metamorphosis over the previous two weeks must have been remarkable to behold. For now that I had India in my life, I had an inner ring of confidence that meant I could talk to girls without being turned into a tongue-tied fool.

Angela and I walked companionably down Judy's Passage, her shoulder occasionally tapping against mine.

"What were you dreaming about?" she asked.

"I was flying," I said. "I was flying over Eton."

"With anyone in particular?"

"Would it make any difference?"

"Well, you know what Freud said about flying in your dreams?"

"What did he say?"

"You'll have to look it up."

"Like when I next go to the library?"

"I've never once seen you in the library." She cuffed me lightly on the arm.

We'd arrived at the end of Judy's Passage, and there on the other side of the road was the dusty elderberry bush under which I had first found love with India. I looked at it and almost felt guilty for being there alone with Angela.

"You'll let me know if you ever go flying with me?"

"Be sure of it."

I had only just come from India's arms and I would be seeing her again that night. But already, here I was, allowing myself to flirt with Angela. Although it wasn't as if I'd actually done anything with her. I had been faithful to India in word and deed, though not, perhaps, in thought.

I know that this – among many other things – does not show me in the best of lights. I could have skipped telling you the incident completely. However, I would be doing you a disservice because what we are observing is not just my frailty but that of every schoolboy. It is not pleasant; it is not savoury. But welcome to the world of the single-sex school, where all relationships with the opposite sex are to be cultivated. Industriously.

That very afternoon I went to the school library, and Freud's *Interpretation of Dreams* duly confirmed my suspicions. Flying dreams are nothing more than 'sexual intercourse'; not so very surprising when you consider that Freud's entire oeuvre revolved around sex.

What indeed was surprising though was how Angela had alluded to my dream in such a risqué manner. Let her know when I flew with her? It was a come-on if ever I'd heard one.

Well, I was not going to take up Angela's offer. I had India in my life, I had sex three or four times a day and I was deliriously in love.

No – what I did was what I believe every other boy on earth does when they're in the midst of a grand love affair, and when they get that first tentative sniff that another girl might be interested.

They may not act, but they store it up, file it into the pending tray. Not, of course, that the grand love affair isn't going to last forever, but, just on the off chance, just in case…

Trust in God, but tie up your camel. An old Arab proverb and I've always liked it because it so pithily expresses a schoolboy's instinctive fallback position when it comes to his dealings with women.

After lunch, I joined the queue to Frankie's study, a dozen boys all in various states of nervousness. We were each waiting for Frankie's signature. Some of us had rips, which were sloppy pieces of homework that had been literally ripped at the top; some of us had show-ups and needed a tutorly pat on the back; some had chits that needed signing; and some, like me, had tickets and would be called upon to explain our misbehaviour.

Frankie's face was always a wax mask when you entered his study, for he never knew whether in the next minute he would be delivering the carrot or the stick.

Except with me, for with me he always had on his face a look of weary resignation.

Frankie's study was lined from floor-to-ceiling with books and there was a large window that overlooked the Slough Road. He had a sofa and armchairs, but for this meeting we adopted the formal positions of Eton combat, Frankie at his antique walnut desk while I stood, hands square behind my back.

"Falling asleep in class?" He screwed up his nose, as if at a noxious smell. "Insolence?"

Silence. The tick of the clock and the sound of boys noisy in the library outside.

"What would you like to say?"

A bluebottle worked its way across the window behind Frankie's head. "I fell asleep in class."

"I see." He signed the ticket. "I see."

He looked up and cocked an eye at me. "So, what's been keeping you up?"

"Revision, Sir. Can't sleep."

Frankie 'hmm-hmmed' to himself and handed back the ticket. "Insolence too?"

"Slipped out, Sir."

"If you start that, it's going to get you into a lot of trouble one of these days, Kim."

As I left, he drummed his fingertips on the desk, wondering if there was anything to be done with his unbiddable pupil. Was that the moment when Frankie had that first kernel of an idea to lay a trap for me? It may well have been.

But, even without the aid of my insolent tongue, I was more than capable of landing myself into any number of hair-breadth 'scapes and disastrous chances.

For, along with our countryside sex and our midnight assignations, that very afternoon India and I were strolling right through the heart of Windsor. Not hand-in-hand, or with our arms tight round each other's waists, but at a school like Eton it is enough – more than enough – for a boy to be seen walking with a young woman for the grapevine to start humming.

We had exercised some caution. We were off the usual schoolboy track and keeping our eyes open as we admired the Georgian houses.

We were laughing at any foolish thing that came into our heads. I'd found a Tabby cat and had bent down to scratch him behind the ear.

"My dad's got a tabby," I said. The cat arched its back as my hand streamed over the length of his body.

India was catching some sun, leaning against the railings, her hands outstretched. It was a beautiful day and she was wearing a short skirt, t-shirt and sunglasses. My watch glinted fetchingly on her wrist. To look at her then, she could have been aged anything from 15 to 30.

"I like cats," she said dreamily. "It's only the control freaks who can't stand them."

"What about dogs?"

"Love them too." Her hair was falling back in a brown spangled waterfall over the railings. "One day, when we have our house in the country, we'll have a whole menagerie."

I looked up at her, silhouetted by the sun. I didn't know if she was joking. But she had voiced my exact thoughts. Already I had started dreaming of our intertwined lives – that we would live together, travel together, have children, make music, and have the most magical sex until death us do part.

But to have her say it like that? I didn't know whether she was playing with me. I looked at India one more time. I could have said something. Instead, I busied myself with the cat.

India then looked down at me and stroked my hair.

"Would you like that?"

She was serious and had taken off her sunglasses.

"More than anything." I held her hand and kissed her wrist, and for one golden moment we were two credulous fools, synchronising our idyllic futures together.

It's funny how life never works out like that. You can have your plans, your dreams and your glorious future together mapped out. Yet fate still comes along anyway and, with haughty disregard, sets you off on a different path entirely.

But this was one golden moment when we both dreamed the same dream.

India held her hand against my cheek. "I love you to distraction." Even as she said it, she glanced uneasily across the road.

"No!" she said. "That boy Savage is coming."

We ran like hares, arms pumping, our breath whistling through our teeth.

India rounded the corner first and, as I followed, I looked behind – and that was what undid us. For it was only then that Savage recognised me.

I was tearing after India still, hard on her heels. We jinked round lampposts and parking meters, turned another corner, though when I looked back I could see Savage effortlessly cruising behind us.

"Jesus!" I said. Already I was imagining what might happen if we were caught. India grabbed my hand and was dragging me down a murky cul-de-sac, a back route to one of the Windsor hotels.

I tried a fire-door but it was locked. We had to hide. India squeezed into a two-foot gap between the industrial-sized bins and I followed.

My lungs were in flames. I tried to catch my breath without making a sound. All I wanted was a rasping lungful of air but I didn't dare breathe.

India had her back against the wall and was peeking behind the bins. "He's standing at the top," she said, her hand tense on mine. "Looking this way and that. Thinking about coming down here. Yes?" Her fingers clenched. "No."

India was then chuckling as she kissed me with relief.

"Close." I looked around, taking in our surroundings. We were in a dingy side road, with four storeys of buildings on either side and just a smear of grey skyline. Vegetables were rotting on the cobbles and there was a stinking haze of decayed food.

"Very close," India replied and kissed me again.

It was as if India and I were on a permanent sexual hair-trigger. We could make love once, twice, and then might be contentedly sipping tea together. But just the slightest word, or look, or touch, was the only spark that was needed to start another blaze in our tinder-dry desire.

She quickly had her hands up my shirt, was pressing herself tight against me. "I hope you're thinking what I'm thinking."

"I just might be."

"I'm so glad to hear that." Already, as she kissed me, she was tugging at my belt and easing at my fly-buttons.

I was hauling at her skirt, my fingers warm on her buttocks, pulling aside the knicker elastic.

With her arms set round my neck, she gripped her knees over my hips, and there, in among the trade waste and kitchen cast-offs, we made love against the wall.

"Beautiful," India whispered in my ear. "So beautiful."

Although our love-making had started out of nowhere, we were taking our time. Not for us the one-minute coupling. No, it may sound sappy but our sex had become the highest expression of our love for each other. It was just as they always say – or at least certainly ought to say: 'Sex, even when it's sandwiched between two industrial-sized rubbish bins, blasts into outer space when you're in love.'

"Oh my darling," India said, rocking her hips against me. She took my ear entirely in her mouth. "I'm so close."

The next moment she let out a little laugh. "There's somebody coming," she said. "It's one of the cooks."

I could hear him, a young man from the sound of it, whistling *Under Pressure* by Queen and David Bowie.

She didn't break stride, gently coasting up to the brink.

"Darling," she said, looking over my shoulder. "He's coming right over to the bin. I can't…" Her knees squeezed tight at my waist, "…stop."

And, to the amazement of that genial kitchen-porter, India peaked as he off-loaded another bucket of slops into the bin.

I could not see him, but there was a tell-tale pause in the whistling.

India kissed me and nuzzled into my shoulders. "I love you," she said.

She always said that when our love-making had ended.

"Did he see us?"

She laughed again as she eased her feet down to the cobbles. "He winked at me."

"Good for him."

The first and indeed only time that India and I were definitely caught in *flagrante delictu*. I hope we made the man's day.

An hour later we were taking our leave of each other when India fished into her handbag. "I've bought you a present," she said, handing me a small box that was wrapped with love hearts.

I gazed at it, gave it a shake. Something rattled inside. "What could it be?"

"The key to my heart?"

"I'd better open it then."

It was not quite the key to her heart. It was the key to her home, small and golden with a brown leather fob in the shape of a love-heart.

"Thank you." I kissed her. "So you won't have to come downstairs at midnight for me?"

"That's right." She kissed me back, nibbling my lower lip. "Let yourself in any time you like."

Oh – indeed I would. But for that little golden key, how different my life might have been.

For you know the story of Duke Bluebeard? He welcomes his new bride to his castle and tells her that she may go wherever she pleases – save for the one room with the locked door. But of course she goes there. She has to go there. And, in it, she finds all of the wracked and tortured bodies of Bluebeard's previous wives.

I too was Bluebeard's bride. For I had been given the key to my love's castle and the only thing stopping me from unearthing her secrets, her skeletons, was my own self-restraint.

And I had none of it.

PRELUDE 19, A Major

It was the night-time jaunts that were my undoing.

I could get away with it for one night, maybe two nights, a week. But there were too many imponderables. Even if every nightly escapade had been planned to the last detail, there were always far too many things that were out of my control. My Economics master, forever banging on about supply and demand, would have deemed that there were too many 'variables'.

There was one night when I was flying back from India's at five in the morning, hurtling like a black wraith down Keate's Lane. To any master with any perspicacity, I could have looked like nothing other than what I was: a schoolboy on the run.

A car was coming the other way and I was locked in its headlights. I flew past, not stopping at the traffic lights by College Chapel for already I had heard the dink of brakes and the revved three-point turn in the middle of the road.

A thrill of terror washed through my body as I realised I was being chased. It felt like I was cycling for my very life.

The car was just yards behind me as I raced past the Burning Bush. I skidded round the corner and pedalled at full tilt down Judy's Passage, laughing with demented glee as the headlights gazed forlornly after me.

I took a wide loop round the school, over the parade ground, the fives courts, and onto Sixpenny before dumping the bike behind some trees.

Yes – I'd got away with it, just as it was my destiny to do, for my love affair with India was not going to be snipped short by an

Eton beak on the prowl.

My luck was to hold for a little while yet.

But I would have a few scares on the way.

It was Friday, nearly midnight, and I had not seen India since I'd left her arms that morning.

I let myself in with my golden key and with light steps walked up to her flat. There was a single candle burning on the piano, but from India's bedroom upstairs I could see a fiery haze of light.

I savoured the moment and the prospect that awaited me.

"Hello," I called softly and walked up the oak staircase to my love.

She was lying on top of the bedclothes, wearing the scantiest of cream silk negligees and reading Walt Whitman. As she saw me, her face lit up, as if just the sight of me could make her day.

We kissed, we made love, roaming wild over each other's bodies.

But it is not the love-making that I wish to detail, it is what happened afterwards, because this is where the rot set in.

It was, I suppose, our first row. Not the full-scale, screaming glut of swear words that I came to endure in later years with other partners. But it was our first bust-up. Unpleasant and unkind. And it would directly lead to the most panicky, gut-churning hour of my entire life.

We were naked, lying in each other's arms, blissed out on love.

But I could tell she was distracted. She wasn't really there; those walnut eyes had glazed and her thoughts were miles away.

"What's up?" I said.

She sighed and kissed me. I loved that about her. Her automatic response to anything was always to kiss me. "I won't be around on Tuesday afternoon," she said. "I've got to go to London."

"Oh yes?"

"Got some things I have to sort out." She said it lightly, too lightly, the last two words catching in her throat.

I was cool, casual, relaxed – just as I always am when my heart starts to quicken and I sense danger. "Anything you want to talk about?"

"Ohh," she sighed. "Just trying to sort out my future."

I tickled her and rolled onto her. "And do I feature?"

She squealed. "Of course you feature. But I'm going to be out of a job in three weeks."

I was staggered. "What?"

"They only ever got me in for the summer term," she said. Careful. Studied.

"But …"

"I should have told you sooner," she continued. "But I didn't know how."

In that moment, all the ivory towers of my future, the dreams that I had so painstakingly constructed, started to crumble. I had genuinely assumed that India would be teaching at Eton for the next year – marking time at the school so that we could be together every night.

"Oh." My veins were icing up. Everything seemed to stop. All the emotion, all the love, seemed to have been frozen down to one single focus-point – that India would be leaving me at the end of the term.

She was talking again, faster. "That isn't to say that I don't love you any less, or that I don't want to be with you. It's just…" She trailed off. "…I can't put my whole life on hold here at Eton."

"Can't put your life on hold for me?"

"Oh Kim," she said and kissed me. "Teaching here at Eton was only a stop-gap while I got my life back together."

Her life back together?

The words struck a jarring discord in my jealous heart.

"Really?" I spoke softly now. Trying to coax her on. Coax it out of her. "Has your life fallen apart?"

"Until you came along." She gazed at the wall. "You are the light burning for me at the end of the tunnel."

"Are you out of it yet?"

"Nearly. Very nearly," she said. The pause hung over us like a black cloud, as she twisted the sheet in her fingers and weighed up whether to tell me, calculating whether I could take it.

And do you know what she concluded? She thought that I, a callow, jealous schoolboy, was still not nearly ready to know.

And how right she was.

She swallowed, stifling back her secret, and, at that moment, I instinctively knew that she was withholding something from me. But would I go there? Would I quiz her?

I couldn't. I remembered my vow never to ask India a single question about her past life.

"Before you came along I'd been thinking about VSO," she said. "But now I'm toying with trying to be a doctor again."

"In London?"

"If they'll have me." She rolled on top of me. "I don't know why I haven't asked you this before. What are your plans when you leave?"

"I had been thinking…" I paused, ran it through in my head. "I'd been thinking about the army."

She didn't say anything for a while. "The army?"

"It's in the blood." I knew it sounded weak.

"The army?" She was deadpan. "I'd never have guessed."

"That's what I'm thinking of, yeah."

"Get to travel the world," she said. "Sexy uniforms."

"I thought you'd like it."

"An army officer?" she mused. "So, it could have been you out in the Falklands?"

"Suppose so."

She never raised a single doubt, a single query, and that, in itself, set off a host of demons in my mind. Would I really be joining up for myself or for my father? But, seemingly more important, did India even care, or was I just a temporary lover?

The conversation was so light, so effortless – and so unnatural. Both of us were just playing at being the carefree lover, for although my words were easy, my brain was going into meltdown. My love was leaving me, was going to London. We would have one of those old-fashioned relationships where we wrote, talked on the phone and met at weekends, until that inevitable day when someone fresh came along to take her fancy.

"Let's go on holiday this summer," she said. "Why not Greece?"

"Great."

It was the first time that I had ever physically shunned India. She wanted to make love, to get everything back onto an even keel, but I was dead down there. I still went through the motions, told her that I loved her, that I was tired. Already my open heart was turning into an icy citadel. Already I was fearing the worst for when she went to London.

We did eventually make love that night. It would have been impossible to resist her. Down she'd gone beneath the covers. All my jealous fears and rages were expunged in that moment. It was my first – and probably my most joyous – introduction to the art of kissing and making up. What a wonderful thing it is, to be able to row and then to come together, seemingly stronger and more united than ever you were before.

We thrashed from side to side, heaving and clawing onto each other, desperate for love. We knocked pillows to the floor, knocked over the light, the table, and only then, only when we were done with each other and had proved our love, did we fall asleep in each other's arms.

It was the sunlight that woke me. Just a little sunbeam worming through the white blinds and raking across my eyelids.

I sat bolt upright, stared at the bright sunshine rippling into the room, and felt a hollow queasiness in the pit of my stomach.

India was still asleep, her arms fast round my waist.

I looked on the floor at the upturned lamp, the now-broken alarm clock and India's Walt Whitman poems. I stretched over to pick up my watch.

It was gone 7.30am. I was in a chasm of trouble.

I was already late for the Saturday Economics division, which would almost certainly lead to another spell on the Tardy Book. But, as I stared out of the window, I realised with incredible clarity that I was trapped in India's flat and there was no way out.

I couldn't get back to the Timbralls.

Eton would be up and awake and her boys and masters out strolling the streets, all of them in their shiny uniforms and with ears and eyes alert and twitching. And, as for me, all I had were my trainers, my sweatshirt, hat and bike. I was stuck.

I tried to tick off the possibilities. Biking back to the Timbralls would have been suicide. Even if I'd made it back to the house, there was no way that I could have returned to my room. My tutor, the Dame, the senior boys – there were any number of people who could have spotted me out of uniform and drawn their own conclusions.

I thought about getting a taxi to the Timbralls, or borrowing a pair of India's shorts and pretending I'd been out for a run.

The more I thought about it, the more I realised that I was stuck like a cat up a burning tree. Either I stayed put, ensuring I was roasted alive, or I jumped to a certain death.

India was waking up. She looked at me dreamily, such love in her eyes. "Mmm," she said. "That feels good."

She caught the worry in my face. "What's happened?"

"I've overslept," I said. "I can't get back."

She was up now, checked the time and looked out of the patio door.

"You need some tails," she said.

"I do."

"Why don't I go down to Tom Brown as soon as they open and buy you some?"

I stared at her miserably. Because I didn't just need tails, I needed a shirt, collar, tie, studs, black shoes, black socks. She'd need to go to about four different shops, and meanwhile time would be ticking by and I would be missing lesson after lesson.

Another nightmarish scenario occurred to me. I remembered the Timbralls' fire-door, with its bolts secured by bits of gaffer tape. The tape was good enough to pass muster in the middle of the night. But in the full light of day?

I squeezed the bridge of my nose. I was in one hell of a hole.

It seemed that I only had one chance – and I'd be lucky to get even that.

I did what preparations I could. I shaved, washed and brushed my teeth. After that, there was nothing for it but to wait – wait patiently and watch the minutes tick by.

India made me some tea and toast, but I was so nervous I couldn't speak, let alone drink or eat. No, all I could do was watch the minutes glide by, and try to maintain a mask of stony indifference as the waves of cold terror lapped at my feet.

India was an angel. She didn't talk, but stood behind me and massaged my tense shoulders.

Finally, eventually, the minute hand ticked round to 8.30am. It was my only shot.

I called the house-phone at the Timbralls. The boys would be at breakfast and, with luck, so would my saviour.

The phone was picked up after five rings. It was one of the fags.

"The Timbralls," he said, in his piping cut-glass voice.

"Good morning," I said, putting on a patrician voice. "This is Jeremy Raikes' uncle. May I speak to him?"

"I'll see if I can find him."

I waited an age. The boy must have scoured the house – upstairs to Jeremy's room and back down to the dining room.

Two full minutes he was gone.

I then heard something that took me a moment to recognise. To my horror, I realised I was listening to the sound of a bellowed boy call, "BoooyUppp!"

Even over the phone, I could hear the drum of the fags' feet as they tore up the stairs. Any thought of my phone call and Jeremy Raikes' uncle would have been erased from the fag's mind.

I waited and I waited.

Over the phone came the sounds of Timbralls life: shouts of boys mobbing in the hall, a whistle as a boy sauntered off to chapel, the thud of books being thrown onto the floor.

And still nobody picked up the phone.

I hung up and tried again. And all I got was the same open line. I started screaming down the phone, hoping that someone might hear me. But there was nothing at all, no one to hear my shouts, just the sound of the Timbralls emptying into the morning.

Oh, I was dying a score of deaths. Minute after minute ticked by and I was helpless. How I cursed the Librarian who had given that particular boy call. I was so mad that then and there I could have yanked the phone from its socket.

India had dressed and she made me more tea, which I watched go stone-cold as I sat in a twitching spasm of impatience by the phone, waiting for someone to pick up.

My hopes lifted. I heard the door of the kiosk. Someone picked up the phone, before slamming it on the hook.

Immediately I dialled back. Now the phone was engaged. Some Timbralls' boy having a morning chat with his girlfriend no doubt. I redialled and redialled and redialled, over and over again for minutes on end. I could think of nothing else but plugging in the Timbralls number. It was my only hope.

I finally got back through, and this time the phone was ringing out again and not one of the swine was answering. I was grinding my teeth with rage.

"Hello?"

It was Archie. My heart sank.

I tried to mask my voice. "May I speak to Jeremy please?"

"Who's speaking?"

"His uncle."

A pause. A deathly pause. "Is that you Kim?"

"It's his uncle."

"Why do you want Jeremy?" he persisted. "Where are you anyway?"

The sweat trailed down my arm. "Just get me Jeremy please."

"Not until you stop putting on that stupid voice."

"All right." I spoke normally. "Now will you get him?"

"Gotcha! I knew it was you!" he shrieked. "What are you doing out of the house? Where are you calling from?"

"Please, please Archie, could you get me Jeremy."

"Only if you tell me where you are." He had me skewered.

"Archie, please, I don't have much time."

"Tell Uncle Archie!"

"I'm stuck in bloody Windsor, now get me Jeremy. Please!"

"Windsor?" Archie cooed. "What are you doing there?"

"Please?" I could gladly have throttled him.

"Will you tell all later?"

"Yes!"

"I'll hold you to that."

Finally he went. Another boy who knew about my night-time excursions. Another boy who might reveal my fatal secret.

I had to endure more time hanging on the phone, listening to every clump and bump of Timbralls life. By now I'd gnawed every one of my nails to the quick.

"Hello?"

"Jeremy, it's me! It's Kim! I need your help."

"Where are you?"

"At India's. I've overslept. I've got no clothes."

"*Fouquet moi!*"

I could hear my teeth as I ground them. "I've been trying to get hold of you for the past 45 minutes."

"What do you need? Tails, shirt, shoes, everything?"

"And my English books." I told him the address.

"Be quick as I can." He laughed. "Get the tea on."

"Why?"

"So we can all have a nice chat."

He must have raced down the High Street because within 20 minutes he was knocking at India's door with a carrier-bag full of my clothes.

I'd hoped he would drop off my uniform and leave. But he was not going to pass up the chance of checking out my love-nest, and I immediately heard him walking up the stairs after India.

His face was wreathed with a huge smile, as though he knew he'd just saved my life and as a consequence could take any liberties with me that he pleased.

"Here you go." He passed me the carrier-bag.

"Thank you." Of the three of us, I was by far the most nervous.

"Would you like some tea?" India asked Jeremy.

"Love some."

I changed upstairs while listening to the pair of them talking in the lounge.

"Lovely day," Jeremy said. "And if I may, a quite lovely flat."

"Thank you," she said. "It was kind of you. I know that you're a very dear friend of Kim's."

"Anything for Kim."

On and on he went and, when I walked downstairs, I found Jeremy sprawled in one of the armchairs, his legs outstretched and a mug of tea on the armrest. India was sitting at the piano stool, a wry look of amusement on her face.

"Very smart," said Jeremy as he appraised me. "I think you should lie in more often."

I stifled the insult on my lips. "Thank you."

Jeremy checked his watch. "We've already missed Chapel. We must away if we are going to make our next div." He stood up. "Thank you so much for the tea."

He waved goodbye to India and left me to my fond farewell.

I kissed India on the lips.

"See you this afternoon?" she said.

"Don't doubt it."

I flew down the stairs, out into the sunshine, out to the High Street and to the humming mass of Eton life in which I longed to bury myself. It had never felt so good to be in my tailcoat.

Jeremy was waiting on the corner.

"Nice girlfriend," he said.

"Thank you."

"I hope you appreciate her."

"Very much."

Jeremy kicked out at a Coke can lying in the gutter. It clinked satisfyingly down the road. "I suppose you've just used up another of your nine lives."

"Quite probably."

PRELUDE 2, C Minor

My life was India and my work suffered for it.

And I didn't give a damn.

My grades had tumbled in both Divinity and Economics. I was even bumping along the bottom in my favourite class, English. But it was nothing I could not handle. I felt that I could take any amount of abuse and raillery from my tutor and my beaks.

Soon enough my indolence would find me out.

For it is not for nothing that Eton has one of the best academic records of any school in Britain. The college's internal exams are known as Trials and the penalties for failure are severe. Failed exams merit the obligatory roasting from your tutors and have to be re-taken at the beginning of the Michaelmas Half. Fail the lot and your Eton career is over.

Trials were due to start on the Friday, a week before the end of term, and I was anxious. Five days to make up for a year's worth of daydreaming.

I'd done monster-cramming sessions before and they had been highly effective. So, with four days till my first English trial, I got down to some heavy work. No music, no photos, nothing ahead of me but my books and three solid hours of revision.

It was hopeless.

With every turn of the *Othello* page, all I could think of was India. Nothing would stick in my mind, even for a moment. Page-after-page would be read and seemingly absorbed, and 20 minutes later I would flick back and realise I had not taken in a single word.

How could I concentrate on *Othello* when India was forever

dancing through my brain, constantly nuzzling my ear, worming her hand in between my shirt buttons?

I hurled the book across the room and tried some Economics instead. I thought the text's turgid style might distract me.

I didn't make it past the first line before I saw India's face beaming out at me. She pouted and blew me a kiss.

Divinity: the same. Even St Paul's letters to the Ephesians and the Romans were nothing more than another India photo-book.

I gave up and grabbed an hour's sleep before getting up at 11.30 for my midnight flit. But all the way down to India's flat, I couldn't get the Trials out of my head. Despite a year of lessons, I'd realised that my Economics knowledge was zip. The exam was coming at me with all the inevitability of a slow-mo car-crash.

I was crabby even before I'd walked through India's front door, like a stressed-out husband after a bad day at work. So when I saw her and kissed her, I was trying to sound carefree but looking for any opportunity to vent steam.

I soon found one.

I'd spotted the formal grey suit and white blouse that India had hung up in the bedroom. They were the clothes she'd need for her interview the next day in London – and for the 'other stuff' that needed sorting out.

Other stuff?

"Got your clothes all ready for tomorrow," I said.

She caught it instantly. I thought it was inflexion-free, that I'd just been making polite conversation. But she immediately discerned its every inference.

"Anything up?"

"Nothing at all," I said. "Should there be?"

She sat down beside me on the bed and gave me a hug. "Kim, I love you and only you."

"I know you do."

India held onto me as she looked me in the eye. "I know you feel left out."

She pecked at my chin, my lips unresponsive.

"But when I'm with you I want to make love, to laugh and be free." She held me secure round the neck. "What do you think?"

"Great." Slowly, so slowly, I could feel the door to my heart closing shut, for I knew that never again would I expose myself to the vulnerability of blind love. She could not trust me with her past, and rightly so as I could not trust myself.

India was fumbling with my belt now. And the sight of her slim fingers working their way into my boxers was – as always – more than enough to temporarily blow away the cobwebs of my insecurities.

We made love, as frenetic as anything we had ever done before, position after position just for the sake of having done them. I marvelled at her beauty. I loved her completely and when I left the next morning I kissed her the very fondest of kisses.

It may not seem much to the outside observer, but it was then as if the courses of my head and my heart had diverged and, ever after that night, the two of them were never in synch again.

When I was with India, alone and walking the fields and feeling her weight bear down on me as we made love, I was brim full of love.

But it was the times that we were apart that would come to dog me. Those times when my yammering jealousy would overrule my heart, when in under a minute I could forget that India loved me and only me. Instead I would obsess about her past and her secrets. And since she did not think fit to tell me about her past, I would invent these fantastic chimeras, would imagine that she'd been a call-girl, or that she was the mistress of some Arab millionaire.

I didn't know and my heart didn't want to know.

But my head?

My head wanted to know everything.

That Tuesday, after India had returned from London, she was as jolly as I'd ever known her. The champagne was already open when I'd arrived and it was the first time I'd ever seen her like a ditzy schoolgirl.

We were up the whole night and, by the time I pedalled back to the Timbralls, I was nothing but a shell. Hollow-eyed and with the light drum-roll of an impending hangover.

We had no lessons that week to give us time to revise. I did the best I could. But my bed was a constant distraction, forever luring me into its snug embrace. For every minute that I spent revising, I must have spent ten sparked out on my mattress.

I was being tugged this way and that – trying to revise yet having lost all ability to learn; yearning for love, yet so desperate to pick our relationship to pieces.

And it all came to a steaming, frothing head that Sunday night. It was the first time that my spell of luck had been broken and, after that, it was as if my every step was dogged by ill-fortune.

I now had my routine down-pat when I visited India at night.

While everyone else was at supper, I primed the fire-door, opening it and sealing down the two bolts. Later, at 11.30pm, all it needed was a slight push and without a sound I was out on the fire-escape and inhaling the crisp night air.

Jeremy's bike was tucked away in the New Schools Yard and with a slap of the Sebastopol cannon I was off into the night and to the delights of India.

That particular night she was playing the piano as I walked into her flat; my old favourite, Prelude 17, the very first piece I'd heard her play.

The wheel had almost turned full-circle.

I sat beside her on the piano stool and gazed at her fingers moving so precisely over the keyboard.

"Still like that prelude?" she asked.

"Of course," I said. "It reminds me of you."

We had a drink outside on her patio, with just a candle for light while all around us was the loneliness of the dark night.

I blew her a kiss and in an instant she was on my lap, kissing me, her fingers raking through my hair.

"Let's make love outside," she whispered.

"Shall I get the mattress?"

"Why not?"

So we tugged out the mattress, the pillows and the duvet, and there with the ramparts of Windsor Castle silhouetted against the stars, we made love on the patio. It was glorious, the very best *al fresco* sex that we'd ever had, and with all the luxury of a mattress.

How she clung to me, her legs cocked round my knees. The breath caught in her throat as a choking sob. Perhaps she had already scented the disaster that was lurking round the corner.

We snuggled underneath the duvet and fell asleep, holding each other tight, locked in our last embrace.

I woke to the jarring shrill of India's phone in the bedroom. It took a moment to remember where I was. It was still quite dark, a trace of dew on the duvet, the stars bright.

India was awake.

"Who's that?" she said.

I didn't know. But already my heart was sinking, for any phone call at 3am can never be anything other than bad news.

She got up and kissed me, and I can still recall that exact picture of India as she sashayed naked over the patio and into the bedroom. It's etched into my chambers of remembrance, so lithe, her hair swinging from side to side.

She steps out of the twilight and into the dark.

I would never see her naked again.

Would never hear her play another Bach prelude.

For we had made love for the last time and our piano-playing was done.

I lay back and looked at the stars. My heart was thumping. Already I had a suspicion of what had happened.

The conversation was brief. India was fluttering at the door. "It's Jeremy," she said, her words sharp with alarm. "There's a fire drill."

I arrowed out of the mattress. No time for words, no time for kisses, for I was pulling on trousers, shirt and shoes and with a farewell wave was thundering down the stairs.

A sprint to the bike and a manic fumble with the lock as I nearly snapped off the key, before the panicked dash back to the

Timbralls. I pedalled like a demon.

On the bike, I had a moment to weigh up my chances.

They were bleak.

Once a year, Frankie would hold a night-time fire-drill. The rules were specific. At the first sound of the alarm, you leapt out of bed, put on shoes and dressing-gown and made certain that your neighbours were up. The fire-doors were flung open and you would troop out to the garden where Frankie would be waiting for the roll-call.

Of course I should have thought of it, should have been aware of the possibility of a fire-drill, but love had made me blind. I was lucky; I'd always been lucky. The fates were with me on this one too.

I tried to concoct a plan as I raced up the High Street. But the closer I got to the Timbralls, the worse it looked.

To evacuate every boy normally took about three minutes. Jeremy's phone call had been about eight minutes ago.

Oh boy.

It was going to be carnage.

I tried not to picture the scene that awaited me. Probably Frankie and a couple of the senior boys waiting for me in my room.

The grand inquisition.

Expelled by noon.

I did have some sort of plan. I couldn't go back up the fire-escape because it was in full view of the boys on the lawn.

But I did know that all the Timbralls' doors would be open. So I'd march up the main staircase and pray that I didn't meet anyone on the way.

I shot through Cannon Yard, and there was the Timbralls, ablaze with light and alarm bells ringing. With her tall chimneys, she struck me as an ocean-going liner plunging into the night.

I dumped the bike by the railings and took the stairs three at a time. The noise of the alarms was deafening.

I didn't know how it was going to end, but I'd play it out to the last card. I'd say that I'd fallen asleep in the lavatory, that I couldn't sleep and that I'd had a cat-nap in the library, that I'd been so dead to the world that not even the sound of the alarms and the stampeding boys had been enough to wake me. Deny, deny, deny. I'd admit to any foolishness or oversight, but I would never confess to being out of the house after dark.

Up one flight of stairs and hurling myself up the next. Then stopped. She had me.

The Dame, Lucinda, was hobbling out of her suite of rooms. Her dog Rufus wagged his tail at the sight of me.

I gawked. "Good evening Ma'am."

Lucinda stared at me, cocked her head to the side, trying to understand why I should be fully dressed and racing upstairs during a fire-drill.

"Good evening, Kim," she said at length.

I held my breath, wondered what to say. Would she call for Frankie now? Report me later?

"Just getting my dressing-gown, Ma'am," I said.

"Really?" she said.

"Yes Ma'am."

She bent to stroke Rufus, fussed over his ears. "I don't think I ever properly thanked you for all your dog-walking," she said. "I'm very grateful."

"Been a pleasure."

"Well, be off with you then," she said. "You'd better be quick."

"Thank you Ma'am." I darted up the stairs. "Thank you very much indeed." Then and there, I vowed that come the end of term I would buy Lucinda the biggest box of chocolates that she'd ever laid eyes on.

Still not a boy in sight. My luck was in – of course it was, because, as with all my dealings with India, everything I touched would turn to gold.

I bolted into my room and barked an astonished sigh of relief. The door was open, the lights were on, but it was empty.

I was hauling off my jeans when Jeremy, ice white, hurried in.

"Get out of here." He was grabbing my dressing-gown and tugging at my elbow. "Come to my room." I followed him down the passage, ripping off my t-shirt as we went. He clicked the door behind.

We heard the drum of thundering footsteps on the stairs.

"Put on the dressing-gown," he ordered, throwing himself onto the ground. "I've had an epileptic fit. You're tending me." He gave my hand a squeeze. "Make it good."

The door cannoned open and there staring down at us was Frankie, Savage and Archie. Frankie was red-faced, breathless, eyes raking over the room. I can even remember the exact clothes that the boys were wearing: Savage in blue silk pyjamas and an immaculate white gown, while Archie was still in the same stained dressing-gown that he'd had since prep-school.

I was kneeling on the floor by Jeremy's stricken body. His face was stuck in a grotesque rictus and his eyelids twitched.

"Jeremy's had an epileptic fit, Sir." I looked up at Frankie. "I've been looking after him."

"A fit?" Frankie said. "Jeremy's had a fit?"

"Yes Sir."

Jeremy shuddered and started to cough. I delicately rolled him into the recovery position, head into the crook of his elbow, one leg straight, the other bent at the knee.

Frankie turned to Savage and Archie. "You two, get those alarms turned off."

The pair left together, Savage with a scowl, Archie with a knowing leer.

Had I missed something? Was there some tell-tale clue that would finish me off?

Frankie squatted down beside me and took Jeremy's wrist. "So, he's had an epileptic fit?" he said again.

"I believe so, Sir."

"Did you know he was epileptic?"

"No Sir." I stood up now. It was uncomfortable squatting knee-to-knee with Frankie.

"Right." He counted off the seconds on his watch. "Pulse is fine. And how did you know what to do?"

"I have an aunt who's epileptic."

"You do, do you?"

The whole conversation had about it an air of disbelief, as if Frankie knew I was lying, was certain I was lying, but couldn't quite figure out exactly what was going on.

He sat on the bed and stared at me, and, while Jeremy lay quivering on the floor between us, he tried to divine the truth.

"So, tell me what happened."

I patted my hair, stared at my knee. Had to keep things simple.

"The fire-alarm went off and I came to check that Jeremy was awake, Sir," I said. "We were about to follow the other boys out when he had a fit."

"And then?"

"I made sure that he couldn't injure himself and I monitored the fit."

"I see."

"I thought that was more important in the circumstances than coming down for the roll-call."

"I see."

But he couldn't see at all. I watched as his brain ticked over all the possibilities, tested my story. But so long as I stuck to my guns, he couldn't pin a thing on me.

"I see," he said again. He looked down at Jeremy, who was breathing normally now. "Very well."

My spirits were lightening by the second. I'd done it! Yet again I'd got away with it. I couldn't resist tugging Frankie's tail. "Do you think I did the right thing, Sir?"

"I'm sure you think you did." He got up. "I'll send the Dame to check Jeremy."

He scrutinised the scene one more time as he stood at the door, his eyes minutely checking over us.

"Nice watch," he said. "Don't think I've seen it before."

"Thank you, Sir."

"What happened to that Heuer your father gave you?"

"Lost it, Sir."

And with a final disbelieving shake of his head, Frankie was gone. Jeremy turned and winked, and I had to bite my cheek to suppress the whoop of laughter that wanted to burst out of me.

The Trials were not a total fiasco. Somehow, some small smatterings of English and Divinity must have lodged into my head during that wild summer. English questions about Othello and his fatal flaw, Divinity questions about Justification by Faith. The exams were yet further evidence of my supremely mediocre academic standards.

But the day after the fire-drill, I didn't have a thought for my exams. I was still on a high from the previous night. I'd come through! Against all the odds, despite all the traps and snares that had been laid for me, I had come through. My Eton career intact and my love affair going from strength to strength.

It felt like a near miss in the trenches, a sniper's bullet fizzing past my face. I had inhaled the stench of death and had lived to tell the tale.

I called India up at teatime, knowing she would be back home by then.

"What happened?" she said. "I've been so worried."

"Well, I'm still here." I was cocky.

"What did you do?"

"Jeremy pretended he'd had a fit. I'd tended him as the rest of the boys fled the house."

"Quick thinking," she laughed. "I was terrified for you."

"You're my lucky charm."

"You're so sweet."

"Though it might be stretching it to come over tonight. I can scent a spot-check."

"What a shame," she said. "It's my favourite time of the day when you come to see me."

"So can I see you tomorrow afternoon?"

"Ahh," she said, and, as she said it, I felt my stomach curdle. "I've got to go to London again."

"Oh, I'm sorry."

"But what about teatime? You could come round."

"I could be there, all tucked up and waiting for you."

"I'd love that," she said. "And I love you."

"And I you." I blew her a farewell kiss.

It was fortunate that I didn't visit India that night for, just as I had expected, Frankie did indeed make a little routine check on my bedroom. It must have been about 2am when I woke to hear a click at my door. I could sense a thin beam of torchlight scouring over my face before the door shut fast.

I smiled at my own perspicacity.

It seemed as if I was out-thinking them at every turn.

But I was not.

For, although I might have deceived Frankie, there was one person who had not fallen for any of my moonshine.

It was such a minor blunder. But it had enabled Savage to perceive everything.

He knew it all – knew that I was seeing India and knew too that I was sneaking to her arms at night.

I'm not sure if he had spotted India that day in Windsor as he'd chased us through the streets, though it might have been a pointer. It's possible, even, that Archie tipped him off about my midnight excursions.

But, either way, it was the fire-drill that finally did for me.

I can picture the scene that night: the fire bells ringing and Savage bawling for every one to quit the house. He rams home the bar on the fire-door – and discovers that the door is already open. He looks more closely; he wonders. And there, at top and bottom, are those two tell-tale pieces of gaffer tape that could only ever have meant one thing: one of his boys was off and away and enjoying the raptures of love in the outside world.

Savage could have passed on his suspicions to Frankie, though much good it would have done him. As long as I stuck to my denials, they were never going to break me.

But why should Savage have bothered informing my tutor when he could dish out his own personal revenge?

For, along with everything else, Savage knew my little

routines, had observed how, just a minute before Absence, I would furiously pedal through New Schools Yard. And that is the inherent problem with routines, for once your enemies have found them out, they can use them against you.

Yes, my time of reckoning had come – the day when Savage would pay me back for that thump in the library, out of nothing more than sheer spite, and when the fates would finally bloody my nose for daring to find love at Eton.

PRELUDE 1, C Major

That Tuesday started well enough. There was only one hurdle left, my Economics Trial, which I was due to sit the next day.

I was doing my best to chug my way through the dreary textbooks. All I had to do was retain the information in my head for 24 hours and reproduce it on the page in a great torrent of verbose knowledge.

Some of it might have stuck. I don't know. I might even have passed the Trial.

It is all rather immaterial now, for I never sat the exam.

Throughout lunch I had an uneasy tension; I knew, oh yes I knew exactly, what was about to happen.

One side of me, of course, wanted nothing more than to buy India a bunch of flowers and some chocolates. I would let myself into her flat, would put the flowers in a vase. I might play the piano for a bit, might leaf through some of her books, and when she came through the door, all sleek and groomed in her grey suit, I would be gleaming with my own virtue.

That was one way of looking at it, that I'd be going into India's flat with the sole object of being there for her when she returned from London.

That was what my heart wanted.

But my head? Even before I had stepped through the door, my head had other designs altogether. Didn't I just know it? As I let myself into her flat, I felt like a burglar come to ransack her home.

It was 3pm. I went through the motions.

I trimmed the roses – white, I remember – and put them in a vase on the piano. I made myself a cup of tea. I played a tune, but my heart wasn't in it.

I started to potter around. It's what you do when you're in your lover's home and you have the place to yourself for the first time.

I had a look at the books in her spare room. Medical textbooks, music books, novels, biographies. Some I'd read, some I hadn't.

That cork noticeboard by the front door. A picture of India with a man. I pulled it off but there was nothing on the back.

To the bathroom and to the kitchen, for a quick poke through the cupboards. A peek upstairs at the bedroom and shower room.

Up until now, my behaviour had – just – been within reasonable bounds. I had been inquisitive, certainly. But I hadn't overstepped the mark.

But, as I walked round India's flat, inhaling her smell, a wild mist descended over me. All thought of love had gone out of the window. For all I wanted to do was dig – find out everything about her. I was like a reformed alcoholic who, after that first whiff of booze, then drains every bottle in sight.

She had secrets and she had kept them from me – deliberately kept them from me because she knew that I had a jealous heart. But I would find them out, would winkle out every last one of them. I was as thorough as any detective.

First the drawers of her desk in the spare room. Then a sweep under the bed, the mattress and the wardrobe shelves. Followed by a look in the kitchen above the cupboards.

I delayed it to the very last. I had searched the entire apartment from top to bottom and had found not a single thing to compromise my lover.

But I was only playing with myself, stretching out the search to breaking point.

For I had known for several days where India stored her secrets.

Where else but under the piano, underneath her music books, her Bach, her Partitas and her *Well-Tempered Clavier*?

I stretched for the chest and hauled it out from underneath India's baby grand. I was detached, like a vet who has the task of putting down a much-loved family pet. It was not going to be pleasant, but it was a job that had to be done.

I placed all of the music books onto the piano, alongside the vase of roses, and for a moment I stared at the box. It was an old seafarer's chest, made of gnarled oak and latticed with black iron. There was a handle at each end and a clasp in front. But no lock.

I think at that stage I was so in the thrall of the terrifying rage coursing through my veins that, even if there had been a lock, I'd have wrenched it off with a crowbar. Yes – I was now livid with anger. I was insanely jealous of India's lurid past and furious with myself at my own lack of self-restraint. And there was guilt too, for I knew exactly what I was about to do, and I knew there could never be any turning back.

I was about to attack my golden Goddess with a sledgehammer, was going to knock her clay feet from underneath her until I had razed her to the ground.

It was the most awful thing I have ever done in my life.

I gritted my teeth, I flicked the latch and I opened India's past.

And there it all was, exactly as I knew it would be and exactly as I had feared.

My heart was beating wildly. At first all I could do was look and stare. A packet of letters, tied up with a pink ribbon; and, tucked into the corner, photo albums, thick leather photo albums, piled one on top of the other; some ethnic jewellery lying loose over the letters; some sheet music; a lock of black hair tied-up with some white cotton; and, filling nearly half of the chest, India's files, lots of files, labelled and in line abreast.

But it wasn't yet too late. It wasn't too late for me to slam the chest shut and replace the music on top of the lid. I could have skulked from her flat and returned when it was safe – when my love had returned, when the temptation was out of sight and when the madness had lifted.

However, it was already far, far too late, for I was no more capable of leaving India's chest of secrets than I would have been of playing *The Well-Tempered Clavier Books I and II complete*. To leave would have been a physical impossibility. It would have gone against my very nature.

So, with my heart turned to flint, I allowed myself a first jealous sip. It was a love letter, dated five years back and postmarked from Bristol. Inside, there were no torrid details of trysts beneath the Clifton Suspension Bridge, or walks in the Botanic Gardens. But I saw that it was from 'Malcolm' and it was signed 'with much love'.

I scanned the letter and tossed it to the side. Not for me the discreet look in India's chest and then the pretence that I knew nothing. For in that moment I was not just outraged but physically repulsed at the thought that my love could have had boyfriends before me, and I was determined to have it out with her. Blow by blow, we would sort it out once and for all.

I read letter after letter, all of them from Malcolm. He was another Bristol medic and in his own way seemed perfectly amenable. They weren't explicitly raunchy, but every word was a twist of the knife in my guts. They seemed to have started during India's first year at Bristol and spanned at least three years. There was hardly even an intimation of sex. They were just loving, affectionate letters. But my vivid imagination, churning at warp speed, could more than fill in the details.

I was coming towards the end of the letters and picked up another crisp white envelope with Malcolm's now familiar scrawl in black ink. This one was from just a couple of years before, with a London postmark.

I scanned it fast and the three words at the end blazed out at me as if they had been written in blood. Just three words and, the moment I read them, I felt queasy with nausea.

For with those three words, the edifice of my beautiful golden Goddess had finally come tumbling to earth and she lay at my feet in a pile of rubble and dust.

My eyes were watering as I read them again, realising their full import. Not the words 'I love you', but something far more devastating.

They were Malcolm's fond farewell. The three words that shook me to the bottom of my soul: 'Your loving husband'.

My hands were shaking with rage. The bitch! The bloody bitch! Married to someone else and she hadn't even thought fit to tell me? She'd used me like some toy-boy lover, while between times she must have tripped back to London to see her husband. I was apoplectic. Then and there I tore the letter to shreds and hurled it across the room.

I was so crazy with rage that I could hardly read the other letters, but they were more of the same – Malcolm eulogizing about his wonderful wife, telling her how she'd made him the happiest man in the world.

I'll bet she had, with all her *houri* bedroom tricks and her insatiable lust.

Photo albums next, and there, if ever I needed it, was the proof of India's infidelity right in front of my eyes. Pictures of a schoolgirl India, winning prizes, clinching teenage loves. Pictures too of her parents and friends, but those were passed over in a moment, because the only thing that I wanted were photos of her with men and, specifically, with her husband.

And there he was. I knew it was him – from the look of love in her face and the way that they were entwined about each other in the bedroom. Malcolm had finally arrived on the scene and the next two albums were devoted to India and him, their holidays and their parties. He had glasses, was about six-foot tall and had wispy receding hair. He was by no means a hunk and all I could think then was that she'd cuckolded me for this gangling geek?

Pictures of the diamond ring too – on India's left hand – as they celebrated their engagement. She was wearing a little black dress, her hair in a short bob. She looked years younger.

I knew they were coming, but it was still a shock when I found them – an album full of wedding pictures, recording the happiest day of her life down to the last piece of confetti. Pictures of India having her hair done, wearing a simple white silk dress as her father led her up the aisle, cutting the cake and kissing her new husband with a look of starry-eyed love. There were honeymoon snaps too, a week in Istanbul from the look of things, with India and Malcolm forever holding hands, clutching at each other's waists, and the smiles never once leaving their faces.

I threw the album across the room with all my might and, as it ricocheted off the wall, its spine cracked. The pages fluttered to the floor.

I picked up the lock of hair, the pieces of gaudy jewellery, and with one sweep they were hammered into the side of the piano. The sheet music – more Bach, I noticed – went the same way.

A small ring-box was at the bottom of the trunk. I opened it – and there was the diamond ring, the diamond that she had so devotedly taken off for me, but which she had tucked away into her box of secrets. How it mocked me as it sparkled.

I'd seen enough, more than enough, and the righteous, vindictive rage was swelling up in me like an unstoppable tide, sweeping away all before it.

For now that I knew the worst – knew that my India was married – I'd started to think and to piece things together.

Of course she hadn't needed any contraception. She'd been on the pill for years, ever since she'd first started seeing Malcolm.

Of course she was a dynamo in the bedroom. Malcolm had taught her every trick in the Kama Sutra.

But then I started to think back, started to remember little details from the previous two months. And gradually I completed my picture.

It seemed so obvious. For she hadn't just been cuckolding me with Malcolm, but with Savage too. I remembered that day when we'd kissed for the first time, how she'd been so eager to run away from Savage. And only a few days after that she'd sprinted through the streets of Windsor in order to keep the two of us apart. And then, the killer blow: Savage in the Tap, openly bragging about how he'd bedded India. At the time, I'd foolishly dismissed it as nothing more than Savage's idle boasting, but now…now I could see it all with crystal clarity. She'd bedded Savage and, after she had tired of him, she had taken up with me instead.

I was crying with rage, the tears pouring down my cheeks and dripping over India's chest of secrets. But yet the pity of it. Oh, the pity of it.

I squatted there amid the torn-up letters and the scattered photos, and I howled for myself and for my shattered love. I'd been abused and India had treated my love with a vileness that defied comprehension.

Eventually the tears dried, but I was so choked with self-pity that I didn't hear the clink of the front door, or the quiet step on the stairs.

And in she came.

She was wearing her grey suit and white blouse and, like me, was red-rimmed with tears.

India stood on the doorstep. Agape.

I must have looked like a mad thing, like a wild animal in its soiled nest, with her box open and her letters, her photos, and all her intimate secrets strewn all about me.

She looked round the room, saw the pictures and the scattered baubles, took it all in, before finally staring down at me. She shook her head and burst into tears, her breath coming in racked sobs. She clutched her hands to her face and sank to the floor.

My heart, my ice-cold heart, did instinctively go out to her a little. But then I remembered that it was I who had been spurned, who had been treated so abominably. And well she might start crying in front of me, but out of nothing more than guilty shame at having been found out.

She cried and she cried, slumped on the floor, her whole body heaving. I quashed every instinct to go to her. I squatted there like a troll in its own filth and watched and waited. I had nothing to say, for now I knew everything. But I would bide my time, would give her as long as she wanted, see if she had anything to say for herself.

And when the sobbing had stopped and she had caught her breath, she finally spoke. "I'm sorry."

She'd apologised. And her apology only strengthened my resolve. I had nothing to be ashamed of. I might have gone through her private papers, but all I had done was expose her infidelity. I might have done wrong. But it was a gnat-bite compared to the outrage that she had inflicted on me.

"I'm sorry," she repeated.

At length I spoke. "You're married."

She could only shake her head dumbly from side-to-side.

"I've seen the pictures of you and 'Malcolm'. Read his letters. Seen the two of you together on your wedding day."

"It's not like that," she said. Softly.

Oh – I could be quite the lawyer when I turned my mind to it; four years at Eton had taught me more than enough about sarcasm and a savage tongue. She'd opened the floodgates, and out it all poured.

"Oh, I'm sorry," I said. "So, it's not like that then? Maybe you were just married to Malcolm at weekends, leaving you free to sleep with me or Savage or whichever other boy took your fancy?"

"*Savage?*" She was horrified.

"I know everything. He was openly boasting about the two of you."

"But…" She was twisting her handkerchief into knots. "But there's never been anything with Savage."

I laughed, laughed at my own folly. "Three weeks back I wondered what you were doing about contraception. I wondered how you just happened to be on the pill." I flicked at some of the torn letters at my feet. "I thought that maybe you were just a good-time girl who was always prepared, always ready for any eventuality. But the one thing I never imagined was that you were actually married."

"Kim," she said, and when she looked at me I could see the tears dripping down her cheeks. "I love you. I love only you."

I was standing up now. I'd said my piece. There was nothing more to be gained by staying. "Funny way of showing it."

"You're right. I was married." Those vile words caught in her mouth. "I'd wanted to tell you. But it had never felt right. I…"

I stalked past her and stood at the door.

She looked up at me. "I didn't know how you'd take it. I thought it might change everything between us."

I laughed in disbelief. "You thought it might change everything if I knew you were married? Well, maybe it just might!"

Her fingers, those long tapering fingers, strayed to several of the wedding pictures on the floor. She picked them up and stared at them. "We split up a year ago." One-by-one the pictures fell from her hand. "He found someone else and he broke my heart. And then I found you." She looked up at me. "And you made me believe in love again."

She blinked back the tears, and, as she sat there in front of me, with her hands in her lap, I felt the cold, raw power of the executioner at the block.

"I can never trust you again."

The tears fell wet down her neck. "We divorced today," she said. A trace of a smile wavering at the edge of her lips. "And I thought that I was free to be yours. Even if you did want to join the army."

She was pleading with me, imploring me to stay, to hold her. She shuffled towards me on her knees.

And with one sharp, scything blow, I severed our love by the neck. "India, you are free to be with whomever you want." My hand rested on the door-handle. "But it's not going to be me."

I slammed the door shut behind me. India's sobs were still ringing in my ears as I stormed down the stairs.

I rode back to the Timbralls with this icy, icy rage clinging to me like a cloak. Oh, I had such malice in my heart that at that moment I was capable of any sort of infamy.

I looked at my watch – her watch – and nearly stopped then and there to toss it into the bushes. I dully registered that Absence was in five minutes, but it made no odds anymore. I didn't care what happened at Eton or with India. As far as I was concerned they could all, all of them, go to hell in a hand-basket.

I was pedalling with psychotic fury, hurtling down the High Street, my feet relentlessly grinding, taking out my anger and my hurt on the bicycle.

Cuckolded by my first love? I seethed with impotent rage. I never wanted to see or hear from her again. I would excise every trace of her memory from my mind.

And as for my searching through her private papers? Compared to India's scheming lies, that had been nothing but a minor transgression.

I did vaguely register that she'd said she'd got divorced that day, and also that she'd denied sleeping with Savage. But my jealousy had turned me into a white-hot supernova, exuding wave after pulsating wave of anger.

I streaked through the traffic lights, past the Burning Bush. The wheels keening faster and faster beneath me, fizzling with sympathetic rage.

The Sebastopol cannon ahead of me. Instinctively, I stretch out my hand to slap its broad, black flank. Only one hand on the handlebars.

Up the little ramp to go through the archway into New Schools Yard.

From behind a pillar, I catch a blur of movement, a glimpse of Savage's bestial face as he thrusts forward.

He stabs a cricket bat into my front spokes. In an instant everything stops and I am flying, flying through the air, pitched heel-over-head. In a whirl I see the arch, the Timbralls, the sky, the cannon, the Satanic glee etched into Savage's face, and the tiles, the solid scuffed tiles of the New Schools archway, coming closer, ever closer, until with a flat thud I crash to the ground. Even as I'm losing consciousness I can hear the crack of brittle ribs being snapped in two and the sickening wrench of bones being wrung from their sockets.

*

The sound of my parents' quiet voices filtered through to me as I gradually regained consciousness.

I could tell I was in a bed.

For a while I lay there, trying to piece together what had happened.

I opened my eyes.

It was the first time I had ever seen my stepmother cry. She saw

209

my eyes flicker. Immediately, her voice was turned into a hoarse cough and she was by my side, holding my hand. Even my father choked up. Both of them were on either side of me, with the tears pouring down Edie's cheeks.

After two weeks, I was back from the dead.

Two weeks? I couldn't believe it.

They told me what had happened. A master had found me out cold in a pool of my own blood in the New Schools Yard. I'd have died if they hadn't got me to Slough hospital in under 15 minutes.

Blood transfusions and hour upon hour of surgery to my head, my shoulders, my ribs and my shattered knee.

They'd put me on drips and, as my muscles had atrophied by the minute, they wondered if I would ever come round, or if I would spend the rest of my days in a coma.

I never told them that it was Savage who'd nearly killed me.

I suppose in part it was because I thought I'd deserved it.

My subconscious had been working overtime, digesting everything that had happened with India and me. Some coma victims can't recall what happened before they were knocked out. But I could remember it all, from those last distraught minutes with India through to that exact moment when I had seen Savage thrusting a cricket bat through the front spokes.

From the moment I woke up, I realised that I had behaved hatefully. I knew that India had been true to me, that she loved me and only me. And so it followed that everything else was nothing but the product of my own jealousy. Of course she was estranged from her husband – because she loved me. Of course she had not slept with Savage – because she loved me.

India loved me and only me and so long as I clasped that one fact to my bosom, then everything else would slot into place.

And I understood too why she'd kept her secret from me. I'd been exuding jealousy from every pore. If she'd told me everything, it would without doubt have been an unpleasant, fraught conversation; I would have behaved badly; our fledgling relationship would have been blighted.

When you can accurately predict your lover's rage, is it any wonder that sometimes you shirk from telling them the whole truth?

India hadn't lied to me. But she had held things back.

It had been for the best. I could see that.

And to anyone who's wondering whether they should furnish their partner with all the tawdry details of their past, I offer but one piece of advice: seal your lips. Keep it close to your heart. For lovers are sensitive plants and they can be choked with too much information just as a flower can be stifled by too much fertilizer.

I'm sure that, in time, India would have told me all. But there at Eton, when we had only just embarked on our voyage together?

She was wiser by far to keep it to herself.

So, as I lay on that bed, with my head and shoulders swathed in bandages, I was contrite. India had said she was sorry – but it was not her that needed to ask for forgiveness. It was me who should have been begging on my knees.

And as for my jealousy, my wild, seething jealousy, it had disappeared like water seeping into the desert from a cracked bottle. So she'd had boyfriends before, had been married before, had made love before? I relished it all, welcomed all the previous men in her life, for they were the people who had made her what she was today. Who gave a jot for the past, when all that mattered was the moment and our love together?

My parents were so pleased to see me come out of the coma. I'd never seen them so happy.

Edie was laughing nervously as she spoke, all the while having to pinch herself that I was up and alive, and that she wasn't sitting next to my corpse.

It was the first time that I can ever remember my father stroking my hand. Tentative, like a young man courting his first love.

As my parents watched over their little nestling, the doctors came and inspected me. I started to take in my surroundings. A small white room with a television. On the shelf and by the window were dozens of cards.

I asked for them to be brought over. Edie swept them all up.

"Shall I read them out?" she asked.

"It's ok," I replied, and she placed them by my side on the bed. My arms were so weak it was a strain to lift each one.

I was touched. Cards from all my teachers, including some from the beaks who hadn't taught me in years, cards from my housemates and from my classmates too. All of them with that deft touch which says we hope you pull through – but please don't hold it against us if you do.

Even a card from my parents. 'Kim, get well soon. Lots of love, Mummy and D.' Three kisses too. The tears stabbed at my eyes. I tried to blink them back.

The number of cards left to read were dwindling and my fingers started to twitch with impatience. I'd scan one, see who it was from, and instantly go onto the next.

For there was only one card I wanted to find.

As the last one fell from my fingertips I knew it was not there.

"What kind friends you have," Edie said.

"Yes," I replied. I could have dissembled, but I was boiling up to know about India's card. "Have there been any other letters? Any phone calls?"

My parents looked at each other, shrugged.

"I think everything's there," my father said.

"Has anyone come to visit?"

Edie perked up at that. "One girl came here twice to see you."

Angela visited the next day, just after I'd finished eating soup and bread. She was wearing another mini-skirt, though a white one this time as it was the summer holidays, and a pink t-shirt. She kissed me on the cheek and sat by the side of the bed.

"Hi," I said.

"Hi."

"Thought you'd seen the last of me?"

"I did," and as she spoke all trace of jocularity was gone and she was wiping the tears from her eyes. "I did."

"Thank you for coming," I said.

She smiled through her tears. "I didn't think anyone else from school would come to see you."

"You were right," I replied. I could have small-talked, but I was too anxious. "Have you been here before?"

"A couple of times."

My brain convulsed, for it seemed that fate was yet again having a joke at my expense. It was slowly dawning on me that India had not written, had not visited; that she might not even be aware of my accident.

"How sweet of you," I said, but already I was scheming. "I wondered...I wondered if you might be able to pop in on my music teacher. Just tell her what's happened. She had some music for me. She might not have heard..." I trailed off. It sounded lame.

I don't think Angela scented anything out of the ordinary. She took India's name and address, and promised to let her know.

She came back the next day, and, while the news was not a disaster, I did get that deadly prickle which apparently so often presages a shipwreck. It's not much, just the slightest tingle, but it's the sinking feeling in your guts when you know you're on the verge of catastrophe.

"There was no one there," Angela said. "The downstairs neighbours said she moved out last week. The flat's up for rent."

I took the news without a tremor.

So India had gone. But I would track her down and beg her forgiveness.

It took me another two weeks to get out of hospital, and from my parents' home I sent India letters to wherever they might reach her. I sent them care of Eton College, care of Bristol University, and even care of London's various medical schools on the off-chance that she might have been continuing her degree.

These days, with the internet, it might have been easier to track her down.

But 25 years back, it was no simple thing for a 17-year-old to find a lost love. I did the best I could, sent a score of love-notes. But as the weeks went by and I received no calls and no letters, there were only two possible conclusions remaining: either my letters weren't getting to India, or she was choosing not to respond to them.

More and more it was the latter option that came to dominate my imagination. She must have received my letters – how could she not? – and, for whatever reason, had chosen not to reply. I conjured up every single scenario I could think of: that she'd seen me at my very worst and couldn't stomach the sight of me again, that I had driven her back into Malcolm's arms, that, following on from her divorce, the last thing she needed was a relationship with an emotionally-retarded teenager.

I don't know. There may have been any number of reasons why she did not write. But by the time I arrived back at Eton for the start of the Michaelmas Half, still with a slight limp from my shattered knee-cap, I had resigned myself to the fact that India did not want to see me again.

I thought that I deserved it, that I had behaved despicably, that I was beyond redemption.

My father took me back to school. It was a Thursday, the second week of September, spitting with rain, and my heart was dead. My love was gone and I felt certain that no woman, no girl, would ever be able to hold anything for me again.

A few boys were milling around. They joshed me as I limped into the Timbralls Hall. One of them took my suitcase upstairs. I followed my father out to the car. The streetlights gleamed on the wet bonnet.

"Well, goodbye old boy," he said. "You look after yourself."

He hovered. For the first time, I realised that he was unsure about what to do next.

"Goodbye," I said, "and thank you." And before he could turn on his heel, I took the two steps to give him a hug. Both my arms round his waist. At first there was no response. Then I felt his arms come up warm around me. It was all a little bit rigid. But both of us were out of practice.

We broke off. My father flushed with embarrassment. "I wish I'd been able to do that before, but…" He trailed off.

"I know."

He paused, his hand on the car door, drawn to me yet desperate to hide any hint of emotion. "I think we should do it more often."

"I'd like that."

He gave a wave, and with a relieved roar the car thrummed off into the night.

I waved till his taillights blinked into the darkness. It was a strange feeling. I think that hug had probably called for more courage than anything else my father had ever done.

I mooched back into the Hall, shaking my head with amused surprise.

My pigeon-hole was crammed with post.

I flicked through the letters. Was I expecting something? Possibly. But I didn't want to start hoping again, because I knew deep-down that it would only cause more pain.

For the most part, they were 'Get Well' cards. But right at the back there was a small white letter, and just the sight of it made my hands tremble, for I knew that copper-plate handwriting all too well.

India.

I hobbled quickly up the stairs, my knee shrieking with every step.

I hardly even noticed my room as I walked in. It was exactly as it had been before the accident. But how much my life had changed in the last two months.

I only had eyes for the letter.

I stared and stared at the letter's postmark and the date.

She had sent it the morning after I'd last seen her; the morning after I had stormed from her flat in a jealous haze of hate.

What I would have given to have taken it all back.

The letter was thin. I could feel the trace of a card. My hands twitched as I slit open the envelope with a paperknife.

This is what she had written.

I'm sorry. I love you. Please forgive me.

The card is in front of me now, though my tears over the years have made the ink fade and blur.

I would never hear from India again.

BOOK 1, PRELUDE 17, A-flat Major

I am not quite done.

There are a few strings yet to be tied, though I am afraid none of this ends happily. No one especially gets their just desserts.

I finished my final year at Eton and passed my A-levels without mishap. As for my Eton companions, I know next to nothing. Jeremy and I soldiered on. But when it came to our final parting, he never even said goodbye, just left and that was that. I have never seen or heard from him since.

Angela, beautiful Angela, would still gaze at me in the English classes, but nothing ever came of it. We never kissed, we also never said goodbye, and, like Jeremy, I have not the faintest idea what happened to her.

It was like we had all served a five-year stretch together in this gilded army camp. And, at the time, just like those poor benighted Argentinian conscripts in the Falklands, we had done the best we could, had made new friends. But once we'd left, we had come to see how those friendships had been forced on us, and that outside Eton it was possible to make companions of our own choosing.

So, I'd like to hear from Jeremy, from Angela, from a few other of my unruly band of Scallies, but it's never happened. It's another era and another world, and it's as if we have all made a silent pact never to return there.

Frankie and my Dame, as far as I know, continued their Eton lives without a blip. They both must be close to retirement now.

And Savage – what of him? I would so love to report that he had met some hideous end. But the truth is, like almost every one of my peers, I have not heard a word of Savage since he left Eton.

As for me...well one thing was quite apparent after my accident – any career in the army was out of the question. My knee was finished, caput.

But my injuries were merely the catalyst. For thanks to the Falklands, I'd already begun to realise that an army career was not for me.

So instead of Sandhurst, I read English at Bristol University; Bristol, of course, because that was where India had been.

I left university with an all too predictable 2:2 in English. That, by the by, is often the way with Etonians when they go to University. There's no one driving them as hard, no tutors to give them a kick up the backside, no beaks shouting with incoherent rage. As a result, the boys suddenly realise that at university they can coast along quite nicely on just a bare minimum of work.

After Bristol, I travelled the world for a couple of years, and then became a journalist. I well remembered my father's outraged reaction to *The Sun* newspaper on that Fourth of June. So I set out to become a 'Red Top' reporter. But not even that could annoy him. It hardly registered a flicker. For my relationship with both my parents had bumped, had jinked off the rails, and was now set on a new course.

They'd thought I was going to die after my accident. And when I lived, it was as if every day was a bonus. My father learned to kiss me on the cheek when he greeted me; my stepmother learned to unbend.

And for me, it was as if a ton of expectation had been lifted from my shoulders. I was left to roam wherever I pleased.

I found new girlfriends and new love, and discovered to my utter amazement that it was more than possible to relive love's first careless rapture.

Girlfriends, many, many wonderful girlfriends, and every one of them has taught me so much about myself and about life. One day, I may yet get round to telling some of their stories.

But, no matter how much I loved them, the one thing I never wanted to know about was their pasts. I was like a schoolboy who'd been caught smoking, and who was then made to puff his way through an entire box of cigars – for my experience with India's chest of secrets was the most profound aversion therapy.

Of course, I still had a part of me which was that infamous, jealous, screaming horror that longed to know everything about my girlfriends' past loves. But that was now so tightly-shackled, locked away in the dungeons of my mind, that it couldn't move a muscle without receiving a savage kick to the ribs.

I know that it is not how the psychiatrists would recommend that you deal with your baser emotions. They would tell you to talk it out, to work it through until you are spent, to understand reasons and motives. Only then, they'd say, can you properly move on.

That is one way, but it is not my way. Not for me weeks of intensive therapy. No – like many better men before me, the matter of my own jealousy is so unpleasant that I prefer to duck the issue altogether.

I used specifically to instruct girlfriends that I did not wish to know anything – not one jot – about their pasts. As for their old love-letters and their photos, you could have waved them all in front of my face and I would have ignored them. My aversion therapy had been so severe that even if I had found an open diary on the kitchen table, I would have left the house rather than read a word.

Every time I felt even the smallest stab of jealousy, it reminded me of my own ugliness and my terrible loss.

India.

I still think it the most beautiful name in the English language.

After I'd received that short note from her, I tried once more to get in touch. I even sent a letter care of the letting agents who had rented her flat in Eton.

I went through the motions, chased up every last avenue that I could think of. Though I knew in my heart that we were done, that our little ship on which we had briefly placed such high hopes had sunk without trace.

I never heard anything more of her.

But.

There is one thing more left to tell.

Gradually my memories of India dulled – as did my piano-playing skills. Eton found me a new teacher for my final year, but I've not had a lesson since I left the school.

For over two years, I couldn't play or even listen to *The Well-Tempered Clavier*. Just a couple of bars would be enough to set me off.

But new girlfriends came into my life and I started to remember the rapture of the music. Listening was always a bittersweet experience, always awash with memories of India. I tried to play some of the simplest preludes. But after a three-year lay-off from the keyboard, I was back floundering in the shallows and the miseries of Grade 1.

Eventually, *The Well-Tempered Clavier* became a memory, a rather awkward memory. I still liked the music but, whenever I heard it, I could not but be reminded of my own repellent nature. It's funny, but the things that haunt me now are never the slights and snubs of other people; rather, the memories that make me shudder are the hideous things that I have done to my friends and to my loved ones.

I married once and we had a son. It ended horribly; again, one day I may tell the tale.

I married again. My second wife is a good woman, a special woman. She cares for me and puts up with my little foibles and the fact that my emotions are kept wrapped in their own icy citadel. We get on well. It is amicable, comfortable. We understand each other.

Of course there is none of the soaring passion that there was with India. But I do not think any couple on earth could sustain that level of passion for more than a few months.

We have three daughters, three adorable daughters. They're the cement that keeps us together. Splitting up is not even an option. There are not, perhaps, as many highs as I might like, but there are also none of those depressing lows when the rows and arguments seem to roll on from one day to the next.

It is a strong, workable marriage. We tell each other that we love each other.

And India – India, like *The Well-Tempered Clavier,* has become nothing more than a blissful, if occasionally painful, memory. Although, like the music, if I dwell on her for too long, she still has the ability to make me cry.

A month back, we were in Edinburgh for the festival, three weeks of cultural mayhem with something to tempt even the most jaded palates. I still like the Fringe, the crazy comics and the mime artists, but as I get older I take fewer risks. I prefer to go for the safe and the steady rather than risk an hour's boredom with something new.

So, instead of bearding the stand-ups or venturing to see the latest gritty drama, I took my wife to one of the late-night concerts at the Usher Hall.

Andras Schiff was playing Bach's *Goldberg Variations*. They are slightly similar to some of *The Well-Tempered Clavier* fugues, but I think they're more highly evolved. I like the variations. Most importantly, I can listen to them without crying.

The Usher Hall is a classic round concert hall – Scotland's version of the Royal Albert Hall. The concert was a sell-out, not a seat left in the house. We arrived, just as we always do, a few moments before the lights went down. There was no time for a drink. It was wet, which was making my bad knee throb.

My favourite part of the Goldberg's is the Aria at the beginning. It's Bach at his tranquil best, and you've got it all to look forward to again at the end, when the Aria is repeated.

I took time to settle down. I stared at Schiff. I could feel the pack of people sitting shoulder to shoulder, smell the moist hum of wet coats. My mind wandered from this to that.

By these days, I was not thinking of India quite so much. She was just my golden Goddess. Whenever I thought of her I mentally genuflected. In my mind she had been returned to her rightful pedestal.

But the Goldberg's, being so similar to *The Well-Tempered Clavier*, had pricked at my memory. I started to remember the times we'd had – not that awful fight at the end, but the good times. That day when I'd first seen India outside the School Hall, a moment cast in amber. Laughing with each other in the Eton practice room till the tears dripped onto the grand piano. The way she'd snatched my hand at Judy's Passage and bundled me into the elderflower bush. A rainy afternoon on the Long Walk and a day that I will never forget. Love in the fields and in the spinneys of Eton. And love, too, sandwiched up against the dustbins of a Windsor hotel.

One of the happiest months of my life.

Had she abused me? Pish and tush. She might, just possibly, have abused her position as a music teacher.

But it wasn't just about the sex.

She'd loved me; I knew it. Maybe it was just circumstance, me being in the right place at the right time. Maybe I'd caught her at a moment of maximum vulnerability during her divorce. And, just maybe, it could have been because, for one single term, we both shared an incredible passion for *The Well-Tempered Clavier*.

Who knows why it started, what made it tick.

Lick up the honey stranger, and ask no questions.

As I stared through Schiff, I started to wonder what had happened to India after she'd left Eton. Had she received any of my letters? Had she quit the country to join VSO?

One final thing: had she ever known how many tears I'd shed for her, how I'd begged for her forgiveness?

Schiff was on the Aria for the final time. I gazed at the Usher Hall's domed ceiling and stretched back.

During the previous two decades, I had seen India many times over. Chance meetings at the train station, the street, or the airport. But always, when I looked for a second, a third time, I would see that it was nearly her, but not quite.

But this time, as I leaned my head back and turned from left to right, I really did see her.

It was as if a pin had been thrust into the back of my neck.

I convulsed.

Out of nowhere, my heart was drilling and I was feeling just like that sweaty teenager who had first stepped into India's music room. I thought it was her. I was sure it was her.

It wasn't just the frame of brown hair, but the way she was sitting – exactly as she'd used to sit when I played *The Well-Tempered Clavier.*

As discreetly as I could, I took another look. She was in the row behind me, about ten seats along.

I turned to the side and stared, not being able to tear my eyes away.

I had envisaged India's face so many times over the years, had got my hopes up so many times. But this really was her; I knew it, from her hair to her clothes, still the same elegant pastels that she'd always loved. Even her hands, clasped in her lap, were a giveaway.

The lights were low, but she looked breathtaking.

My palms were clammy with sweat.

Should I go up to her at the end? Greet her? Would she be pleased to see me?

I snatched one more look over my shoulder. She was leaning now towards the man next to her. He was whispering into her ear. She threw her head back and laughed, and as she did so I had a good look at him too. Well-built, I could see, youngish with a full head of hair.

What to do, what to do?

The Goldberg's had come to an end and we were applauding, cheering as well, because the more we cheered, the better the chance of an encore. Schiff came on again, went off, and I am clapping with demented frenzy. I don't know what else to do.

A lull in the applause and I take another look behind. It's India, without a doubt. With the auditorium lights up, I can see her in all her glory, and it's as if that same woman whom I loved 25 years ago has been transported to the Usher Hall; although her hair is shorter, she has not aged a single day.

I don't care what my wife thinks I'm doing. I just have to look again.

India was still talking to the man next to her.

Just a little dart of jealousy? Of course. For India was with another man and it should have been me by her side.

Her sixth-sense must have told her she was being watched.

She was talking to her partner but she suddenly broke off and looked at me, looked directly at me, and my world shattered into a billion pieces.

She was as serene as I had ever seen her. For a moment her fingers strayed to her lips.

Then she waved. Just a simple wave. But it was not a wave of hello. There was an air of finality about it, as if after 25 years she had at last been given the opportunity to say goodbye.

The man looked at me too, looked me square in the eye. A lean face with a snub nose, thin lips, and hooded eyelids that drooped over slightly bulging hazel eyes.

I had to turn away.

Schiff was back on stage to play the encore.

And I was undone.

The Well-Tempered Clavier, Book 1, Prelude 17 in A-flat Major. It was my first love, the first prelude that India had ever played me. Instantly, I was back in that small music room with lime-green walls and a scuffed upright Steinway.

My shoulders heaved. I buried my face into my hands. The tears streamed through my fingers.

My wife leaned over, touched my shoulder. "Are you all right?"

The pain was in my heart and in my head, but the hurt was physical.

Although it wasn't just the music, that ethereal Clavier music that Bach had written more than 280 years ago.

I had also recognised the man beside India, that tall man with the thin lips and the lean face; the man who, two decades ago, I had once used to see in the mirror.

I wept and cursed myself for a fool.

But my tears were not just for the son I'd never known.

There had been one thing more.

I had seen something else.

As she had waved, I had recognised that watch, that classic Heuer that I had given to India on her birthday all those years ago.

She was wearing it still, an ever-present reminder of her lost love.